Life Is A
Boomerang

Life Is A Boomerang

Jenny Guest

authorHOUSE®

AuthorHouse™
1663 Liberty Drive
Bloomington, IN 47403
www.authorhouse.com
Phone: 1-800-839-8640

Published by AuthorHouse   08/07/2012

ISBN: 978-1-4772-2172-3 (sc)
ISBN: 978-1-4772-2173-0 (e)

This book is dedicated to my family.

"AUTHOR'S NOTE"

I believe that just as the earth goes around, until it does a full circle, so do our lives. How the circle ends depends on what we throw in the air while it is turning.

This story begins at the end of the nineteen sixties and turns a full circle by the twenty-first century.

The characters are a composite of many different people in real life but none is a real person.

CHAPTER ONE

John hesitated a few minutes by the door, trying to locate a familiar face. He saw at the other end of the room a group of his newly made friends, but what caught his attention was the gorgeous brunette to whom they were talking.

He went across the room. "Hello, John," they all said in unison. "Have you met Bea? She is an old Tokyo hand; she has been here for ages."

Bea smiled and extended her hand. "I am Bea Alvarez."

John was completely taken by this beauty who had an accent to beat all accents. He managed to shake her lovely soft hand and say, "I'm John Fellow."

One of his friends explained to Bea, "John has just arrived, but he is a fluent Japanese speaker."

"He has been sent to check on all of us," another added with a laugh.

John turned to Bea and said, "Would you like to dance?" Bea was taken by surprise by this sudden invitation and replied: "My mother told me that it is already difficult for a young man to gather up courage to ask you for a dance so you must always accept."

Everybody laughed at this and said: "Did you have to gather up courage to ask Bea for a dance, John?"

John smiled at them and without saying a word took Bea to the floor leaving the others with gaping mouths. "He is a fast worker," one of them said in a jealous tone.

"So, how long have you been here?" John inquired, looking into Bea's brown eyes.

"Oh, not that long; about three years; but once you get to know the people and some of this impossible language, you are considered a native."

"I will not find it too difficult, then."

"Where did you learn Japanese?" she asked him.

"In England, the company wanted me to learn a difficult language, and I chose this one. What brought you to Japan?"

"My father was sent here for work, like you."

"And what do you do?" John asked.

"I was determined to study Japanese, but this is a very special country. They are fascinated by foreigners; one day I was pursued on my way to see my father. You can imagine I was quite panicky and almost ran into the building."

"What did he do?"

"He took the lift with me and handed me his card; I was not used to the Japanese custom of exchanging cards with anyone they meet, and I did not know what to do. But he very politely said he had a modelling agency and that he wanted me to work for him."

"Did you accept?"

"Not at first; I told him I was going to see my father and that he could ask him."

John was amused. "Did he?"

"Yes, he did. He followed me to my father's office and stood outside while I explained to my father what was going on. He wanted to call the police, but I convinced him to talk to this man before he did so. In the end my father was convinced that he was genuine; the man showed my father a catalogue he was carrying with him and explained that foreign faces were very much in demand, and that he already had quite a few. He also told my father that he could check him out."

"Did he?"

"Yes, he did."

"And?" John asked.

Bea grinned. "Well, two days later I received a call asking if he could come to our house to take my photograph and to add me to the catalogue. Again I had to ask my father, and to my astonishment Dad told me to tell him that he could come the next evening when all my family would be there."

"I would love to meet your father," John said with interest.

"He is great fun," Bea said. "He's always telling jokes."

"So what happened next?" John prompted.

"This man—Hiroshi is his name—arrived with a whole lot of equipment and took my photograph sitting down, standing up, looking at him, looking at him sideways, and then looking at him from over my shoulder. It was quite amusing and a bit embarrassing. Then my sister came down, and he wanted to include her in his catalogue, too."

"How funny; I am already learning quite a lot about this country."

"It is a very special place," Bea commented. "Everybody is very kind, and they give the impression of being cold and quiet, but when you get to know them, they are not at all like that. They love to have amusing things to do; you must come with us to one of our outings one of these days. They love singing and playing games."

At that moment one of John's new friends came and tapped him on the shoulder. "You two have danced enough; it's my turn now."

John had no alternative but to let him take his place. He returned to the group, and another friend commented, "You are a fast worker, buddy."

"She is great!" John said.

"You are not the only one to think so, mate. Everybody is in love with her."

John smiled and said to himself, *We shall see.* Then he asked, "Where is she from?"

"You were talking all that time, and you didn't ask her where she is from?"

"I don't like asking people where they are from; it might offend them."

"She is from Argentina, and you should wait until you meet her sister. She should have been here tonight, but she is modelling somewhere."

"So I hear. I find that most incredible, though not because they are not beautiful—I'm sure her sister is, too. But the way it happened; in other countries, models queue for days in order to be interviewed, and here they are actively discovered."

"You will find many things incredible in this land, my friend."

After that John was not sure what to do. He had lost interest in meeting anybody else and would have gone home, but he wanted to talk to Bea again. She was either dancing or talking to her friends, and he did not want to be too obvious. He pretended to be interested in what people were talking about around him, but he kept an eye on her all the time. He waited until he saw her going to get her coat. He sprinted to the door and said, "Are you leaving, too? Can I give you a lift?"

She smiled and answered, "I live around the corner, but if you like, you can walk with me."

The others saw what was happening from the other side of the room and laughed. "We must watch him," they said.

John said to Bea, "So you are from Argentina? I was born in Africa."

Her curiosity was stirred. "Oh, I thought you were English."

"I am British, but I was born in Rhodesia—my grandparents live there."

"Do you go and see them often?"

"I'm afraid not. My work keeps me busy, and when I go on holidays, I tend to go with friends, or I pop in to see my mother in the country every once in a while."

"What about your father?"

"I never met my father; he was killed during the war, two months before I was born."

"That must have been very hard for your mother. Didn't she remarry?" Bea asked.

"No, she went back to England and stayed with her parents for a while, but then she went to South Africa, where she had friends. My mother is quite a free spirit and found it difficult living with her in-laws in Rhodesia, and even with her own family. So she took off, and I was brought up in the Cape. I had a wonderful time until I was ten and was sent to boarding school."

"Here we are; this is where I live," Bea said. "Next time, you must tell me more about your adventurous life."

"May I call you?"

"Sure; here is my card. I have taken up the ways of this country."

"And here is mine. In my line of work we are always exchanging cards, but not so often with the girls I go out with."

"Do you go out with many?" she teased.

John laughed and gave her a peck on the cheek while she was opening her door." "I will call you tomorrow."

The following day John arrived early in the office, cleared his desks from some papers left the evening before, sorted out his day, and then called Bea.

"Alvarez residence," a voice answered at the other end of the line.

"Could I please talk to Bea?"

"I will see if Miss Bea is available. May I know who is calling?"

"John Fellow," replied John, baffled by the answer he received. He had no idea how formal Bea's household was.

"Hello, how are you?" Bea said after a short delay.

"Have I called too early?"

"No, not at all; I have to go to work soon."

"How about dinner tonight, are you free?"

"I'm afraid I'm working late today. I also work for a television studio, and we are shooting all day."

"Well, can't I pick you up from work, and then we can stop somewhere for something to eat?"

"I won't be free before midnight, and we are fed in the studio. It is not great food, but I wouldn't last until midnight without a meal."

John was determined. "All right, then, I'll pick you up from the studio and take you straight home. How is that?"

Bea laughed. "The studio sends me home in one of their cars when I'm working late."

"But can't you tell them that tonight you already have a lift?"

"Yes, yes, I can," Bea said, laughing again.

"Right, that's settled then. Where are the studios?"

Bea gave him directions and said good-bye. She was inwardly flattered but anxious at the same time. She realised that John was keen on her, but she had not dated all that much before.

When she had arrived in Tokyo three years previously, she had been seventeen and was just out of school. She had had a boyfriend in Buenos Aires, but it had not been serious; he had been a best friend more than a boyfriend. She had just finished her secondary education and wanted to learn Japanese in Tokyo. Then Hiroshi had followed her to her father's office that day, and from that moment her life had changed completely. She had a good social life, but her work and the Japanese lessons that she took whenever she was free kept her from any steady dating. She did not want little affairs here and there—and her father would not have allowed it, anyway.

For his part, John was thrilled. Although he had had other plans for that evening, the mere thought of seeing Bea again exhilarated him. He had not had a serious relationship, either. Many short affairs, yes, but he had not felt like this before. He had a lot of work to do but kept looking at his watch. Finally at about nine he left the office and went to get something to eat. He then went home and watched television until it was time to meet Bea. He showered and shaved and was at the studio doors at the agreed time.

Bea did not make him wait long. She was even more beautiful than he remembered from the previous night.

"Hi, have I kept you long?" she asked him.

"I just arrived—perfect timing. So, where do we go now?"

"Would you mind taking me home, please? I'm dead tired and have to get up early tomorrow again."

"Oh, are you working all day?"

"No, no. Tomorrow is just a photograph session, and then I am free."

"Great; will you have dinner with me tomorrow night, then?"

"I think so." Bea said, but she sounded unsure.

John looked at her quizzically. "Am I putting too much pressure on you?"

Bea tilted her head and with a grin said, "A bit; I have lots of friends, but I have not dated all that much."

"I promise I will not do anything you do not want me to do. I just want to get to know you better."

Bea said, "My father will want to know who I am going out with, so come and have a drink at about seven and then we can go out."

John did not sleep well that night. Bea was not like the other girls he had met. Her father might be amusing as she had said, but he also seemed to be strict and he could see that Bea was a respectful daughter. He should be careful if he wanted to continue seeing her.

He took great care in his appearance and presented himself looking immaculate when a woman opened the door. He recognised her voice from the telephone call and suddenly became nervous, but she smiled when she showed him into the sitting room, where Bea's father and mother were having a drink.

Bea's father got up and extended his hand. He had a kind face, and his handshake was firm. "You must be John Fellow. Bea has told us that you have just arrived in Tokyo. How are you settling in?

"I am still finding my bearings, but I will get there," John answered, feeling a bit more relaxed.

"My name is Alberto, and this is Mercedes, my wife."

Bea's mother did not stand up, but she smiled warmly and extended her hand, which was just as soft as Bea's. "What would you like to drink, John?" she asked.

John had noticed that Bea's father was drinking whisky, and he asked for the same. He did not want to start on the wrong foot and ask for something that they did not have.

"Please sit down. Where are you going tonight?" Bea's father said.

"I thought I would show Bea my culinary achievements and cook myself." John said confidently.

Bea's parents looked at each other, and the smile disappeared from their eyes. "Who else have you invited?" Mercedes wanted to know.

"Nobody; I thought I would cook for Bea," John replied without thinking.

Alberto was now grave. "We do not allow our daughters to go to single men's homes by themselves. Why don't you stay here? I am sure there is enough food for all of us, and it will give us a chance to get to know each other."

John realised that he had made a great error of judgement. Bea's family was indeed old-fashioned! He did not know what to say.

Bea came in looking as marvellous as ever. Her father put his arms around her and informed her, "We have invited John to stay for dinner. I hope you don't mind, darling."

Bea obviously knew better than to disagree, and she asked for a drink.

It was not the evening that he had had in mind, but he was surprised at how much he enjoyed himself. Bea's family was formal but in a demure way. They were visibly well off but were not ostentatious. And Alberto was funny—one could tell that he liked a good laugh. He recounted some of his adventures that his family knew well, but for John it was all new.

"I did my masters in London," said Alberto. "Where in England do you come from, John?"

"I was born in Rhodesia. My great grandparents went to live in South Africa in the middle of the nineteenth century. My grandfather was born there."

"That is most interesting. Did he stay in Africa all his life?"

"Almost; when the Boer's War started, he had just finished high school and lied about his age in order to be enlisted. He was taken prisoner but managed to escape by jumping off the cart that was taking him. He ran for several days until he found the headquarters of his regiment. He was decorated for his bravery."

"How fascinating" Mercedes said. "Did he stay in the army?"

"He went on fighting until the end of the war, and then he studied law in England before he went back to South Africa. When he finished his studies, he was recruited by a law firm in Rhodesia. But then he was recalled during the First World War. I believe it was at that time he met my great grandmother, who was born in Singapore."

"Was she of Chinese origin? You look very English."

"No, she was English," John said with a laugh. "Many English people were born in the colonies, and that is why many of them enlisted in the army during the war."

"Where they married during the war?"

"I'm not sure; I must ask my grandfather to explain that one day."

Bea had not told them about John's father, and they asked, "Where was your father born?"

"He and his twin brother, as well as his two sisters, were born in Rhodesia. Both of the boys were killed during the Second World War, my father was in the Royal Air Force and my uncle in the army. It was very tough for my grandmother to lose two of her children a few months apart."

"Absolutely horrible," Mercedes uttered in shock.

Alberto said, "Obviously, your father was already married when he died. How old were you?"

"I was born two months after he was killed."

"Your family has suffered a lot!" Mercedes said, horrified. "You said that your mother's family was in England. Where did your father meet her?"

"In England, to be more precise, in Yorkshire; her family owned a textiles company. My father was on his way to England when he met some people on board ship, and they invited him to stay in Yorkshire. It was through them that they met. I think that during both wars, people did not waste any time in marrying; they did not know whether they would live through it. I believe that he took my mother to stay with his parents after they were married. He left her there, but he never went back for her because he was killed soon after. After I was born, my mother took me back to England. By then my grandfather was already into politics, and he eventually became an MP."

Mercedes repeated, "An MP?"

"A member of Parliament," John explained. "I believe he was knighted after that."

"What a fascinating family!" Alberto exclaimed.

"We would love to meet your mother when she comes to visit you. I imagine she will want to know where you live." Said Mercedes knowingly.

"Oh, I am sure she will," John said, laughing.

CHAPTER TWO

That night while getting ready for bed, Alberto said to Mercedes, "I think John will fit well into our family."

"Don't you think you are getting a bit ahead of yourself?" Mercedes said, amused.

"Why?"

"For goodness sake, Al, they've just met, and we don't know their feelings towards each other."

"Oh, but I do!" replied Alberto, winking at his wife. "I have seen the way our daughter listened to him while he was recounting his family history—and the way he looks at her. I do know, I do know. He waved a finger at her on his way to the bathroom.

On his way home, John thought of the unexpected turn his plans had taken. He liked Bea's family. Gaby, Bea's elder sister, arrived halfway through dinner, kissed her parents, and apologised for being late. The sisters were quite similar in looks, but for the fact that Gaby had light brown hair and hazel eyes; otherwise one could not tell the difference. Perhaps Gaby was a bit more self-assured than Bea, but she was two years her senior. When their father was posted to Japan, Gaby was in her second year of art studies at university. She had not wanted to go with her parents, but her father had organised for her to go on studying in Tokyo. "There is no better place for your subject," he had said. Now she was happy to have accepted. She had learnt the language and went to school in between jobs. Like her sister, she had a great social life, but it was not always with the same friends. She had friends that she had made through school, and she preferred to hang out with them rather than the more formal friends her sister had.

In her room, Bea smiled to herself while she got ready for bed. Her father always got what he wanted, but she was sure that the evening had gone on well. John laughed at all the stories her father recounted and every once in a while, John looked at her with a smile while he talked about his family. She wondered what he had thought of Gaby, she was always so charming, and what Gaby had thought of him. She knew her parents had liked him. She almost laughed at John's face when she entered the sitting room, and her father had just informed her that they were having dinner at home with the family. She could not imagine that John had ever had such an experience before. She was still smiling when she turned her light off and went to sleep.

The following day, as soon as he got to the office, John wrote a very polite letter to Mercedes thanking her for having him to dinner and for the wonderful time he had. He was afraid to ring Bea too soon, especially at the thought of their housekeeper Martina, picking up the phone. By lunch time he could not wait any longer and dialled the Alvarez's number, but Bea was not in; she had gone to her Japanese lesson and would be back after five. He had a meeting at five and left a message that he would call her that evening.

He rang again as soon as the meeting was over. Bea was there this time, but she said she was going out with a group of Japanese friends. "Come with us. I think you'll enjoy meeting them; we all belong to the same club."

"What club is that?"

"We raise funds for different charities, mainly children's charities."

Here was a new thing about Bea that he had not known. He had not picture her raising funds for anything. "I would love to come, but one day you must come to dinner with me alone."

"I promise." Bea giggled and hung up.

Reluctantly he had to ring again to find out where they would be meeting, because she had not told him. She replied, "Why don't you come to collect me in half an hour; is that convenient?"

"Sure." John was going to have at least a few minutes alone with her in the car!

"You are very punctual," Bea observed while John opened the door of his car.

"I was told that I should never be late in Japan."

"So true; we all learn to be on time here. I think I will be in trouble when I go back to Argentina; nobody keeps time there."

"We are quite punctual in England, too, but if you happen to be a few minutes late, it is not a big deal. In fact it is polite to be up to fifteen minutes late when you are asked to dinner, just in case the hostess is delayed by some unexpected problem."

"I am fascinated by people's cultures and habits, but it is not easy to always know what to do, and what might embarrass or offend them."

"How did you get involved in this club of yours?"

"Oh, that had a lot to do with my father. He came to Tokyo first, by himself. My sister and I had to finish the school year; my mother stayed with us and organised the packing. We arrived on Christmas Eve. My father had invited some of the junior members of the office for dinner, as well as some of the sons and daughters of the contacts he made. My sister and I were invited to go skiing with them just after New Year, but neither my sister nor I had ever been skiing before. In fact I don't think we had seen snow before! My mother insisted in coming shopping with us; she did not think we would buy clothes that would keep us warm enough. She made us buy cagoules that went from the tops of our heads to our necks, with just two holes for the eyes."

John laughed at the image. "What did your friends think?"

"They were polite enough, but you should have seen the people on the slopes. We did not know how to ski, but our new friends insisted that we should rent skis, and they made us take the lift to the slopes. My sister was braver than I and gave it a go, but I took off my skis and walked down with this red cagoule on my head and the skis on my shoulders. The snow came almost up to my waist, and it was very difficult to move. Everybody around yelled, 'Obake, obake' as I was passing by."

This time John could not stop laughing. "So they thought you were a ghost?"

"That's right! I was teased nonstop from that moment onwards. But it helped to break the ice in more than one way. We were taken for soba at lunch time—I love those noodles—and they taught us how to use chopsticks. We had a great time."

"But how did you meet your Japanese friends?"

"They were in the group; some were business acquaintances, and others had been at university with my father's staff in the office. It was a large group, and they took up the whole of the hotel. In the evening we danced and played games."

"Wow! What a fantastic way to integrate into life in Japan."

"Yes, it was. We have never looked back; we love it here."

"I think I will like it very much, too," John told Bea as they arrived.

"I hope so. I don't think there are many people who don't like it."

Bea's friends were waiting at one of the tables, sitting on cushions on the tatami floor; they had left their shoes at the entrance. Bea and John waved at them as soon as they saw them, and the men behind the counter yelled, "Irasshaimase," which means "Welcome". Bea waved back and took John by the arm. "Hi, this is John; he has just arrived," she said in Japanese.

"Nice to meet you," said John in Japanese.

His response made everyone laugh and exclaim, "What a surprise! How come you speak Japanese?"

"I studied in England, but I'm afraid I still have a lot to learn."

They were a relaxed and jolly bunch, and they chatted away while they ate their yakitori, a dish of grilled chicken and vegetables on sticks.

On the way back to Bea's house, John thanked her for introducing him to such a nice group of friends. He assured her that it would have been difficult to have met this kind of people through his work. "In my line of work, everybody is more formal."

"Don't be so sure. When the Japanese let their hair down, they *really* do. You will see."

"Am I ever going to be able to take you out to dinner?" he asked her.

"I am free tomorrow evening. How about you?"

"At what time shall I pick you up?"

"Is seven all right?" she said with a smile.

"I will be here on the dot. Tell your parents that I am taking you to a restaurant; they can reserve a table for us wherever they want, so that

19

they can be sure we will be there," John said while she opened the door.

This time Bea laughed and gave him a peck on the cheek.

Bea recounted the evening to her parents over breakfast the following morning. Bea's father burst out laughing when she told him that he could choose the restaurant for that evening. "So, where do you want to go?" he asked.

"Daddy, don't you think you are being too hard on John? I think he is very confused by our family. You have to admit that we are a bit old-fashioned."

"My darling girl, I might be old–fashioned, but at least everybody knows that they have to respect you and your sister. I know that in England everything is more lax than in our country, but in Japan the parents are just as strict as I am."

"Fine; reserve the restaurant, then, but don't choose an expensive one."

John again took great care in his appearance, but Bea was dressed in jeans and a pullover.

"I'm sorry, John," she said. "I should have let you know in advance about the restaurant my father chose. You are looking so smart, and look at me. My father made a reservation in a very simple restaurant."

"Is your father in?" John asked.

"No, they have also gone out to dinner, to a friend's house."

"Do you have their number?"

"Yes, I do. Why?

"I will not take you to a simple restaurant on our first date. I will call and tell him that we will go to the Copacabana. I have reserved a table there."

Bea looked at John with her mouth agape. Up to know he had agreed to do everything on her father's terms.

John was not a pushover; he was going to establish his territory. The previous night when he told Bea to ask her father to reserve a restaurant, he hadn't really meant it. He had not expected Bea's father to do such a thing. He was always going to take Bea to the best restaurant in town.

Bea gave him the telephone number and ran upstairs to change.

She came down looking like a million dollars and with a huge smile. "What did he say?"

"No problem; he told me that he also liked the Copacabana and wished us to enjoy ourselves."

Bea was surprised but felt relaxed and happy. She had not seen this side of her father. Although he was a great joker and liked a good laugh, he did not like to be disobeyed. She had never been to the Copa and knew it was the in place at the moment. One could have dinner upstairs and then go down for a drink, a show, and dancing. She had dressed for the occasion and was looking forward to this new experience.

When they arrived at the restaurant, a porter opened her car door, and a very stiff maître d'hôtel guided them to their table.

"Would you like a drink, Bea?"

"I would love some wine with dinner. I'm quite hungry; I had a very small lunch."

"Let's order, then. What kind of food do you like?"

"I am not too fussy, I like almost everything."

"Do you like lobster?" John asked.

"I love lobster!"

"So do I. And to start with?"

"Could I have a salad, please?

John called the waiter—who was with them in the blink of an eye—and ordered the food and a bottle of Sancerre.

They had a lot to say to each other. John recounted to Bea his years at boarding school and how difficult it had been in the beginning to get used to it. He had missed the days on the beach, when he and his mother lived in the Cape, but slowly he became adjusted to his new life. He liked sports and had gone to Oxford on a scholarship.

For Bea, boarding school was for maladjusted children, or for those in dysfunctional families.

John explained that most children went to boarding school in England. "Perhaps it has to do with the fact that in the past, many of the parents lived in the colonies, and they sent their children to be properly educated in England."

"I think my mother will be horrified when I tell her this. She would accept finishing school, but boarding school? No, no, no."

John laughed. They were so different, and yet the attraction that they had for each other was visible. He thought that Bea felt comfortable with him, and he already felt something for her.

They went down and watch the show, which was perhaps a little risqué for Bea, but she took it well. Then they danced until closing time.

CHAPTER THREE

Bea went with just a glass of orange juice the following morning. She had overslept and had to rush to be ready for mass with her family at noon. They always went together and then had lunch at the club. The afternoon was free for everyone to do what they liked.

"Tell us about last night," Mercedes asked, though it sounded more like a demand.

"It was a great evening. I had never been to the Copa. John likes lobster and dancing, just like me!" Alberto looked at Mercedes as discreetly as possible with a twinkle in his eyes. She looked away as if she had not noticed. Bea went on. "You know, in England most children are sent to boarding school—some as young as seven!"

"That is barbaric," exclaimed Mercedes. "How can a mother let a child of that age go away all on his own!"

"John told me that in the past, some children did not see their parents for years, but that they were made to write a letter every week."

"Poor children—no wonder they say that the English are cold."

"Oh, but John is not cold!"

This time Alberto could not stop himself from laughing. "And how do you know that?" he asked.

"Because of the way he talks," responded Bea, turning slightly pink in the cheeks. She was beginning to feel uncomfortable by her parents' questioning. She could not hide that she liked John—perhaps too much for her own liking. She was looking forward to meeting him again that afternoon for a walk in one of the peaceful gardens of a shrine, not far from her home.

Gaby as usual ran to meet her friends and Alberto and Mercedes took advantage to have a rest from their hectic life. Tokyo was a busy place for everybody and yet the Japanese were very calm and took their time in doing whatever they had to do. One of the things that annoyed some of the foreigners was the time they took wrapping anything you bought, especially if it happened to be a gift. But they had to admit that they did it beautifully.

"I have not been to this shrine yet."

"I come here most of the time; it's quiet and allows me to concentrate on my books."

"What books?"

"They are mainly my Japanese study books, but I also like to read translations of famous Japanese authors; I love Kawabata."

"I have not had the chance to read any of his work, although I do know that he is supposed to be one of the greatest Japanese writers. I love old French literature; I studied French as an A level."

"What is an A level?" Bea asked.

"We have quite a different education system from other nationalities. We go to primary school more or less like in any other country, but at the age of thirteen or fourteen we have to choose several subjects which are called O level, for ordinary. In a way it's a good thing because we start specialising on those subjects from an early age, but in other ways we miss out completely on the subjects that we have not chosen. The clever ones choose enough subjects to make them well educated, but the lazy ones might only take five or six. For A levels, the advanced level, you choose immediately after your O level, and then you can choose as few as two. I chose four, among them French literature."

"So you are an expert in French literature?"

"Not an expert, but I enjoy it and did well in the end."

"What did you get?"

John was now embarrassed—he had been taught not to boast, but he did not see why he should lie, either. "I got an A."

Bea smiled and held his arm. "Congratulations. I thought you were clever."

John took the opportunity of her proximity to turn around and hold her in his arms. He looked into her eyes and then kissed her, first very gently, but then he could not control his passion.

Bea had not been kissed like that before but spontaneously she let herself go. She then pulled away, feeling confused.

John put his arm around her waist and murmured in her ear, "I think I am falling for you."

Bea looked into his eyes and answered, "I think I am falling for you, too, but I do not know where this is going to lead."

"We do not have to hurry our relationship; let's get to know each other better first."

Bea smiled again, held his arm, and put her head on his bicep since his shoulder was a bit too high for her head.

CHAPTER FOUR

"Bea, my mother is coming for Christmas," John said. "I've told her about you; I think she is wondering what you are like—she doesn't trust my judgement."

"Oh dear, I am already nervous!" Bea confessed.

"She is not an easy person, but I am sure she will like you almost as much as I do."

Bea gave a chuckle, not knowing how to reply and feeling that her mouth was dry. "I will tell my parents. Do you think she might want to join us on Christmas Eve? In Argentina we celebrate Christmas on Christmas Eve, because it is usually quite hot during the day. Then we go to church either after dinner, at midnight, or on the twenty-fifth."

"I will ask her, although I am sure she will not go to church—or at least not with you. She is Church of England."

"What is that?" Bea asked.

"It is what Henry the Eighth formed after he was kicked out of the Catholic Church. It is almost the same, with only a few exceptions."

"I think I have a lot to learn before I meet her. I am terrified."

John laughed, but he was inwardly just as anxious. He knew his mother and she did not like foreigners. She had lived in South Africa and had

had servants there, but for her they were not foreigners; they had just been members of the household. She had also taken him on many trips to different parts of Europe, but those were educational trips, and she had to interact with the natives because she had no choice. Bea and her family were a completely different kettle of fish. Although John had been as discreet as possible about his feelings, she had guessed that this time John was serious about a girl.

Bea waited until that evening when they were having dinner to tell her parents about John's mother.

Mercedes asked, "What is her name?"

"I have no idea—I forgot to ask him. He just calls her Mother, and I was so nervous that I didn't care about her name."

Alberto said, "Why are you so nervous?"

"I have the impression that she is not going to like me," Bea said worriedly.

"For goodness sake, darling, why wouldn't she like you? We like John." By then John and Bea had been seeing each other for nearly three months, and he had been completely accepted. She was allowed to go out with him with hardly any questions asked. "If you think like that she is not going to like you. You must think positively and find out what she likes doing so that you can talk about it."

Bea reflected and agreed that her parents were right. She should find out more about John's mother, starting with her name.

John and Bea had arranged to meet the following afternoon. Although it was Saturday, she had to work in the morning. As usual they went for a walk in the gardens of the shrine, which had become their meeting place.

"John, I don't know your mother's name. You know almost everything about me, but I hardly know anything about you."

"That's not true; I've told you about my grandparents and my father, and even my mother's family, but you have never spoken about yours. But I know I have not told you my mother's name. It is Katherine."

"That's a beautiful name. What does she look like?"

"She is small, quite a lot shorter than you."

"Oh, but you are so tall!"

John explained, "My father was very tall, but he was dark; my mother is fair."

"So you are a mixture of the two."

"In looks, maybe, but I don't know what my father was like. I've seen his photographs, and my grandparents have sometimes mentioned certain things that he liked doing, but I think it is too painful for them, and also for my mother, to talk about him."

"I understand. Could you tell me a little about your mother's likes and dislikes?"

"She likes a good argument."

"Do you mean she likes arguing?" Bea asked.

"Not for the sake of arguing; she likes to play the devil's advocate, to bring the other side of the coin into conversations."

"Oh dear, I'm not very good at that."

"It takes practice; I am beginning to learn, but you have not had this kind of experience up to now."

"Thank you! I might not have had this kind of experience but I have had others," said Bea feeling that she had been put down."

"I know but you have lived a sheltered life. Perhaps you should go travelling by yourself to learn about the world."

"You are being very patronising, today!"

"I'm sorry; I did not mean it in a bad way. It is just that in England, girls of your age are more worldly than you."

"You should be going out with them, then." Bea was hurt; she knew that she had had a sheltered life, but she was working in the advertising and show business industries, and she had seen a few things. She had remained untouched by them because of her upbringing, but what John had just said meant that he thought she was a baby. "The fact that I don't have sex with you does not mean that I'm stupid."

"Oh, darling, it's not that. It is that you are one of the purest people I have ever met, for you everybody and everything is good. The world out there is quite different, and I am sure that when you have to face it, you will cope very well." He turned around and kissed her with the passion that she always provoked in him.

CHAPTER FIVE

Mercedes asked Katherine to tea as soon as she arrived. John had taken a few days off, and they arrived at the suggested time. Unfortunately on that same day, Bea was called by the studios, asking her to go back to retake a scene that needed a few changes. Bea had no alternative but to go. She managed to be there when they arrived, but then she had to excuse herself. John knew that she had to go and had told his mother, but nevertheless Katherine did not take it well.

Mercedes tried her best to engage her in conversation, but Katherine was monosyllabic. John ended up answering all the questions that Mercedes asked and carried on as well as possible.

In the car on their way home John, asked: "What is wrong, Mother? You hardly said a word."

"I think Bea was rude, leaving like that."

"I told you that she had to work."

"What sort of work takes her away in the middle of the afternoon, when we had been asked to tea by her mother?" Katherine complained.

"She has a contract with these people, and if a shoot goes bad, she has to go back and do it again."

"Could she not have said that she would do it in the morning or at some other time?"

"No, I already told you—she has to go when it is convenient for them."

"I do not understand why you have to get involved with this girl. Sarah is so nice. Why did you have to break up with her?"

John sighed at the old argument. "I did not break up with her; we decided that we did not care for each other enough to get married. She would not have come with me to Japan. This is my job and I like it. And I also happen to like Bea."

"She does not seem to like you very much."

John asked, "What gave you that impression?"

"I don't know. I think she is very polite and proper, but I found her rather cold."

"Cold? Bea is one of the warmest and kindest people I have ever met."

"Well, you are entitled to your opinion," Katherine said dismissively.

John did not think it was worth going on trying to convince his mother. She would find out by herself on Christmas Eve, when all the family and some other friends would be at the Alvarez's. He changed the subject. "Would you like to try some Japanese food, tonight?"

"No, thank you. I've had enough of foreign things for one day."

John inhaled deeply but did not comment. Instead he said, "How about a steak? Japanese beef is delicious."

"Fine; I will give you my opinion once I have tried it."

John took another long breath but said nothing.

During dinner, once his mother had tried some of the food, the conversation veered toward home and what Katherine had been doing during the months that John had been abroad. She was a skilled horsewoman, but now that she was in her late fifties, she did not ride as much; mostly she judged events, especially children's pony events. She was well-known and well respected in that field. She also had a good social life; she had got used to living by herself and entertained as often as she was invited out. It was probably because she had made such an effort not to fall under depression when her husband was killed, that she had become the way she was. The mother and son relationship would have been so much better if she had allowed herself to be human, but she had been brought up to hide anything that was upsetting. The problem was that by doing so, she was constantly upsetting John.

But she was interested in John's work and the new friends he had made—as long as he did not talk about Bea. She was also a keen bridge player, and John had organised a dinner and bridge night in his house the following evening with an English couple that he had met recently.

"How did you meet them?" Katherine asked.

"Through work; he works for one of the companies with which I deal. One evening they invited me to dinner, and we found out that we liked bridge. I have not asked them back yet, and I thought that you would enjoy meeting them."

"Thank you, John. I am looking forward to tomorrow night."

"How is your steak?"

"You were right; it is very tender and tasty. What is this sauce you made me put on it?"

"Soya sauce; the Japanese call it 'soyu'."

"I might take some with me when I go back."

They did not talk much on the way back home; the day had been long and they were both tired.

"Thank you, John, I have enjoyed tonight. Tomorrow morning I will go to the market with you to see what other things I do not know about. Would you like me to cook?"

"This is your holiday, Mother. I shall be doing the cooking; it's what you have taught me."

"Good night, darling. Sleep well," she said before heading to her room.

John poured himself a drink and went to the study. He was happy that he had been able to cheer up his mother, but he did not know what she was going to be like at Christmas. He had agreed with Bea not to see each other as often as they usually did, so that he could spend time with Katherine, but he was already missing her and almost picked the phone to ring her—but it was late.

That same evening at the Alvarez's while having dinner, Alberto asked Mercedes, "How did it go this afternoon?"

Gaby turned to her mother. "Yes, how did it go? What is she like?"

Bea also turned to face her mother but was quiet.

Mercedes replied, "She is not very talkative; in fact I ended up talking to John most of the time."

"Perhaps she is shy," Alberto commented.

Bea knew Katherine was not shy; John had told her enough about his mother for her to realise that things had not gone well that afternoon. She felt uneasy and longed to call John, but they had made a pact, and she was not going to break it.

CHAPTER SIX

In Argentina people did not decorate their houses as much as in other countries, but the Alvarezes did have a wreath on the door made of fresh pine cones with red bows. In the large entrance hall there was a beautiful and almost life-size nativity set; next to it the Christmas tree reached the ceiling and was decorated with red bows and silver lights. The star on the top of the tree was also silver like the lights.

This was what John and Katherine saw when they entered that evening to celebrate Christmas in a "foreign manner", as Katherine put it. Katherine had not been too sure about accepting this invitation, but John had convinced her. "You cannot refuse this invitation, Mother. They know we are free tonight, and it will offend them deeply if we don't go. We can celebrate Christmas here the way we always do tomorrow."

They were a few minutes late on purpose. John wanted the other guests to be there before they arrived so that Katherine could concentrate on them rather than on the Alvarezes.

As usual, Martina opened the door. She was very cheerful and said, "Merry Christmas, sir."

"Merry Christmas, Martina; remember my mother?"

"Yes, of course, sir; Merry Christmas, ma'am."

Katherine looked at Martina for a second. Martina came from Singapore, and her English was perfect. Reluctantly Katherine answered, "Happy Christmas."

Martina showed them into the sitting room.

Both Mercedes and Alberto approached with their hands extended. "How are you, Katherine?" Mercedes greeted them. "This is my husband, Alberto."

Alberto said, "It is a pleasure to meet you, Katherine. We are very much looking forward to hearing what you have been doing these days. What have you shown her, John?"

"We have driven around a bit. I took her to the Ginza yesterday, and the night before we went to Shinjuku."

"I don't like Shinjuku; it is too noisy for me. But I did enjoy going shopping because everything is clean and tidy." Said Katherine

"Yes, it is," said Mercedes. "They do everything to perfection." She smiled. "Let me introduce you to Vanessa and Edward Fisher." She took Katherine by the arm to where the Fishers were talking to Gaby. "This is Mrs Fellow, John's mother. But you have not met John, either; here he is. He is now a friend of the family." At that Katherine turned to John with an inquiring look. John paid no attention and shook their hands.

"And this is Gaby, our elder daughter."

Gaby extended her hand and said, "We are so happy that you can join us tonight."

Katherine smiled for the first time and shook Gaby's hand. She was much more to her liking than Bea: she had lovely hazel eyes that sparkled when she spoke and she seemed more relaxed than her sister.

John left Katherine and went to look for Bea, who was in the kitchen.

"Oh, you are here," she said, cleaning her hands and giving him a peck on the cheek. "I will be there in a minute. I have been making a dessert; I hope your mother will like it but I am not a great cook"

John wanted to hold her in his arms, but the cook was there, and he was sure that Bea would not appreciate it. Instead he said: "I am sure we will all love it."

Soon after, they went together to the sitting room. Bea thought of giving Katherine a welcoming kiss but thought better and extended her hand. Katherine had to admit that she was very beautiful and had a very gentle voice . . . but Katherine was not going to be persuaded. She shook her hand but said nothing. Fortunately at that moment the Argentine couple that had been invited arrived, and Bea went to meet them with her parents. John was left to talk to the Fishers, who wanted to know from where in England they came.

Alberto introduced the last guests to the Fishers. "These are our good friends, Angela and David Campos. We met three years ago, soon after we arrived in Tokyo." Then as Alberto guided the Camposes away from Vanessa and Edward, he added, "This is Mrs Fellow, John's mother, who is visiting him for Christmas; John has not been long in Tokyo."

Mercedes had left her husband while he did the introductions and served the drinks to supervise what was going on in the kitchen. All looked fine; even Bea's Pavlova was impressive. She then went to the dining room to check on the placement. Alberto wanted to sit in the middle of the table with her opposite him; Katherine would be on his right and Vanessa Fisher on his left, David on Mercedes' right and Edward on her left. The girls would sit at both ends of the table and John would be between Bea and Vanessa. She went back to join the others, feeling relaxed and ready for a last drink before dinner; it was going to be a long evening, and they could take their time.

Both Angela and Vanessa commented on how lovely the table looked, with the silver candelabra and the beautiful flowers. Mercedes had been learning Ikebana, and she loved making her flower arrangements.

Katherine did not comment, but her body language showed that she was also impressed by the display of leaves and flowers that covered the centre of the table.

Smoked salmon with capers, lemon quarters, and buttered bread was followed by the traditional turkey that Mercedes had found out the English liked for Christmas. But it was not brought to the table whole; the cook had already carved it in the kitchen and surrounded it with several kinds of vegetables. In a different dish there were roast potatoes, and in individual bowls were cranberry and bread sauces. Katherine raised an eyebrow when she saw that the bird was already carved, but she kept quiet. Nevertheless, she could say that it was delicious, as did everybody else. For a while they were quietly enjoying the wonderful meal. When the desserts were brought to the table, there were again exclamations of delight. Guests praised Bea's meringue covered with cream and strawberries, as well as the apple tart with homemade vanilla ice cream that the cook had prepared to end the meal. It had not been the usual Christmas dinner, but it had been excellent, and Katherine congratulated Mercedes and even Bea.

They had a couple of hours to kill till midnight, during which time they played games suggested by the Fishers, John, and the girls. When the bells started to ring, they were still behaving like children, but they stopped immediately as soon as they heard the bells and went to hug each other. John whispered, "I love you" in Bea's ear and Bea responded in the same manner. They would have loved to have been alone, somewhere far away from there.

The girls ran to the Christmas tree and brought the presents that everyone had placed under it. Bea had bought John a pair of plain gold cufflinks with his initials engraved on them. John gave Bea a jade and gold bracelet, which she put on her wrist immediately. Katherine had brought presents for the Alvarezes, as had the others, but not for anybody else. She gave Bea a pair of old silver shoe buckles, and Bea exclaimed, "They are lovely! I will make them into a belt." She went to kiss Katherine, who was surprised and inwardly happy, but she was still resisting liking the girl. Bea gave Katherine a beautiful lacquer box.

Katherine appreciated that Bea had good taste, and she said so to John on their way back home.

"Do you still think she is cold?" John asked her.

"Perhaps I was too quick to judge her. It was a good party," Katherine conceded.

John smiled inwardly.

CHAPTER SEVEN

"Hello, John," Bea said. "It has been a long time. How are you?"

"Yes it has, Bea—too long. Mother left last night. She enjoyed herself; we went to Sapporo over the New Year. She wanted to see as much of Japan as she could in the time she was here. What have you been doing?"

"The club is preparing for the annual bingo party in aid of the Red Cross. Since we always do it in the same place, there is not much work to be done—we just have to make people come. Will you?"

"Of course! I would not miss it for anything in this world."

Bea smiled. She had missed John, but she was uncertain of their relationship. Before his mother's arrival in Tokyo, she had thought that they were more or less an item, but when Katherine arrived, everything changed, and she had not seen John in the way she used to for a least a month. "Good; I will find something for you to do," she said cheerfully.

"What are you doing tonight, Bea? I'm dying to see you."

"We have a meeting about the party. You can come with me, if you like."

"If that is the only way to see you, so be it!" John sighed.

Now Bea laughed; he sounded so dramatic. "You are funny, John. We can go and have something to eat afterwards, if you like."

"I'd like that very much! When shall I collect you?"

"The meeting starts quite early, at five thirty. But I know that you work long hours; it might be better if you collect me after the meeting, and we can have dinner together."

"Great! Give me a call when you are about to be finished, and I will go wherever you are."

"I will do that. I'm glad you called," Bea said, and she hung up.

That year was particularly cold. By February Tokyo had snow almost every day. On the morning of the bingo party, they woke up to see a thick carpet of snow. The Alvarezes' driver had taken precautions and had put on chains. John had also bought chains in expectation of going skiing in the near future. Some of the members of the club were not able to arrive on time for the party.

"John, we need your help," Bea told him.

"What is wrong, Bea?"

"We are short of members. Will you call the numbers?"

"I have never done a thing like that."

"It does not matter, we have a little booklet on how to do it; I am sure you can memorize it in a short time."

"How do I get hold of it?"

"I have it here. I can ask the driver to get it to you."

"All right, Bea. I am doing this for you."

"Thank you, John. I will see you there."

Bea had to go early, and the driver took her first and then went back to the house to collect her parents and sister. Despite the weather most everyone who had bought tickets managed to be there. They gathered in the hall, queuing to buy the bingo cards. John had asked Bea's mother to look after his. He thought that although he was working, he should contribute to the charity. He was not at all sure that he would be able to call the numbers in a professional way; all this business of "twenty-two, two little ducks" and so on was new to him. He remembered playing bingo as a child at school, but that was a long time ago.

All was going well when suddenly there was a commotion at the Alvarezes's table. Mercedes was making funny gestures that John could not interpret. He had no alternative but to go on calling the numbers.

As soon as it was all over, the Alvarezes almost ran to meet John. "You won!" they all said at the same time.

John was still disorientated. "What did I win?"

"A set of *Encyclopaedia Britannica*; I tried to signal it to you," Mercedes said cheerfully.

"Ha ha, I can't believe it! I never win anything. You bring me good luck!" John answered while giving Mercedes a hug.

The organisers were going to go out to dinner together, but because of the weather they decided to go back home as soon as possible. John was invited to have dinner at the Alvarezes, which he accepted with the anticipation of being able to talk to Bea alone, even if it was for a short time.

Despite the fact that his mother had not taken to Bea completely, he was sure that she would with time. But he had been thinking that perhaps Bea should go to England and see for herself what life was like there before he proposed to her. It was not going to be easy to convince Alberto to let her go, and he was not sure that Bea would want to go even with her parents blessing. She was busy with her work, which she liked, and she had never travelled by herself before. However, he loved her so much, and he was almost sure that Bea felt the same for him. But for some reason he was worried about their future together; she was so different from anyone that he had ever met before—so different from all the girls he that had met before.

CHAPTER EIGHT

It was not until Bea's twenty-first birthday party that John gathered up enough courage to ask her to marry him. It was late, and most of the guests had gone home; only a few of them, Bea's closest friends, remained on the dance floor. Bea had her head on John's chest, and John had to lean over to whisper in her ear, "Bea, I love you so much. Will you marry me?"

Bea did not move, and John thought she had not heard. Then she lifted her head and, with tears in her eyes, said, "That is the best birthday present." She then got on her tip toes to reach his lips and kissed him with a passion that John had never experienced.

All those around them, including Gaby, saw this and stopped in their tracks. Bea was not known for this kind of demonstration, and they guessed what was going on.

When they finally separated, John said, "I think she said yes!"

Gaby was the first one to run and hug her sister and future brother-in-law; she was followed by all the others who surrounded them, wanting to know the wedding day. Gaby whispered in Bea's ear, "I think you'd better stop this until you talk to Mummy and Daddy."

Bea realised that although she was sure that her parents liked John, she was not sure whether or not they would get their blessing. "I think I'd better talk to my parents before we decide on the date," she announced.

"I think *I* should talk to your parents, too," John said.

It was time for the guests to depart, except for John, who stayed a bit longer.

"Bea, can I come tomorrow and talk to your father? Will he be at home?"

"You know that we go to church in the morning, and then to lunch at the club on Sundays. I think the best time for you to come is at about six, when we usually have a drink before supper."

"Will you tell them first?" John asked.

"I don't know. What do you think I should do?"

"Ask Gaby; she will tell you what the best way is."

"I love you," said Bea as she closed the door behind John.

The next morning, after a rather short and restless sleep, Bea went to wake Gaby, who was a bit disoriented to start with but paid attention when her sister asked, "What shall I do? I don't know whether to tell Mummy and Daddy, or to leave John to do it."

Gaby shook her head for a minute or two. "Perhaps it might be better that you tell them first, just in case. They like John but marriage is different. Spare him a bad time."

"You are right. Will you come down with me?"

"All right; just let me have a shower and I'll be dressed in ten minutes."

Both girls showed up in the dining room where their parents were having breakfast.

"Hello, girls, we did not think that you would come down for breakfast today. Did you enjoy yourselves last night?" their mother asked. Alberto and Mercedes had gone to bed after Bea had blown out her candles.

"It was a great party; thank you, Mummy," Bea said as she and Gaby kissed their mother. "Thank you, too, Daddy," she added before sitting down. "I have something important to tell you."

"Is there something wrong, darling?"

"No, Daddy. John proposed to me last night."

Alberto turned to Mercedes and winked at her. Mercedes got up, and this time it was her turn to kiss their daughter.

"Are you happy? Do you want to marry John?" she asked.

Bea's face said it all, but nevertheless she answered, "Yes, it is!"

Her father walked over and kissed Bea on her forehead. "We are very happy for you, darling. John is a wonderful man."

"John is coming this evening to ask you for your blessing; is that all right?"

"Of course; there is some champagne left in the fridge from last night," replied Alberto.

As they were going back to their rooms to get ready for mass, Alberto said to his wife, "Was I right?"

"You win. I was not sure that this was so serious. But there are a few things that worry me."

"What is it now?"

"John is great, but we saw what Katherine is like. Bea will have to deal with people like her in England. Here in Japan we are all foreigners, but in England she will be the only one."

"I am sure there are plenty of foreigners in England, darling."

"No doubt, but not in John's family. And there is also the question of the Malvinas."

"You should call them Falklands. Nobody knows what the Malvinas are."

"Don't be silly, Al; we know what the Malvinas are, and if there is a conflict, everybody will know about them."

"Why should there be a conflict? They took them over one hundred years ago, and there has been no conflict up to now."

"Still, it worries me." Mercedes' father had been a general in the army and had also been very patriotic—as was all his family. He had passed away a couple of years ago, but Mercedes' brother was in the air force and was even more patriotic than his father. The Malvinas was the one thing that separated them from being friendly with the Brits.

"Today is a great day for our daughter. Let's leave it at that," replied Alberto, kissing his wife.

It was very difficult for Bea to concentrate on the service that day. Mercedes was not much better than her daughter; she wanted her to be happy, but there were so many differences. She had seen that Katherine did not take to her, and although she was polite to Bea, she had made no effort to talk to her and had kept her distance. Neither Katherine nor John was Catholic—what sort of wedding were they going to have? She could not stop worrying.

Alberto and Gaby kept the conversation at lunch going. Bea's thoughts were on John and their future. She was not worried; she knew there were differences, but by now she knew John, and she knew they would overcome any difficulty. The most important hurdle had been telling her parents, and the fact that they were happy for her was all that counted.

On the other hand Mercedes wanted to talk to John about her qualms.

John was surprised by Alberto's welcome. "My good man!" Alberto said, giving him a hug. "We are delighted by the news." John would find out with time how affectionate the Argentines were. Men hugged and kissed each other if they knew each other well. Because Alberto had studied in England, he knew that one did not do that there, but now the John was going to be a member of his family he was going to be treated in the Argentine way.

"So Bea has already told you?" John asked.

"This morning at breakfast, we have been looking forward to this evening all day."

Alberto was making John's life very easy. John had been practicing what he was going to say for hours, but Alberto seemed to have given them his blessing already.

"Come in; Mercedes will be down in a minute."

Mercedes's welcome was warm, but John felt that she was not herself.

"We are very happy with the news, John, but I have a few things to ask you."

At that moment Bea arrived and kissed John on the lips. She had decided that now that she was twenty-one and engaged, she would not hide her feelings for John.

Her parents looked at each other a bit surprised, but Alberto continued smiling.

"Thank you for telling your parents; I was not sure what I was going to say," John said.

Bea replied, "I spoke with Gaby as you told me to, and we thought it was better like this."

John put his arms around Bea and said to the Alvarezes, "I love your daughter very much, and I hope that we will be married soon."

They sat down, and Alberto went to get the champagne that was in a bucket on the side board.

Bea went out of the room to call Gaby, who was waiting impatiently upstairs in her room.

When everyone gathered again, Alberto raised his glass and said, "To a very long and happy life together." They all drank to the new couple.

"Thank you, Alberto, I promise to look after Bea," John said.

"I'm sure you will," Alberto said as he sat down.

Mercedes could not hide what was troubling her anymore, and she repeated what she had said to Alberto that morning.

John said, "I understand your concern. I have also been wondering how Bea would take to living in England. Perhaps she should go there before we set a date for the wedding."

"I know I have been protected all my life, and I have never lived alone, but I am not a child and will make those decisions myself," Bea said firmly. Again she had surprised everyone. She would have never spoken like that in the past. She went on. "The club is organising a charity ball; it was my idea, and I must help as much as possible. I will think about going to England before we get married, but first I will do what I have to do here. If I got used to Japan, I can get used to England, too. John will help me."

"Darling, in Japan we are all foreigners, but in England you will be the one who will stick out," Mercedes told her daughter what she had said to her husband.

"I am used to sticking out, Mother. This is why I got the job I am doing—it is what they want."

Mercedes gasped for air; she could not make her family understand what she meant, but she thought that John did. "What about the Falklands?" she asked.

Now John laughed. "I do not think many people in the UK know what the Falklands are or where they are."

"Don't they?" Mercedes was surprised.

"What are the Falklands?" asked Bea, not knowing what they were talking about.

"The Malvinas," clarified Alberto.

"Ah! What is wrong with them?"

"They belong to the British."

"But they are in our territory," said Bea, surprised by this news.

"You see?" Mercedes continued. "What will happen if there is a war?"

This time it was Gaby who spoke. "Don't say that, Mother. Why should there be a war?"

"True," agreed John. "They have been in our possession for over one hundred years, and nothing has happened up to now."

"And if something does happen, what will you two do?"

"I imagine that we will have to overcome many hurdles in our married life. If there is a war between our two countries, we will deal with it then."

Mercedes could not let go of her misgivings. "Are you going to marry in the Catholic Church?"

"That will be decided by Bea," said John, looking at Bea.

"We can get married in both churches, if you like," Bea answered.

"There is no need for that." John said.

"What will your mother say?"

"I know she is difficult; I have already said that to you. But I don't think she will interfere," John said.

"Good! Let's have more champagne," Alberto said, and he got up to go and fetch it, apparently relieved that this conversation was over. "Who would like sushi?" he said while pouring the champagne.

"That is a wonderful idea, Daddy," Bea said. "What do you think, John?"

"I'm all for it," he replied, hugging her.

CHAPTER NINE

That night it was Bea who could not sleep. She did understand her mother's misgivings and wondered what would happen if indeed the UK and Argentina went to war, but she could not believe that that would happen. What really worried her was Katherine. She had been brought up to respect her elders, and she was going to have to be strong to make this marriage work; she loved John too much not to try. Perhaps she should go and see for herself what the English were like in their own land.

The charity ball was scheduled to take place in the next six months; Bea's responsibilities included looking for prizes for the raffle or auction during the ball, as well as selling as many tables as possible. With her job and her Japanese lessons, she did not know when she would have time to go on this trip. She finally went to sleep.

In the morning she called John. Up to now it had always been John who rung Bea. "I am sorry to ring so early, but I must go to work in ten minutes. Could we meet tonight?"

"Of course; is there anything wrong?"

"I have been thinking, and I would like to share my thoughts with you."

"Are you sure there is nothing wrong?"

Bea laughed. "Of course there is nothing wrong!"

"I will see you tonight, then. I love you."

Bea worked all morning at the studio and then set out to visit all those who were on her list. It included companies, embassies, ministries, and of course all her friends. They needed at least five hundred people to make the ball a success. She was going to leave her friends until the end; Bea was sure that they would go to the ball even if the tickets were not cheap.

She started by trying to get prizes for the raffles. Since "airlines" began with an *a*, and she had no idea of how to start with the task that she had been given, she chose to visit as many as possible that afternoon. She succeeded in getting two tickets to Istanbul with a Turkish airline and two tickets to Rome on Alitalia; one of her friends who worked there introduced her to the marketing manager. They also bought tickets for the ball; in exchange they had asked for advertising and the logo of their airline on the raffle tickets.

John was waiting for her when she finally got home.

"I am so sorry to have kept you waiting; I have been looking for prizes for the raffle and trying to sell tickets at the same time."

"How did it go?" John asked.

"Great. I got two tickets to Istanbul and two tickets to Rome."

"From the same airline?"

"Nobody is that generous! A Turkish airline gave me two, and Alitalia gave me the other two."

"Do they know this?"

"Who?"

"The two airlines, you silly girl."

"Of course they know—they gave me tickets; I have it written down," Bea said matter-of-factly.

"I mean does Alitalia know that the Turkish airline has given you tickets, and vice versa?"

"No. I did not think it was any of their business to know what anybody else was giving."

"What have they asked in exchange?"

"They both want advertising and the logo of their airline on the raffle tickets."

"I think you might get into trouble."

"What do you mean?" Bea asked, not feeling as confident as she had been a few minutes before.

"When companies that do the same thing give you something, they expect to be the only ones. You should tell them what you have done."

"Oh, no! They might take the tickets away!"

"Let me see what you can do for each one in a different way. You should also talk to your father," John suggested.

Bea realised that she did not know many things and her good spirits were collapsing—why couldn't she even do this simple task well!

John saw her face and hugged her. "Darling, how could you have known that? I do because I work in a company, and this is the way we operate. Don't worry, we will find a way. Now, what was it that you wanted to share with me?"

Bea did not feel like sharing more things with John at that moment; she felt stupid and wanted to go and hide in her room. "I'll come down in a minute. I would like to have a shower and change, if you don't mind. You know where the drinks are; get yourself one." She gave him a kiss and went up.

Under the shower she let go and cried. "I am not even capable of executing my own idea. Am I going to spend the rest of my life relying on other people?" But then she composed herself. "How was I to know about the airlines? They never said I could not accept tickets from any other company. Of course John knows this because of his company, but I am not working for a company—I am trying to make money for a charity. I will go tomorrow and tell them. I don't need John to do it for me."

She felt much better after the talk she had with herself, and she looked as lovely as ever when she went down. "I'm sorry I have taken ages, but I needed to freshen up."

"Don't worry, this is the first time you have ever kept me waiting."

"I don't like to keep people waiting—as I don't like to be kept waiting either."

"Where would you like to go, my darling?" said John as he moved closer to her.

"Anywhere were we can talk; somewhere quiet."

John looked worried again, but he did not seem to want to press her. "I know just the right place."

In the car they listened to the radio. Both of them had a lot on their minds, and they wanted to wait until they were seated comfortably before embarking on a long conversation.

Not until their drinks were brought to the table did Bea have the presence of mind to say, "I know that you want to help me, but I have been working in the club for over two years now. The airlines never said that I should not get tickets from any others. We will put their logos and advertise both airlines as being very generous towards this charity."

"I'm sorry, Bea. I should not interfere with your work," John admitted.

Bea smiled and changed the conversation. "John, I know you think like my mother. You want me to go away so that I can mature, but—" John interrupted. "It is not that I want you to mature—I know you are. It is just that England is so different from Argentina and Japan that I believe it would be good if you went to stay with my mother for a few days."

"No, I will not stay with your mother. I am not marrying her. But perhaps it would be good for me to travel not only to England but to other countries on my way there. I have not been to Southeast Asia or to Europe. I will make a plan. The problem might be my father, but I am twenty-one now. By the way, have you told your mother about us?"

"I was going to call her tonight, but when you rang this morning, I decided I would wait until we had our talk."

"Do you want to tell her, or do you want to wait until I come back from my trip?"

"Do you think you are going to have second thoughts once you have been abroad?" John said, looking worried.

"John, I want to marry you. I love you and do not think that going on a trip will change my mind . . . but you might change yours."

"No way! I think about you all the time; I want to live with you, have children with you, and grow old with you."

Bea burst out laughing and held his hands across the table. "I want all that, too. As soon as I finish with all the preparations for the ball, I will go away. In the meantime, if you like we can set a date so that my mother can start the preparations for the wedding."

"But don't you want to take part in the preparations?"

"In Argentina, it is the mother of the bride who organises everything."

"In England, the bride always has a say."

"Perhaps I will choose the music. No, we will choose the music together. How is that?"

"If you like, I will, but I sincerely would like you to choose it."

"I love Shubert's 'Ave Maria'; I would like to enter the church while they are playing it," Bea said, looking up as if she was already seeing herself going down the aisle.

"Anything you like, my darling," John said, but he suddenly realised that his mother was not very enthused about the Virgin Mary. He was not going to have an easy time, and he was not sure he wanted to tell Katherine about the wedding yet.

CHAPTER TEN

Bea arrived that day at lunch time full of beans. She announced proudly to her family, "I have sold three tables today."

"That is great, darling; to whom?" Asked Albert

"To start with, I went to the Cuban embassy."

"You didn't!"

"Of course I did! They were charming."

"The Argentine embassy will never talk to me again. We do not have diplomatic relations with Cuba." Added her father

"Well that is too bad, because they have also bought a table."

"No!" Alberto shouted.

"Yes, Daddy, they did."

"Do they know you are my daughter?"

"The Argentine ambassador does; I had coffee with him."

"You spoke to the ambassador?"

"Who else?" Bea said.

"You must make an appointment before talking to the ambassador."

"If he could not have seen me, he would have said so. As it was, I had a really nice chat with him over a cup of coffee. The Cuban ambassador offered me a glass of sherry, but I decline because it was too early. They were both charming. Then I went to the Foreign Ministry, but the Foreign Minister was not available, so I talked to several other people who decided to share a table among themselves."

Alberto and Mercedes were staring at her with their mouths open, looking at their youngest daughter. Gaby burst out laughing and hardly controlling herself. "Daddy, I hope you have some savings, because you might be out of a job very soon. Ha!"

"I do not know why you and John make such a fuss about things," Bea said.

"What did he make a fuss about?" Albert sounded very nervous now.

"He told me that companies who make the same products and donate one want to be the only ones doing so."

"He is right," Alberto confirmed.

"I'm sorry, Daddy, but I do not think that is right. Nobody who has donated said anything of the sort. I am working to make money for the children's charity; I thought they were doing it for charity, not only for their benefit. I know our club has never done anything like this before, but we are going to get there. As soon as I finish with this, I will go abroad."

This time Alberto and Mercedes were completely thrown off balance: "Where are you planning to go?" they asked without even thinking of objecting.

Bea replied, "Mummy and John have said that I should go to England before we get married. But the trip to England is very long, so I am planning to stop off at all the places where the plane lands. There are many different routes, so I will have to check them out."

Alberto and Mercedes looked at each other again and asked, "With whom are you going to stay?"

"No one—I will stay in hotels. I have saved a lot in three years, and I can afford my ticket and good hotels."

Her parents were quiet for a while, but Gaby was very excited for her sister. "That is great, Bea! I wish I could go with you."

"That is a great idea! Why don't you plan this trip together?" Mercedes suggested.

"I'm sorry, Gaby, but I have to do this by myself. Everybody thinks I am an innocent child who does not know anything about life. I have to prove to myself that I can do this."

Alberto said, "Will you at least let us give you some names and addresses? You never know, they might come handy."

"Fine, Daddy, if that makes you happy."

Everybody became quiet after that.

Bea had already been planning her trip in her head and was going to get in touch with a travel agent whom she knew that very afternoon.

Alberto was surprised but also proud of his younger daughter. She was finally showing that she was not a baby anymore.

Mercedes was regretting having said that Bea should go to England; she had thought, as John had, that she would go and stay with Katherine.

Gaby was over the moon and thanked her sister in her mind for having had the guts to do what Gaby had wanted to do for a long time. She said to herself, *Now I will do it.*

That afternoon Bea rang John: "Hello, darling." It was the second time that Bea had rung him, and it still surprised him. "I have told my parents that I am going abroad as soon as the preparations for the ball are ready."

Now John was really surprised. "Didn't they object?"

"They did not say anything."

"I can't believe it!"

"I just told them what my plans were, and they only asked me if I would let them give me some names and addresses."

"Well, that really surprises me." John was beginning to realise he had underestimated Bea.

"You shouldn't be. Up to now, I have done everything I have been told because I should respect my parents and I live in their house. But now that I am twenty-one, I should start being more independent. Besides, I am not asking for money; I have my savings and shall pay for this trip myself."

"Of course, darling; we all forget how hard you work. You must be quite well paid."

"As a matter of fact, I am, but I will not tell you how much I earn because you might get jealous," Bea teased.

"All right, all right; I am going to have to be a bit more careful with you."

"I think you will." They hung up, she feeling contented and he bewildered but happy.

CHAPTER ELEVEN

"Hello, Martin. It's Bea here."

"Hello there, how are you?" her travel agent friend replied.

"Fine, thank you. I am calling you because I would like to go to England, but I would like to stop in different countries on the way. What do you recommend?"

"Come and see me, and we can work it out together."

"Are you free this afternoon?" Bea asked.

"I would be around five. Can you come then?"

"I'll be there."

She had time to go and visit other embassies before that. She said to herself, "I wonder how many more blunders according to John and father I will make this afternoon!"

A bit past five o'clock, she arrived at Martin's office. "Hi, sorry I'm late," she said.

"That suits me fine, Bea; it gave me time to put a bit of order on my desk. So when do you want to go on this trip?"

"In about three months, if possible; I have to be back for the ball."

"What ball is this?"

"Ah, I had forgotten to ask you—would you buy a ticket?"

"A ticket for what?"

"The ball."

"But you have not told me what ball this is!"

"Sorry. The club is organising a charity ball in aid of orphaned children, and I have to sell as many tables as possible and also get some donations. By the way, perhaps you can also donate a trip somewhere?"

Martin laughed. "You cannot stay still, can you, Bea? You are always running here and there."

"Am I?"

"Yes, you are. You came to buy a trip to London, and here you are asking me to give you a whole lot of things."

"I only asked you if you wanted to buy a ticket for the ball, and donate something," Bea said defensively.

"I know, I know; you are great. Let us start with your trip. You can go via Hong Kong, and from there you could make a jump to Cambodia and then go to India, Greece, Italy, France, and finally London."

"It sounds wonderful! How long will it take?"

"It depends on how long you want to stay in each country; you might want to go sightseeing in some of them."

"I have a month; that will give me time to be back in plenty of time for the ball."

"Let me work it out for you. Do you want hotels, too?"

"Yes, please—good ones. I will be on my own."

"On your own?" Martin repeated. "What does your father think of that?"

"I am twenty-one, remember? You were at my party."

"You have changed in a few weeks, Bea. What has got into you?"

Bea smiled but did not answer. She did not want to disclose her engagement to John before talking to him. "Please call me when you have worked this out. I am open for ideas. And don't forget the ball."

Martin laughed again and got up to give her a kiss on the cheek. "I will be in touch soon."

Bea's duties for the ball were over; she was free to go on her trip and come back before it took place.

Mercedes said to her husband, "Darling, please call them and let them know where Bea will be staying. I am sure she will not ring anyone."

"Fine; I have connections in almost every country she is visiting. Has Bea given you the dates when she is going to be in each place?"

"Yes, I have it all here."

"Let me have them, and I will send a telegram to everyone I know. Are you happy now?" Alberto asked.

"Yes, thank you." Mercedes gave him a peck on the cheek and went to check on Bea's packing. When she arrived in her daughter's room, she said, "You should take one or two warm outfits, too, darling. It will not be that warm in England."

"I only have twenty kilo allowance."

"Put your shoes in the hand luggage."

"It will weigh a tonne."

"Don't take so many. Let me see what you have packed."

Bea took a deep breath and stepped aside; she knew her mother meant well, and she was going to miss her a lot.

Once Mercedes had rearranged the suitcase, they weighed it again.

"Mother you are a genius! I still have a kilo left. I will take another pair of shoes."

Mother and daughter embraced. Then Mercedes said, "Darling, I am going to miss you so much. You will look after yourself, won't you?

"I will; please don't worry. I will be fine and will be back in no time at all."

That evening she was going to say good-bye to John; her parents would be taking her to the airport the next morning.

"Are you all packed up?" John asked her.

"Thanks to my mother. She found a way to make my suitcase lighter. I know I have a lot to learn, John."

"We all have a lot to learn. I don't think we ever stop learning."

"Have you told your mother that I am going?"

"Yes. Here is her address and telephone number. She lives about three hours by train from London; you might want to stay one night with her."

"No—I will go to see her, but I will not stay. I have an uncle in the embassy in London and some Japanese friends as well, but I have made reservations in hotels everywhere."

"I hope you have a wonderful time. I am going to miss you so much," said John, holding her hands across the table at the restaurant where they were having dinner.

Bea shed a little tear but soon composed herself. "I am very excited about the trip, but at the same time I can't wait to come back. Mother is arranging everything for the wedding—she has also designed my wedding dress."

"Don't you mind?" John asked.

"No, I quite like it. Our dress maker is making it; I shall try it on when I come back. There is plenty of time for her to finish it."

"Are you happy with the hotel my parents have chosen for the reception?"

"It is great; I could not ask for more."

They kissed across the table and ordered dinner. Soon it was getting late, and Bea went home because she had to get up early.

Alberto, Mercedes, and Gaby took Bea to the airport and helped her with all the formalities. "You will have plenty of opportunities to do this yourself; let us help you just this once," her father said, lifting the suitcase onto the weighing machine.

Bea was now tense—it dawned on her of all a sudden that what she wanted to do was happening, but she had not really understood up to this moment what it meant. "Daddy, I love you very much, and I am very grateful for everything you have done for me."

Alberto hugged his daughter and held back a tear. He could not say anything and felt a ball in his throat.

Unexpectedly, Mercedes took over. She held her daughter in her arms for a few seconds and said, "I know you are sensible, Bea, but please be careful any way."

Gaby kissed her sister. "Thank you for opening the door, little sister. I am planning my own trip, but with friends—I don't think I would enjoy myself alone."

These words made Bea even more edgy, but she could not show them that now. She waved good-bye as she disappeared through the departure doors.

CHAPTER TWELVE

In the plane seat next to her sat a priest. This only increased Bea's anxiety; she wanted to turn back and be pampered by her parents. She also wanted to be with John; she promised herself to ring him as soon as she got to Hong Kong—that was, if nothing happened to the plane. She prayed until she was interrupted by the stewardess offering her lunch. It was the distraction she needed. The priest next to her asked, "Have you been to Hong Kong before?"

"No, this is my first time."

"I go there often on my way to other Southeast Asian countries. I was trained as an architect before I became a priest, and now I deal with housing complexes for the poor."

"I never thought that priests could do that."

"Oh, we do many things that nobody thinks we do. Many of us join our congregations after we have studied for another career."

"Why is that? I would have thought that you studied that career because it is what you wanted to do," Bea said.

"Yes, but sometimes we are not completely fulfilled by it; something is not completely right. Then, as it happened with me, you feel the need to help others in a different way."

"How do you make the change?"

The priest said, "In my case, I went to see my doctor because I did not feel happy, and he sent me to a counsellor. After talking to him, I went to confession, and it was then that I realised that it was what I wanted to do. I went to the seminary for seven years; I have only been a priest for three."

"Your life is most fascinating," Bea said, feeling more relaxed and cheerful.

At the first airport she saw two familiar faces and ran to them. "What a coincidence to meet you here!"

"It is no coincidence; your father sent us a telegram, and we want you to stay with us."

Bea said, "Oh, but I have a hotel reservation."

"You don't anymore—we cancelled it." Bea looked at them, not knowing what to say. "Don't worry, you will be completely independent. You will have your own room with a bathroom, and we will give you a key to come and go as you like. By the way, your father did not ask us to cancel your reservation; we just did it."

"I don't know what to say. I mean, thank you very much."

On the way to their home, Bea wanted to see everything around her, and the Garcias pointed out one or two places of interest that she could visit. "There are many tours that you can take, but you can also take public transport to see the sights," said Florencia.

"I have a friend who used to work in Tokyo and is now in Hong Kong. He knows I am coming; he has probably been wondering where I am," Bea said.

"You'd better give him a ring when we get home. You can also ring your parents if you like; I am sure they will want to know about your trip."

The flat was enormous, on the hills overlooking the bay with a magnificent view. Bea had been given a beautiful room with a sitting area and en-suite bathroom. She also had a telephone by her bed.

"It is lovely! Thank you very much. I am sure I will be much more comfortable here than in the hotel."

"If you want to have dinner with us, we will have it at seven thirty, but if you want to go out, please do so."

Bea smiled and hugged Florencia and Nicolas.

She rang her friend Chris, who had indeed been wondering where she was. "I rang you at your hotel, but they told me you were not there," Chris said.

"I know; some good friends of my parents cancelled my reservation and collected me at the airport."

"Would you like to go out to dinner?"

"I am little tired, but if you are free tomorrow, I would like to see you."

"Sure! We can go sightseeing. Would you like to go to Macao? We could have lunch there, have a look around, and try our luck at the casino."

Bea said, "I have never been to a casino."

"Macao is famous for it. Shall I collect you at about ten?"

"That sounds great. Thank you, Chris, I will be waiting."

Bea thought that it would be impolite not to have dinner with the Garcias that night. She went to tell them, "I have arranged to see my friend tomorrow. We are going to Macao."

"What a good idea. Macao is a Portuguese colony; its architecture is beautiful, and the food is delicious. There are quite a few gambling places, too," Said Nicolas

"That is what Chris said; we might try our luck at one of them."

"Just don't get carried away."

"Oh, I do not think there is a chance that I will. I have never been to one, and I will be very careful."

Bea then went to call her parents. "I am at the Garcias', they cancelled my hotel reservation, and I have a beautiful suite here."

"That is very kind of them! We never asked them to have you to stay," Mercedes said.

"They said so and told me that I can come and go as I please. I am going to Macao tomorrow with Chris."

"Does John know you are going out with him?"

"I never thought of telling him," Bea admitted.

"You should, Bea—you are engaged to him."

"There are a few things I have to get used to, Mummy."

Bea hung up and immediately dialled the operator's number. "I would like to make a call to Tokyo, please." She gave the number and then waited to be connected. "John?"

"Hello, darling, did you have a good trip?"

Bea told him all about it, and then came the difficult part. "Would you mind if I go to Macao with a friend tomorrow?"

"Why should I mind? You are there to see as much as possible."

"This friend happens to be a man I met in Tokyo a couple of years ago, and he is now working in Hong Kong. I should have told you before, but I completely forgot. If you mind, I will cancel."

"Don't be silly! Go and enjoy yourself; just don't do anything that I would not do," John joked.

"I promise!"

After she put the telephone down, she wondered what John had meant but shook her head. She went to wash and change for dinner.

"Did you have a good time?"

"Look!" Bea said to Florencia while raising her arm to show her a beautiful gold bracelet formed with squares displaying Chinese characters and flowers.

"Did you get that in Macao? The city is well-known for having affordable gold."

"Yes, I did. We had a great time. First we went for a walk, then we ate in a wonderful old-fashioned Portuguese restaurant, and after another walk we went to the casino, where I won a lot of money!"

"So you bought yourself this lovely bracelet?"

"Chris told me that Macao's money was useless in Hong Kong, but it was very difficult to change it back to Hong Kong dollars. Since there was a jeweller next to the casino, I went in and asked the man what I could buy with my money, and he showed me the bracelet. I fell in love with it; it is so different from anything I have."

Florencia gave Bea a hug. Bea was such a sweet girl and seemed so innocent despite her years that Florencia felt very maternal towards her. "What are you doing tonight, sweetheart?" she asked.

"Chris has invited me to a party a friend of his is having."

"We are also going out. I was going to ask you if you wanted to come with us, but since you already have plans, we won't press you. Do you have plans for tomorrow?"

Be said, "I meant to ask you—is there a church around here?"

"No, there is nothing but a few houses around here. We are going to church at twelve, and then we will have lunch at the club. Would you like to come with us?"

"I would love to. That is exactly what we do every Sunday at home."

"Good. After lunch we can take you to have a look around the island. On Monday, if you like, I could go with you to Kowloon; it is not as pretty as Hong Kong, but you could do some shopping."

"It will have to be something that I can take in my hand luggage because my suitcase is quite heavy already. I would like to buy something for my future mother-in-law."

"Are you getting married, Bea?"

"I'm sorry, Florencia—it just came out. We have not told anybody yet. Mother is sending the invitations soon."

"That is wonderful!" Florencia said, giving her another hug.

"It is the reason of my trip. John is English, and he wants me to go and see for myself if I want to live there."

"I do not know how long you are planning to stay in England, but I do not think you can give yourself an idea in a short time. What is important is that you and John are happy together."

"That is exactly the way I think, but Mother is also worried about the Malvinas."

"Ah! Yes, that might be a worry, but you cannot base your marriage on those islands. I hope you are very happy, darling."

"Thank you," answered Bea, giving her a kiss. She was very fond of Florencia.

Bea had the chance to see a bit of the old Great Britain at the club. They seemed to be very relaxed in their sport outfits, but it was all a show. They talked in such a way that it was difficult for Bea to understand what they were saying; it was as if they had something in their mouths. They also kept to themselves and hardly nodded when they greeted a face that was not British. The Garcias were used to that treatment and paid no attention.

Bea was leaving on Tuesday, so she had only the Monday to see the rest of Hong Kong and do some shopping in Kowloon.

"I need another table cloth and twelve napkins," Florencia informed Bea in the car.

"I am not sure what I want to buy yet, but it has to be small. I might buy a few presents to take back, if they are small enough."

"I will take you first to my usual shop, but if you cannot find anything there, there are many shops all over the place."

Florencia ordered her table cloth and napkins, having chosen the material and motifs while Bea looked for something, without knowing what she wanted.

"How are you doing?" inquired Florencia after having finished her shopping.

"I am totally undecided, I like everything, but I do not know what I want."

"Let's have a look in other shops."

"Thank you. I hope I won't keep you too long."

"I have all day, darling; it is a pleasure having you with us." The Garcias had no children of their own and took every opportunity to see their friends' children.

In one of the shops Bea spotted a delightful square box made of rosewood with a jade inlay. She remembered that Katherine had been pleased with the lacquer box at Christmas and thought that she would like this one, too. "What do you think, Flor?"

"Oh! It is lovely."

"I love boxes; I collect them and also like to give them to people."

"This one is particularly beautiful."

"I like these two little Buddhas as well," Bea said to the attendant. One Buddha was made of jade, the other of ivory. Very quietly she added, "Please wrap another box."

"What is your mother tongue?" the Chinese clerk asked her.

"Spanish," Bea replied. "Why?"

"I have a letter here from somewhere in Spain, but I do not know what it says."

"I can read it for you," Bea volunteered.

The clerk went to fetch the letter while one of the others wrapped the objects that Bea had chosen. "Here it is."

Bea read quickly. "This person would like to order two lamps in the same style that they bought before; it says that you have the record under the name of Pascual."

"Yes, yes, I remember. Thank you very much!"

When Bea went to pay, she found that one of the figurines was not in the bill. "Excuse me, you have forgotten to bill me for the ivory figurine."

"I have not forgotten; it is a present for you, for reading the letter," said the clerk, who happened to be the owner of the shop.

"That was nothing," Bea said while smiling.

"For you, maybe not; for me, it was a lot."

Florencia had joined them at that moment and explained to Bea, "They are always very generous. You must accept the gift; it will make him happy."

Before leaving for her next flight, Bea hugged Florencia and Nicolas and said, "You have been so kind to me. I would have never been able to do everything I did without your help. I hope you will be able to come to the wedding."

"We would not miss it for anything," they replied, still embracing her.

Bea waved good-bye as she had done a few days before to her parents and sister.

She fastened her seat belt and leaned back, feeling relaxed and contented. She was grateful to her parents for what they had done, even when she said that she wanted to be independent.

CHAPTER THIRTEEN

Bea went through security and customs at Bangkok airport, and she looked around to see if there was anybody waiting for her, but she could not see anyone. She suddenly felt lost but took a deep breath and went to look for a taxi to take her to the hotel. She paid what she saw on the meter when they arrived at what looked like a palace. She was used to grand hotels in Tokyo, but this one seemed to have been covered in gold.

Martin had chosen well. Her room was spacious, and the bathroom had all sorts of different lotions, soaps, and shampoos. The telephone by her bed was flashing, and she picked it up. There was a message from the Argentine ambassador inviting her to lunch the following day. She smiled to herself; her father had been at it again. She dialled the ambassador's number.

"Argentine Embassy, how can I help you?" a woman answered.

"My name is Bea Alvarez, and I have just arrived in Bangkok. I found a message from the ambassador asking me to lunch tomorrow."

"He is out right now, but I will transfer you to his social secretary."

After a minute's wait, Bea heard, "Hello, this is Federico Miranda."

Bea repeated what she had said.

"Oh, yes. His Excellency told me to ring you. Can you come tomorrow?"

"Of course; it is very kind of him to invite me."

"I will be there, too," Federico said. "If there is anything I can do for you, please let me know."

"Thank you very much. I am looking forward to meeting you."

Bea hung up and dialled the operator. "Hello, I would like to place a call to Tokyo, please."

"What number?"

Bea gave her the number and waited to be connected.

"Hello, Martina; how are you?"

"Oh, Miss Bea, how nice to hear from you! Are you having a good time?"

"Wonderful, Martina. Everybody is being extremely kind and hospitable. Are my parents in?"

"They have not come back yet."

"And my sister?"

"I am afraid she is out, too. I will tell them that you rang."

Bea tried to call John, but he was in a meeting. She suddenly felt very lonely and did not know what to do. She went to the window; the sun was shining even though it was past five in the afternoon. She said to herself: "What is wrong with me? Here I am touring half the world, and I am sitting in my room like a fool." She took her hand bag and her room key and went down to change money. Then she went for a long walk, felt hungry, and for the first time in her life had dinner all on her own.

Again the telephone was flashing when she returned to her room in the hotel. She had three messages.

"Hello, this is Federico. I'm calling to let you know that I will pick you up at your hotel at twelve thirty tomorrow. Have a good evening."

The second message was her father: "Hello, darling. We are so sorry to have missed you; we will call back tomorrow at nine in the morning, your time."

The third message was from John. "My darling Bea, how are you? I got your message. If you are not back too late, call me; I shall be waiting."

Bea called her fiancé. "John?"

"Oh, my darling Bea, I miss you so much!"

"I miss you, too."

"How was Hong Kong?" he asked.

"The Garcias were wonderful, and so was Chris. We went to the casino in Macao, and I won; I bought myself a gold bracelet with the money. Chris said that I would not be able to change the Macao currency back into Hong Kong dollars. I had no other choice but to buy something."

John laughed. "You are great, Bea—you always find life wonderful."

"But it is! Florencia—that is Mrs Garcia—took me shopping in Kowloon. I bought a present for your mother."

"That is very thoughtful of you. Did you do any sightseeing, or did you just go shopping?"

"Don't be silly; of course I went sightseeing. The Garcias took me to lunch at their club. According to Nicolas—Mr Garcia—there are mainly British members, but I could not understand the way they talked. It was as if they all had something in their mouths."

John laughed and said, "We say a plum in their mouth. It means that they are posh."

"What does posh mean?"

"Upper class."

"I see. I hope we will meet people that talk normally when we go live in England."

"Don't worry, darling, you might end up talking like that, too."

"I hope not!"

"What are you doing tomorrow?" John asked.

"I have been invited by the Argentine ambassador to have lunch; his social secretary is coming to collect me."

"Well, that is posh."

"I suppose it is!" Bea said, and she laughed.

"Sleep well, darling."

"I love you," Bea said, and she hung up.

Bea was dead on her feet, and she hardly had the strength to take a shower before going to bed. She had not unpacked before going out, so she went to sleep in the robe that she found behind the door in the bathroom after turning the air conditioner up.

She slept until the telephone woke her up. "Hello, Bea. Are we waking you up?" Alberto asked.

"Daddy! It's great to hear you."

"How are you, sweetheart?"

"Everything is great. I had a super time in Hong Kong, and now I have been invited to lunch by the Argentine ambassador."

"I'm glad, sweetheart. I have known him for years; give him my regards. Your mother is longing to talk to you. I will pass you to her."

Bea wanted to know how her father knew the ambassador, but her mother was already on the line. "How are you, Bea? Is the hotel all right?"

"Everything is just perfect, Mummy. I was beautifully looked after in Hong Kong, and I am going to lunch in a little while with the Argentine ambassador. We must not forget to send invitations to everyone for the wedding."

"Of course—they are all on the list. I saw your dress yesterday, and it is coming out beautifully."

"Don't tell me, Mummy, I want it to be a surprise! I must rush now; I haven't even unpacked yet."

"You must go, then. I hope you find something suitable to wear."

"Don't worry, Mummy, I will."

Near lunchtime her phone rang; it was Federico. "Hello, Bea, I am downstairs."

"I will be there in a minute. How will I recognise you?"

"I am wearing the Argentine colours on my lapel."

"That is very patriotic."

"I am," Federico said simply.

She was completely ready. She had unpacked carefully, had taken another shower, and washed her hair. The dress she chose to wear was free of wrinkles, and she thought she looked presentable for the ambassador.

"Hello, Federico, I am Bea."

"Hello," said Federico, apparently impressed by Bea's looks. "Let's go to the car; I left the keys with the porter."

"How long have you been in Bangkok?" Bea wanted to know.

"I came here about ten years ago, backpacking. I did not know what I wanted to do with my life, but as soon as I saw this country, I felt like staying. I was able to find a temporary working visa, but then I found a job in the embassy, and I am now allowed to stay for as long as I work there."

"Do you speak the language?" she asked him.

"I do now; I was allowed to take lessons while working for the ambassador. I have served three ambassadors."

"Are you planning to stay forever?"

"Probably; I am not sure," Federico said. "I go back to Buenos Aires every two years, and it is great to see family and friends, but after a while I am happy to come back to Thailand. Here we are—this is the residence."

They were shown into the sitting room, where the ambassador joined them a few minutes later. He came in with a broad smile, and his hand was already extended. He greeted Bea warmly. "It is a pleasure to meet you, Bea. May I call you Bea?"

"Of course, Mister Ambassador."

"Ricardo, please. I met your father when we were both at university. We were great buddies then but lost contact until last year, when he came to Thailand on business."

"I see; I was surprised by your kind invitation to lunch. By the way, he sends regards."

"Thank you. Alberto sent me a telegram telling me that you were coming."

"How embarrassing to be imposing on you," Bea said. "I am sure you are busy."

"I am never too busy for friends and Federico is a great help on this occasions."

At lunch they discussed Bea's plans for her days in Bangkok.

"Federico could show you some of the sights, and if you want to go shopping, he is an expert," Ricardo said, looking at Federico.

"I would be delighted," Federico said. "If you like, we can take a boat down the river this afternoon, and tomorrow we could go to the palace and go shopping."

"That is really too kind. Are you sure you want to do this? I was going to take a tour," Bea said.

Federico smiled and said, "Tours take you where they want to take you. I will take you where you want to go."

Bea laughed. She was again grateful to her father for helping her from a distance. She promised herself to ring him as soon as she went back to the hotel.

That afternoon Bea saw for herself how the poor lived in Bangkok. The river was very beautiful indeed with wild vegetation on both sides, but there were also so many little huts and so many people that it was difficult to count them. Some of them were selling fruit, vegetables, hats, and even snakes. Despite their poverty, they looked happy and waved at Bea and Federico as they went by. Federico had been down that river many times and explained to Bea that many of them were not as poor as they looked. "It is just the way they live," he added.

It was almost dusk when they got back, and Federico offered to take Bea out to dinner.

"Haven't you had enough of me for one day?" Bea said.

"Not at all—I find your company most pleasurable."

Bea laughed. "You are very formal."

"In Thailand, everybody is formal in an informal way. I have become accustomed to their ways."

"I am grateful for your invitation. Where are you planning to take me?"

"Have you had Thai food before?"

"Not really; I went to a restaurant near the hotel last night, but it was not a Thai one."

"I will take you to a typical Thai restaurant. Are you hungry now?"

"Now that you mention food, I think I am."

"Great! Let's go and have an early dinner so that tomorrow you are not tired for sightseeing."

The restaurant was amazing. There was a little lobby where they went to ask for a table, but then they entered into what looked like a jungle with little streams intertwined among the tables. On each table there was a vase with orchids.

"What a fantastic place," Bea exclaimed, almost overwhelmed by what she was seeing.

"I'm glad you like it; I find the food pretty amazing, too. I hope you like it as much as I do."

"Could you order for me, please?" Bea asked.

"With great pleasure; I will order several dishes that we can share. Do you like spicy food?"

"Yes, I do."

Federico ordered, and then they chatted nonstop until it arrived. But while they were eating, they kept quiet, savouring the different tastes. Sometimes the dishes were a little too hot for Bea, but she solved the problem by drinking the wine that the waiter kept pouring in her glass. She felt elated by it and exclaimed, "All this is perfect."

Federico was amused by this remark; he thought that Bea was lovely and fun, and he was beginning to feel sorry that she was going to leave the day after tomorrow.

"What shall we do in the morning?" He asked.

Bea said, "You mentioned the palace."

"That is a must!" he confirmed.

"All right. Let's go to the palace, and then I will invite you to lunch, wherever you want to go. After lunch I would not mind going shopping as you suggested; I would like to take one or two small souvenirs. But please don't feel that you have to come with me"

Federico smiled. "Ricardo has given me all day to look after you. I am at your disposal."

"Thank you very much for your company and help, Federico. It would have been impossible for me to do all the things I am doing without you."

Federico felt like holding her hand, but he controlled himself. He took her back to the hotel and arranged to meet at her at ten the next morning.

Bea went straight to her room, and before doing anything else she phoned John; she had intended to ring her father but she felt like talking to John: "Have I woken you up?" she asked.

"Darling! Well, yes, I had fallen asleep, but I was waiting for your call. Did you have a good day?"

"Wonderful!" She recounted all the things that she had done and her plans for the next day.

"I see, I see. You seem to be meeting an awful lot of men . . ."

"Wasn't that what you wanted?" Bea asked, confused.

"Not exactly; I just thought it would be a good idea for you to go to England and stay with my mother."

"I am going to England, just not exactly the way you and my mother wanted me to go."

"Well, in any case I am glad you are having a good time."

"And you?"

"My life is exactly the same as it was when you were here, but without you."

Bea teased, "Shall I come back?"

"You are naughty, Bea."

"I know, sorry. Sleep well, my darling. Despite all the things I am doing, I miss you."

CHAPTER FOURTEEN

The plane landed in Phnom Penh, and Bea hurried to get on the bus that was going to take her to the plane bound for Angkor Watt. It was very hot and humid, and the anxiety that she felt when arriving in Bangkok had returned; suddenly she felt like turning around and getting on the first plane to Tokyo. But then she heard her name being called, and she went to see the stewardess. Behind her a man said, "I am Mr Bee."

She went back to her seat feeling not only anxious and lonely but also humiliated. She kept her head down and then looked out of the window. The man seating next to her said, "Hello, Bea."

"How do you know my name is Bea?"

The man explained, "You got up when you heard that name. My name is Andrew, by the way."

She could not help but turn a deep red colour. "I'm afraid I made a bit of a fool of myself. I did not hear the 'mister'."

"I don't blame you; it was not easy to understand. Is this your first trip on your own?"

"Does it show that much?" she asked.

"I don't think anybody else noticed. It is just that I have been sitting next to you for a while, and I saw that you were a bit tense. Are you also going to Angkor Watt?"

"Yes."

"In that case, we will be staying in the same hotel; there is only one."

Bea asked, "Have you been there before?"

"No, but I checked it out. I am really looking forward to seeing the ruins."

"Me too—the photographs I have seen are magnificent."

"Did you know that it was a French explorer that found them?" Andrew said.

"No, I didn't. How do you know that?"

"My mother told me; she was Burmese and knew a lot of the culture of this part of the world. Apparently this explorer, feeling tired when it got dark, fell asleep not knowing where he was. When he woke up, he found that he was surrounded by monkeys in the middle of the jungle among the ruins. But when he went back to civilisation, nobody would believe him and thought he was mad. Finally one of those who heard him describe what he had seen decided to go and investigate for himself, and here we are."

"Amazing! Thank you for the introduction; now I am even more eager to see it all."

The flight to Angkor Watt was chaotic; it took only twenty minutes in the air, but in that time they were given a full tea and balloons for the few children that were on the plane. The stewardesses managed to start serving as the plane took off; they were hardly able to balance the trays and were still collecting them as the plane landed, but everything was done with a smile and good humour. Bea felt more relaxed.

She and Andrew chatted together. "Why did you choose to travel now?" he asked her.

"My fiancé and my mother wanted me to go to England before John and I get married."

"You are quite a way from England."

"I know. I agreed to do it if I visited all the countries where the plane landed."

Andrew asked, "Is your fiancé English?"

"Yes. He is worried I will not adjust to life over there, and he wanted me to go and stay with his mother."

Andrew looked at her with a worried expression on his face. "Are you really going to stay with her?"

"No—I have agreed to go and visit her, but that is all."

"You are wise. My father is a Scot, and so am I, but my mother was not. She adapted to life there, but I know it was not easy for her in the beginning. The cold weather affected her."

"Hmm, I am going to try not to think about it."

"Good for you; be optimistic!" Andrew said with a smile.

The hotel was a complete contrast to the one in Bangkok; there was no gold here. It was a one-storey grey building in the middle of an unkempt garden. Several elephants roamed around, ignoring everyone that went past them. Bea's room was simple but large; it had two beds with a little table and a lamp in between. Next to it there was a huge bathroom with an old-fashioned bathtub standing on brass legs. Both the room and bathroom looked clean.

The telephone rang, and Bea rushed to answer it.

"Hello this is Tokyo calling," a man's voice said at the other end of the phone.

"Is that you, darling? I was about to ring you."

"I'm sorry, Bea—it was a bad joke. It's me, Andrew."

"Oh, I seem to be making a fool of myself all the time, nowadays."

"No, you are not, but I could not help teasing you."

Bea smiled. "Well, you have succeeded."

"Will you have dinner with me? I don't like eating alone."

Bea thought for a moment about John's comment on the amount of men she was meeting, and it suddenly dawned on her that he was right: up to now she had not met any girls. But she did not like eating alone, either. "Are you going to the hotel dining room?" she asked.

"There is nowhere else to go, Bea."

"Fine. I would like to have a bath and change; I'll meet you in the lobby in an hour. Is that all right with you?"

"Perfect! See you then."

Bea picked up and dialled John's number. It took a while to be connected, so she started unpacking; she did not like to waste time. When she was finally connected she was getting impatient because she wanted to ring her parents, too.

She asked him, "Have I woken you up again?"

"It does not matter, Bea. I love to hear your voice."

"I love to hear your voice, too, darling." Bea recounted her trip to Angkor in detail.

"So you are having dinner with yet another man . . ." John said.

"Darling, there does not seem to be many other women alone on this trip."

"I am just teasing you, darling."

"It seems that I am prone to be teased," Bea said with a slightly sad voice.

"Now, now, just go and have a good time. I think this trip is a wonderful experience for you."

"As a matter of fact, I think so too! I must rush to get ready. I love you."

After John hung up, he was not completely sure that it had been a good idea to let Bea go alone halfway around the world. She seemed to be enjoying herself too much.

After dinner, the only thing that Bea wanted was a comfortable bed with a soft pillow. She washed, but it was too hot for a nightie, so she stripped the bed and lay down on it. She was going to open the window but decided against it when she thought of the elephants; she was afraid to be taken away by one of them with its trunk! She was asleep in no time at all but woke up again feeling like a prickly blanket was on her. She turned on the light and saw that she was covered by what looked like beetles. She jumped from her bed and went to the other one, turning the light off, but as soon as she did this the beetles returned to her. She left the lights on and saw how the beetles quieted down, but some of them were still on both beds. She sat on a chair with the light on and dozed all night.

She was brought out of her half sleep by the telephone: her mother called. "Hello, darling, how are you?"

"Oh Mummy, how lovely to hear your voice!"

"Is something wrong, Bea?" Bea told her mother about her night. "You must leave immediately. It is not a safe place—you might get something."

"Mummy, I have just arrived here, and I want to see the ruins. I will tell them when I go to breakfast. I am only spending one more night here."

"Please look after yourself."

"I am; please don't worry. I should not have told you, but I feel better now that I did."

"Good-bye, darling."

"Good-bye, Mummy. Give my love to Daddy."

Bea showered and dressed and was down for breakfast at seven thirty. She told the concierge about her night, and they immediately went to put a mosquito net over her bed, apologising profusely. "We are so sorry. You should have had one last night. How can we make it up to you?"

"Is there a Catholic church around here?"

"There is one about half an hour away. The mass is at six thirty in the evening. We can take you there."

"That will be great; I shall be here before six."

As she was having her breakfast, Andrew appeared in the dining room. "You are up early," He noted.

Bea recounted again what had happen the night before, and she inquired about his night.

"I slept like a log; I had a mosquito net."

"I should have called and asked for one."

"Live and learn, Bea," Andrew said with a smile.

"Thanks," said Bea in a sardonic manner.

After breakfast they set out to discover what they had been longing to see since they arrived, and they were not disappointed. There were so many temples with trees growing in and out of them, and the monkeys were there, too, not only in real life but also in carvings all over the walls. Andrew explained, "According to what my mother told me, the monkeys invaded this area and fought the people that were here; they won the war, and this is the reason why they are still here."

"It is of course a myth. Isn't it?"

"I don't know. Look for yourself—there are monkeys everywhere."

Bea smiled and shook her head. It was good having Andrew tell her all these theories; whether true or not, they were fascinating.

They had taken sandwiches for lunch, which they had under a tree inside one of the temples. There were not many people around. "This is so peaceful; I can imagine what the man who first saw these ruins must have felt," Bea said looking around.

"It was enough to make people think that he was mad. Nobody could imagine a place like this could exist."

"Well, I feel I am dreaming all this, too."

They hardly had time to get back in time for Bea to change and be ready for the Jeep that was going to take her and a few other people to the church.

There were benches under a few trees, and the altar was a simple table covered by an immaculately clean white cloth. It was already packed with local worshipers. They started to sing in a very melodious voice as the priest approached the altar. For Bea it was only possible to follow the mass because she knew the order of the service, but otherwise she did not know what they were saying. At the end the priest greeted all those who were not Cambodian in perfect French. Bea's French was not so good, either, but she was able to thank the kind man with her limited vocabulary.

Bea told Andrew that night, "I would be prepared to sleep on a chair every night in order to see all the marvels that I have seen today. I could not understand a word they said in the mass, but it was one of the most uplifting moments of my life."

Andrew leaned across the table and said, "I think we will remember these moments for the rest of our lives."

They parted company the following day after dinner back in Phnom Penh.

Andrew said, "If I ever go to Tokyo, I will give you a ring."

"You must!"

CHAPTER FIFTEEN

Bea went back to Bangkok but did not stay; she took the plane that was going to take her to India. Now she felt more assured and did not feel as nervous as she had felt on the previous flights.

The plane landed in Delhi at exactly midnight, and the anxiety came back to her. There were so many people around that it was difficult to reach the exit. Then she did not know what to do. She did not want to take a taxi all on her own and asked an attendant to direct her to the bus for the city centre. "Oh, miss, there is no bus now. But maybe in hour it will be back."

Bea sat on a seat by the door and waited. Slowly the area became deserted, and she found that there was nobody around. She went looking for someone who might be able to tell her when the bus was coming. "Oh, miss, the last bus left an hour ago; I can find you a taxi," a worker said.

Bea realised that she could not stay in the airport all night and accepted the offer. The driver had a friend sitting with him in the front, and she was filled with apprehension. It was dark everywhere—not a single light was to be seen. She looked in her hand luggage for something to defend herself with, in case she was attacked, but the only thing that she could find was a pair of nail scissors. The two men were very kind and talked to her nonstop. Nevertheless, she did not relax until she was told that they were getting close to the hotel, and they asked whether she would want to be collected the next day to go sightseeing. She was still unsure and thanked them. "I don't know what I will be doing tomorrow, but thank you very much anyway."

"We will be here at ten, and if you want we can take you sightseeing."

They were not going to let a prospective customer get away. But Bea was going to ask the hotel if there were any tour buses; she wanted to be with other people.

An obsequious porter took her luggage to her room that was beautiful and overlooked the swimming pool. When she tried the door, she found that it was not locked. She panicked and called the front desk. "The door leading to the swimming pool has no lock."

"No, ma'am, it does not."

"Could you give me a room with a lock to the outside, please?"

"The only rooms available are the suites in the top floor, ma'am."

"In that case I would like a suite. Could you send a porter to collect my luggage, please?"

"Right away."

She was escorted to the top floor. Her room consisted of a large sitting room with comfortable sofas and arm chairs, and a table with six chairs. The bedroom had an enormous bed, and next to it was a bathroom made of marble with golden taps. There were telephones in every room, including the bathroom. The view from the window at that hour was nothing but darkness, but Bea imagined that it would be beautiful in the morning. She felt lonely and uneasy and decided to run a bath. While it filled up, she placed a call to John and unpacked a few things.

The call came in when she had just about finished. John asked, "Where are you, Bea?"

"I have just arrived in Delhi. I have so much to tell you, John. I never imagined there could be such wonderful things to see in this part of the world." As she said this, she felt that she was standing in water—she had completely forgotten about the bath that had overflowed and was flooding the whole suite. "Oh my God!"

"What is it?"

"I believe I have just flooded the room; I forgot I was running a bath. I must go now. I love you."

She hung up, leaving John bewildered.

She called the front desk and explained what had happened. "I am so very, very sorry!"

"Don't worry, ma'am. We will fix this in just one minute."

True enough, a few minutes later came a man with a water vacuum cleaner. "It will be dry in no time at all," he said as he shut the door.

By now it was past three in the morning and Bea was dead on her feet. She forgot about having a bath and took a shower instead.

She slept until the telephone woke her up. "Ma'am, there is a taxi here to collect you to go sightseeing."

"I am sorry, but I have just woken up. Please tell them that I am not sure what I will be doing today."

"Sorry, ma'am, they say they will wait for you."

"Please tell them that I am very grateful, but I will not need them."

"All right."

Bea took a deep breath and sat on the edge of the bed. She had no idea what she would be doing, and the anxiety was there again. She had had no communication with her father's friends; she was alone for the first time in her trip. She had been lucky to have found Andrew in Cambodia. But she had to keep going, and she got ready to go down for breakfast. She wanted to go on a tour afterwards.

The tour bus came at midday; there were people from other hotels on it already, and she was the last one to be collected. She heard Spanish being spoken in the back of the bus and thought it was Argentine Spanish. She waited for everyone to descend at their first stop; she wanted to see the people who spoke Spanish. She was sure now that they were Argentines, and she went up to them. "Hello, my name is Bea. Are you from Argentina?" she asked in Spanish.

"Yes, we are," the couple replied, looking a bit unsure of what she wanted.

Bea went on. "Do you mind if I walk with you? I am not very comfortable being on my own." It was difficult for the couple to say no, but they were still not totally forthcoming. Bea could hear it in their voice, but she did not care; she preferred to be a pest than to be alone. "My parents sent a telegram to their friends about me, but they have not contacted me yet. The taxi that brought me from the airport last night wanted to take me on the tour. Although they were very nice, I do not feel safe alone with them."

The couple did not have time to answer because the tour guide had started the explanation of the history of the place they had just entered. It was a Muslim temple, and they were asked to take their shoes off. The floor felt hot, and Bea did not like walking barefoot. Some of the worshippers were sitting and praying in groups; the mosque was the biggest in Delhi, and there were several rooms connected by arched doors. Bea did not think it was beautiful; after the wonders of Thailand and Cambodia, she found this place imposing but not attractive.

They were taken to several other temples and gardens. The gardens were beautiful with wonderful tropical vegetation, and it felt peaceful;

there were young and old resting in the shade of the trees. Bea had no time to feel lonely during the tour, and she left the couple in peace after her first spontaneous need for company. At the end of the tour, they asked her if she wanted to dine with them, but Bea wanted to go back to the hotel and phone John before he went to bed.

The first thing that Bea saw as she entered her suite was the telephone light flashing. There was a message from her parents' friends inviting her to dinner.

She called the number. "Hello, this is Bea Alvarez."

"Hello, this is Marcela. Can you come to dinner tonight?"

Bea had not expected such a welcoming answer and replied, "I would be delighted. How do I get there?"

"I will pick you up at eight."

"Thank you very much. See you later, then."

Bea hurried to place her call to Tokyo, making sure that she had not left any taps running. "John, I have just been on a tour all by myself."

"What do you mean? No strangers to meet?"

"Yes, I did meet a couple from Argentina."

"Unbelievable," John said.

"Why?"

"There has not been an occasion when you have told me that you have been completely alone for more than a few minutes."

"Well, come to think of it, that is true."

"What happened last night?"

"I left the bath running, and I flooded the room."

"Oh, dear!"

"There was no problem; they came with a machine, and the carpet was dry this morning."

"So what are your plans for tonight?" John asked.

"As a matter of fact, I have been invited to dinner by some friends of my parents."

John could not help but laugh. "You are great, darling. I don't think you will have problems adjusting anywhere."

"I am glad you are finally coming to that conclusion. I hope my mother will, too."

"I will call them now and let them now that I have just spoken to you."

"Thank you. I must get ready—I will be picked up soon. I love you."

"I love you, too, darling Bea."

Marcela, the daughter of Bea's parents' friends, arrived a few minutes after eight to collect Bea, who was waiting in the lobby. The girl went straight to her and said, "You must be Bea."

"Yes I am—how did you know?"

"You look Argentinean."

"Are you from Argentina, too?"

"I am half Argentine; my mother is American."

Marcela looked younger than Bea, maybe still in her teens, but she was sophisticated and beautiful. She had long blond hair and bright blue eyes, and she was dressed casually but elegantly in an Indian shirt dress.

"Do you know how my father knows yours?" Bea asked.

"I think they went to school together."

"It seems that my father's school friends are everywhere in the world."

They arrived at Marcela's magnificent house in less than ten minutes. Her parents were waiting for them on the veranda and met them as they approached. "We are so happy to have you here with us," said Victor, Marcela's father.

"How are you, dear?" said Nancy, Marcela's mother, in perfect Spanish.

They were eager to know all about Bea and were delighted when they found out that she was getting married. "When is the happy day?" Marcela asked.

"In two months. I will have just enough time to try my wedding dress and see the last preparations."

Nancy said, "How very exciting for you; we wish you all the best."

"Thank you. I hope you will be able to come."

"We certainly will try," answered Nancy.

Victor intervened. "What are your plans for tomorrow?

"I thought I would take another tour and then have a rest before I leave. The plane is due to depart at three in the morning."

Marcela suggested, "Why don't I collect you in the car and take you wherever you want to go? Then after you have had a rest, my friends and I will take you to a wonderful tandoori place. We can take you to the airport after dinner."

"That will be a very long dinner!" Bea said with a laugh.

"We could pick you up at ten, or even later if you like; people don't keep time in Delhi."

"That sounds great, thank you."

The following morning, as arranged, Marcela took Bea sightseeing; the family driver took them in Victor's car. After lunch Marcela took her to the market. "I have never been to a place like this. There are so many shops!" Bea said.

"Yes, some sell rubbish, but you can also find valuable jewellery and beautiful saris."

"I would love to see those. Are they heavy?"

"No, they are pure silk, and you could fold them into a rather tiny package."

"I would like to get one for my mother and another one for my sister."

Bea and Marcela spent over an hour looking at saris. Finally Bea decided on a blue one with tiny gold stars and a gold embroidered border for her mother. For Gaby, she chose one the same colour of her eyes with a silver border."

"Thank you, Marcela. I think my mother and sister will be happy with their presents."

"Are you getting something for your father?"

"I am not sure yet what I will get him. I might find something in England."

Marcela and two handsome male friends arrived to collect her just after ten in the evening. Bea had had time to pack, rest, and have a long bath and be ready for her departure; she was taking the suitcases with her to the restaurant.

"Wow! This is a very unusual restaurant," Bea exclaimed, surprised at the fact that the cooking was done in an enormous round oven that looked like a gigantic well in the middle of an open-air restaurant. She wondered what they did when it rained. The cooks attached whatever they were cooking to a piece of wire and then threw it in the flames; they fished them out and served them with different sauces, yogurt, vegetables, rice, and Indian bread that they used as tools for eating. It was delicious.

After dinner they had time to go to a club and dance. Bea was overwhelmed by their kindness; especially when she commented on one of the young men's watches. "That's a beautiful watch you are wearing."

He took it off and handed it to her. "Oh, please, let me give it to you."

Bea was horrified and said, "No, no, I couldn't possibly accept it; I just thought it looked good on you."

Marcela laughed. "Bea, in India everyone is very generous; if you tell them you like something that they have, they will give it to you."

"That is generous indeed. I will never comment on anything I like again!"

They all laughed at this as they got up to take Bea to the airport.

CHAPTER SIXTEEN

By the time she boarded the plane bound for Turkey, Bea could hardly keep her eyes opened. She wondered why they had to travel at such an inhospitable hour. Again she thanked her father for yet another introduction; without them she did not think she could have enjoyed her trip so much. Gaby was right; travelling on one's own was lonely and definitely not as enjoyable as it was sharing it with other people.

She woke up as they landed in Istanbul. She had not planned to stay there, but she had five hours to kill before her plane to Greece was due. She decided to go through passport control and ask if she could wander around the city for a few hours. The young man was apparently taken by Bea as she showed him the ticket she had for her destination. Finally he agreed to let her go on the condition that they would meet in three hours on the terrace of a well-known hotel; he gave her the address.

He was already waiting for her when she arrived, and he looked nervous. "I have done something illegal by letting you leave the airport—you don't even have a visa. But I am happy that you are here; we must go now."

"Can't I have a cup of tea? It is very nice on this terrace—we can see the city and beyond from here."

"Fine, but I must take you back as soon as possible; I am going to have to get you through the crew door. I have a friend there."

Bea was going from adventure to adventure, and this time she had been all on her own. Now she was looking forward to Athens.

The hotel was not the most luxurious that she had ever seen, but it was adequate. It was an old, refurbished grand house converted into a few suites, and breakfast was included in the cost. She had just finished looking around when the telephone by her bed rung.

"There is a lady looking for you in the lobby," said the concierge in an uncertain voice.

"Could you ask her who she is?"

The answer came in the voice of the woman who was looking for her; she sounded stressed. "My husband is a friend of your father's. We received a telegram that you were coming to Greece a couple of weeks ago but did not know how to contact you. I am here to take you to our house."

"I am very grateful, but may I know your name, please?"

"Yes, yes, of course; you never know nowadays. It is Magdalena Montalban."

"My father did give me your name and telephone number; I was going to ring you as soon as I unpacked."

"Don't unpack—it is not safe for you to stay alone in a hotel. You must come to our house; I have prepared your room."

Bea found herself in a dilemma. She wanted to stay in the hotel, but if she declined this woman's invitation, she might have a fit. "Thank you very much, Mrs Montalban. Could you ask the porter to come and collect my luggage, please?"

"I will go up with him."

A few minutes later, Bea found herself in front of a tiny woman with a huge mass of hair and bright eyes. She approached her ready to shake her hand, but instead Magdalena embraced her around her waist because she could not reach any higher.

In the car Bea said, "I am touched by your kindness, Mrs Montalban."

"Please call me Magdalena. I would not want a child of mine staying by herself in hotels."

"I am twenty-one," Bea said defensively.

"Nevertheless, you are young, and I can see that you are attractive, too. You should not be on your own."

"I had planned to go on a cruise around the islands."

"That will be fine—I will talk to the captain to keep an eye on you."

Bea smiled and thought, *This woman is even worse than my parents!*

That evening Bea was left to have dinner with the Montalbans' children while Magdalena and Carlos, her husband, went out to dinner. They were all very nice, but she felt trapped. She wanted to escape, but because they were her parents' friends, she did not dare. Instead she placed a call to her parents.

"Daddy, how are you? I have not spoken to you for ages!"

"I am fine, but what is most important is, how you are? You must be in Athens now. How is the hotel?"

Bea laughed. "I hardly had time to see the hotel. Your friend Magdalena Montalban has brought me to her house."

"Oh, I see. Is she the way I remember her?"

"I do not know how you remember her."

"I should have warned you—she does mean well, though."

"I know. Tomorrow morning I am going on my little cruise around the islands, and I already know that the captain is supposed to keep an eye on me."

Alberto chuckled. "I hope you enjoy them; I did that when I was about your age and was studying in London."

"I am looking forward to seeing as much as possible. Could you ring John, please, and let him know that I am here?"

"Of course, darling; sleep well."

Bea thought that she would be the first one to get up the next morning, but Magdalena was already preparing breakfast with the maid. "Good morning, Bea. I have prepared a good hearty breakfast for you."

"Thank you, Magdalena, but just a little juice and a piece of toast would be fine for me."

"No, no. You must eat. What will your parents think of me if I don't feed you properly?"

"They know I don't have a big breakfast. Would you mind calling a taxi for me to take me to the docks?"

"Of course I would. I will take you to the docks and speak to the captain myself."

Bea thought that it would be better not to answer. She sat down and had as much breakfast as she could, and then she went to get ready.

True to her word, Magdalena made her way to the desk at the dock and said, "Good morning. I have this girl with me, and I am very worried that she is travelling alone. Could I please speak to the captain?"

"I am afraid he is already in the ship and it will be impossible for him to see you now."

"Could I please write him a note explaining the situation?"

"Yes, of course; here is some paper and a pen."

While Magdalena was writing, the clerk winked at Bea, who was standing just behind Magdalena and felt quite embarrassed.

Magdalena then took Bea to the stairs leading to the ship, and she told her to send her a telegram if she needed anything.

Bea hugged her, thanked her for her hospitality, and almost ran to the deck. Her cabin was comfortable, and she could see the sea from her little round window. By the time she left the room, she felt finally free. She never thought that she would actually want to be alone.

Bea wandered around and inspected every corner of the enormous vessel. Then she saw a young man walking towards her. She had a look at his shoes and immediately recognised them as Argentine moccasins. In her usual manner she could not help asking in Spanish, "Are you Argentinean?"

The young man, who had seen Bea looking at his shoes, replied in Spanish, "No, I come from Chile but my shoes are from Argentina."

Bea was embarrassed for a few seconds and apologised for her curiosity. "I am sorry. You must think I am very nosy?"

"I think it is a good way to meet."

Bea was now completely confused and would have run back to her cabin, but she did not think he would think any better of her for it. "I did not mean to be forward," she stated.

He laughed. "We would have met sometime during the cruise. My name is Ernesto Sanchez."

Bea extended her hand. "I am Bea Alvarez."

They walked together for a while and then parted company. "See you at dinner," he said.

"See you then," Bea responded.

She lay down on her bed, still feeling annoyed with herself but she did not dwell too long on it because she saw a piece of paper being pushed under her door. She got up, filled with curiosity, and picked it up. It read: "The captain will be delighted if you could join him at his table for dinner tonight." Bea could not help but laugh. Magdalena had succeeded in her aim.

Bea had not inspected the bathroom yet and went to see it before deciding on a bath or a shower. It was a good size and looked clean. There was a door on the wall opposite hers. Thinking it could be a cupboard, she opened it. To her surprise and horror, she saw Ernesto Sanchez in his underwear, standing in the middle of his own cabin.

She closed the door immediately, but he had seen her. He said, "I knew that I was sharing the bathroom with somebody; I just did not know who it might be. I should have locked my door. Please don't be embarrassed."

Bea did not dare open the door again but said, "Thank you. I did not know that I would be sharing a bathroom. I will keep my door locked also. Do you want to use the bathroom now?"

"That depends on how long you intend to use it."

"I think you should use it first. I can take my time."

"I will only be fifteen minutes," he said.

"Thank you."

Bea went back to her bed, feeling that she was not going to be able to face this man again. She thanked Magdalena from the bottom of her heart for making the captain invite her to his table.

A little while later she heard through the bathroom door, "I have left the bathroom clean for you, Bea. Give me a minute, and you can come in."

"Thank you, thank you," she called. She wondered how John and her parents would take this adventure. She opted to keep quiet; they did not have to know everything she was doing.

The next morning they got off the boat to visit the island of Delos. There were no inhabitants in this island, only remains of ancient Greece. There were mosaics that had survived the passing of time with hardly a scratch, but many of them were cracked. There were also an uncountable amount of monuments. It was fascinating trying to imagine how they had lived so many years ago. Bea tried to remember what she had been taught at school, but except for one or two legends, she had forgotten most of it; her time in Japan had replaced her past.

Among the other islands that they visited was Mikonos. Here there were lots of inhabitants and many young tourists amusing themselves in one way or another. She loved the little light blue houses that seemed to be piled up one on top of the other.

Magdalena was waiting for her at the dock. Bea ran to hug her. "I am so grateful to you; the captain invited me to his table every night."

Magdalena's answer was two huge tears running down her cheeks from her shiny eyes.

"Are you tired, Bea?"

"No, no, why do you ask?"

"Would you like to see some of the sights in Athens?"

"That would be great, but don't you have chores to do?" Bea asked.

"I have left the day free for you."

"You are a wonderful person, Magdalena."

Again Magdalena kept quiet and just smiled. "I will take you to a few places like the Acropolis. You can see it from here; it looks small but is very large. Greek history is so vast and also so unreliable; you do not know whether it is a myth or real history. What is certain is that it is fascinating. Did you study ancient Greek history at school?"

"Yes, I did, but not in great depth."

"Unless you specialise in it, it would be very difficult to appreciate its depth."

Bea left the following afternoon having changed her mind completely about Magdalena. The woman knew so much and had so many interests; it was important to get to know her to really appreciate what a kind person she was. Bea was able to almost see how different civilisations had lived on that high plateau thanks to Magdalena's explanations.

CHAPTER SEVENTEEN

Bea was getting closer to England; she was now in Rome, and the distances were getting shorter. She fell in love with this amazing city on the way to her hotel and decided that because it was the middle of the day, she would go for a walk. She did not need company here; everything was there for her to see. She visited churches and the Coliseum, and she saw so many squares with magnificent fountains and gardens. She did not get back to her hotel until it was almost dark—too late to call Tokyo. But she felt connected to her parents through the presence of their many friends around the world: she had a message from the Argentine ambassador inviting her to lunch the next day. She had been collecting souvenirs from all the places she had visited, and she chose a little jade figurine to take to the Ambassador and his wife as a present the next day.

The ambassador and his wife were as charming as all the other people that she had met through her father. Silvio and Liliana Echeverria thought that Bea was a well-brought-up young woman who was most interesting to talk to.

"Have you plans for this evening Bea?" asked Liliana.

"I had thought of going to an open air concert in a park near the hotel."

"That sounds like something not to be missed."

"There is so much to see that I will have to come back one day—hopefully with John."

"The Peruvian ambassador to the Vatican is giving a cocktail party tomorrow evening. Unfortunately we will not be able to go. Would you be prepared to represent us? There will be many young people like you. Who knows, you might meet someone who would like to go sightseeing with you."

Bea was uncertain about this invitation, but the Echeverrias had been kind, and she thought it would be rude to decline. She agreed.

"Our driver will pick you up. Don't worry about getting there by yourself."

There were indeed lots of young people at the party, and Bea found herself enjoying the evening much more than she had imagined. She met a Peruvian girl named Sara who was also travelling on her own, and they made plans to go sightseeing the following day.

"What would you like to see?" asked Sara.

"Everything," laughed Bea, and then she added, "I have not seen the Vatican yet."

"Would you like to go to Venice?"

"It was not in my plans, but I could do that. My trip has been planned, but I can always change it."

Sara explained, "I have a Euro rail pass."

"I have a plane ticket from Rome to Paris and then on to London."

"I can go anywhere with my train pass."

"Very well; I will buy a train pass, and we can travel together. I can change my plane ticket from here to London."

Bea had a friend in Venice; his father had worked in Tokyo for a couple of years, and they had met on many occasions at parties. She decided to send him a telegram to see if he would be free to see them. The response was immediate: "How wonderful, Bea. I am expecting you."

Two days later Bea and Sara were met at the station by Giorgio Veneto. He had his car with him and suggested driving them around the north of Italy. But just as they arrived in Verona, he was called back to Venice for work.

Bea and Sara found themselves alone in a place they had not thought of going to, but there were flyers everywhere advertising *Aida* in the Arena that evening. Neither Sara nor Bea had been to the opera very often; Bea preferred the ballet. But the opportunity was too great to be missed—they only hoped that they could find seats.

They were lucky enough to find seats not too far from the stage and in the middle of the arena; it was so big that that if they had been any further, it would have been difficult to see. They bought little cushions and a pair of binoculars from a tenor who was singing while selling his wares. Bea and Sara could not stay still; they turned around in their seats to absorb the magnificence of the place. The night was balmy, but they had brought shawls anyway, just in case it got cooler. The sky was completely clear, and they could see the stars and the moon above them. Their impatience grew by the minute; it was so exciting.

Then their attention was completely taken by the performance, which was just as magnificent as the place. There were even elephants and other animals in some of the scenes, and the women shed a tear at the end when the lovers decided to bury themselves alive in order to remain together.

They left in silence and arrived at the hotel that Giorgio had reserved to find that it was a room with a double bed; that morning they had left their luggage in the front desk and had gone sightseeing straight away. Now it was too late to change it—the new friends had to share the bed. But they were so tired that they did not mind and went to sleep right away.

The next evening they took the train that was to take them to Barcelona. Sara had convinced Bea that it would be great to go to the beach. Bea accepted, thinking that she was going to have to cut short her stay in Paris. They went to the dining room, and as they were having their dinner, the waiter started making passes at them; by the end he had become annoying, and the girls left as quickly as they could. As they were going to their cabin, an inspector was coming the other way and demanded to see their tickets. At that moment Bea said to him, "One of your waiters was most cumbersome." She explained what had happened and went their way. Half an hour later, as they were beginning to get ready for bed, the inspector came with the waiter and asked them if this was the one who had bothered them.

"That is him," Sara confirmed.

"Very well," said the inspector, now holding the young man by his ear and pulling him away.

Sara and Bea looked at each other, and Sara said, "I read in the paper the other day that a girl had been strangled by a waiter in her cabin on this very train."

In reply Bea started collecting her things. "I am not staying here—when is the next stop?" she said.

"In about ten minutes, I think," replied Sara while collecting her things, too.

As they finished, they heard, "Next stop, Monte Carlo."

They jumped onto the platform with all their belongings and realised that it was well past midnight, and they had nowhere to go. A faint light on the other side of the station read, "Hotel Monaco." They went across and inquired if there was a spare room. Fortunately for them there was a room with two beds; this time they made a point of demanding that. It was a very peculiar room, and they had to reach it via a bathroom with a shower in the middle of the room. But they did not dwell too long on what it looked like; they were not planning to stay there for more than one night.

Two days later Bea found herself in very different accommodation to what she had planned. Sara had very little money, and wanted to go to a 'pension'. It was full of young people, and the landlady was very kind; she knew how hungry some young people were, especially boys, and there were four courses on the menu. Bea only managed to have two, which left the landlady worried. "Look at you! You are just skin and bones; you must eat better."

"I have never been able to eat too much, but I am healthy, I promise," she said putting her hand on her heart which made the woman laugh.

They found out that the following day the first man was supposed to land on the moon, and they arranged to be back at their pension in time. They were not the only ones—all the other guests were there, too, and there was standing room only. Bea said to herself, *I wonder if my parents and John are watching this; I cannot believe that I am here and seeing history being made. I will never forget this trip! I never imagined that it would be so amazing.*

The train from Barcelona to Madrid was fully booked, and they stood up most of the time, but in the end they decided to sit on the floor with the other many young people travelling cheap. Bea was happy for the company, but she was missing her comforts; she would have liked to make a reservation in a good hotel in Madrid, but she had to accommodate to Sara's means. By the time they got to the pension, Bea's ankles were swollen, and the only thing she wanted was sleep. Because of the detour they had taken to get to Madrid, she was going to have only one day of sightseeing in Paris.

When she talked to John, he sounded worried. "Darling, where are you? We were worried—the hotel said you had cancelled your reservation."

"Oh, John, I am having all sorts of adventures, but it will take too long on the telephone. We have lots to talk about when I get back."

"You have not told me where you are. Your parents will want to know, too."

"I am about to take the train to Paris. I am in Madrid."

"Train? I thought you had all your flights booked."

"Yes, but I met a girl who cannot afford to travel by air, so I changed the flights from Rome to London and have been all over the place."

"I can't wait for you to get back. Please take care of yourself," he said, and they hung up.

This time there was room to sit in the compartment, but they were pretty squashed in between labourers who were going to France looking for or going back to work there. The labourers had all sorts of food to share among themselves: salami, ham, cheese, bread, and fruit. They were jolly and offered Bea and Sara some of their goodies, but the girls turned them down as politely as possible. What worried the women was the fact that all the labourers had knives that they used to cut the food and peel the fruit. Night fell and they prepared to sleep. Bea could not find a comfortable position, and the two men sitting next to her offered to go outside and sleep on the floor.

"No, no, please, you mustn't," she said.

"It is all right for us, ma'am. We'd rather lie down on the floor than sit here. You go ahead and make yourself comfortable."

The men on Sara's side also thought that they would let the girls sleep in peace and left the cabin. Bea and Sara found themselves alone, able to stretch out on the seats, and they fell asleep. Bea would remember these kind men for the rest of her life; not only they were prepared to share their food, but they were also true gentlemen.

The brief visit to Madrid and Paris left Bea with the intense desire to go back there. When she lived in England with John, they could holiday in Europe at leisure. It had been an experience having a new acquaintance for a travelling companion who had helped Bea see how other people lived.

Sara did not ask Bea to change her hotel reservation in London; Sara said that her boyfriend was coming to join them and that she would reserve a double room for them. Bea did not like this; she had made an effort to accommodate Sara, and now she was more or less being dismissed. But Bea had to go and see Katherine, and she took the train to the southwest of England.

Bea had not been paying attention to the stations being called; she was engrossed in a book when she suddenly felt the train starting again and saw with horror that Katherine was standing on the platform. It was too late for her to get off, and she had to wait until they got to the next station. She went to the station master and told him what had happened. He offered to ring the other station and see if they could page Mrs Fellow.

"Katherine, I am so sorry I missed the station. It will take about forty-five minutes for me to get there, but if you prefer, I will come another day."

"I will go home and come back in forty-five minutes," was the answer.

Bea was not happy with herself. She had felt the icy tone of John's mother, and she did not blame her. The weather in England was not as warm as in Spain and France, and in this station it felt even colder.

"I am so sorry, Katherine," Bea repeated while giving her a brief kiss on the left cheek, as she was told to do. In England one should kiss the left cheek, John had instructed her.

Katherine took her to her house and offered her tea with bread and butter and scones with cream and strawberry jam. Bea was hungry because she had not had any lunch, and she complimented Katherine on the delicious spread.

"It is all homemade; I like to know what I am eating."

"I hope one day you will teach me," Bea answered.

Katherine was taken by surprise; she did not think that Bea was the type to be interested in cooking. Then she remembered Bea's Pavlova at Christmas, but still she thought Bea was too sophisticated for domestic chores.

"I brought you a little souvenir from Hong Kong. I hope you like it," said Bea, handing her the rosewood box with its jade inlay.

"It is beautiful, Bea. I will put it next to the one you gave me at Christmas."

Bea was pleased that at least Katherine had liked the box. "You might end up with a whole collection—I love boxes, and I like to give them as presents, too."

It was late by the time Bea got back to the hotel, and she found a note waiting for her at the front desk: "Sorry, Bea, my boyfriend reserved a room in another hotel. I am moving there with him. Have a good trip back to Japan."

Bea and Sara had arranged that morning to have dinner together. Now she found herself alone at night in a cold city. For the first time on her trip, she felt like crying. She could not ring John or her parents—it was the middle of the night in Japan. She ordered room service and went to have a bath.

The next morning she took a tour and fell in love with London, as she had with Rome. Despite the cold breeze, the sun was out, and

119

the magnificence of the old buildings and so many green spaces gave her the feeling of living a fairy tale. She would not mind living in this city.

Just before the end of the tour, they were taken to Bond Street Market, where Bea bought two beautiful wool scarves, one for her father and the other for John.

CHAPTER EIGHTEEN

Bea had lost a lot of weight during her trip. "Darling, you are so thin," said Mercedes when Bea's parents picked her up at the airport. "I hope we won't have to alter your wedding dress too much."

"I might get back to my normal weight by then, Mum," said Bea as she hugged her mother.

The ball took place one week after Bea's return to Tokyo and was a great success. They achieved their goal of selling five hundred tickets. They were also lucky with the donations they received, among them a car!

Then Bea wanted to know what her wedding was going to be like. She had six weeks to make any changes, but everything seemed under control. The only thing that she was organising was the music. A friend had put her in touch with a nun from the Sacred Heart Convent, who had suggested that her nephew should play the organ while she sang.

Katherine arrived one week before the wedding to take part in the rehearsal. Everything was going well until she heard "Ave Maria", and she was not happy with the performance. According to her, neither the organist nor the singe were up to scratch.

Katherine said, "John invited a couple to play bridge with us last time I was here. I heard them sing at Christmas in our church, and they were superb. I could ask them to sing for your wedding, if they are not busy."

"But who is going to play the organ?" Bea said.

Katherine replied, "I could ask them to ask the organist of the church to come and play here."

"I think you'd better ask them before we get rid of our people," Mercedes said cautiously.

Bea had not been asked what she thought, nor had John, who said to his mother, "Bea made arrangements for the music."

"I know, darling, but it is not suitable."

"Mother, Bea likes it."

At that moment Bea said, "It is all right John; let your mother call your friends."

Katherine did not waste a minute. She went back home and rearranged the players and the music that was going to be played.

That night the nun rang Bea to tell her that she was going to be very unhappy in her marriage. Bea had not been happy with the change, either, but she did not want any complications. She had thought that she could still have her "Ave Maria," but Katherine had taken over and had chosen the music that she liked.

Then John, who had been so eager to marry Bea, began having second thoughts. He was afraid that his mother would indeed make Bea unhappy. He went to see Alberto. "I am sorry my mother is meddling with the wedding preparations at such short notice."

"It's all right John; there are always changes and problems at the last minute for this kind of occasion."

"I do not think that this will stop at the wedding itself. My mother is a very determined person, and I fear that she might make Bea's life difficult."

"John, that will depend on you; you yourself said to us, when you got engaged, that you would look after Bea."

"I know, but now that I see my mother with her, I do not know what to do."

"Do you want to call off the wedding?"

At that moment Bea entered the room and saw the two men that she loved most. She approached them.

John jumped up and hugged her. He kept her close to him for a long time and then said to Alberto, "Everything will be fine."

Alberto put his head on the back of his arm chair, shut his eyes, and breathed deeply.

"What were you talking about?" Bea asked.

"Nothing, darling; just a man-to-man conversation," Alberto said to his daughter. He could hardly control his tears.

But one problem followed another. The church service was under control, but in Japan they did not go to the Sacristy to sign the marriage certificate like one did England after the wedding. In that sense Japanese law was similar to the law in Argentina: they had to have a civil ceremony before they married in the church. John went to the British embassy to ask if they could marry there, and they said yes at first, but then they changed their minds when they heard that Bea was not British. Alberto asked the Argentine embassy, and the answer was the same. They were going to have to be married under Japanese law in a civil court. So two days before the religious ceremony, both families trooped down to the grey old building and signed a piece of paper that read from right to left in vertical lines: the kanji—the Japanese characters—that would unite their lives in matrimony. Then they went to a Japanese restaurant and toasted with sake.

Alberto was still a bit shaken by what had happened not even forty-eight hours previously but he was not going to tell anyone about his conversation with John, and he put on a brave face. He said to himself, *I hope Mercedes has not been right in thinking that this marriage might not work.* Mercedes, Gaby, Bea, and John looked happy. Bea and John held hands and kept very close to each other the entire evening. Katherine, on the other hand, did not approve of this strange way of doing things and said little, but she changed her mood after a few sakes, and they all had a jolly good time—and some of them had a headache the next morning.

The following day the guests started arriving from Argentina, England, and all the places where they had friends. Everyone had to make a very special effort in order to look their best because there was going to be yet another party that evening at the Alvarezes'. Mercedes had organised little stalls of different kinds of food to be placed all over the garden, which was lit by Japanese lanterns; only the dessert was served from a buffet table in the dining room. Mercedes and Alberto were very good hosts, as were Bea and John who went around introducing their friends of many different nationalities. They all seemed to be having a good time judging from the sound of laughter, sometimes provoked by the confusion from lack of understanding of each other's language.

The next day was supposed to be Bea's day, but it did not start well. Mercedes was again worried, and this time Alberto was, too. Gaby was the only one who joined Bea in her room and told her sister, "I am so happy for you. I should be the one to be married first, but you are the sensible one in this family. I am sure you are going to be very, very happy."

Both girls embraced, and Bea said, "I hope you will come and visit me as often as possible; I am going to miss you so much."

"You are not leaving yet, dear sister. Daddy has some time here still, and John has not been here that long, either."

Mercedes came to tell them that lunch was ready. The ceremony was due to start at five in the afternoon, and it would take Bea a while to get dressed in her wedding dress; it was already hanging in her room, and she had tried it a dozen times.

The vast cathedral overflowed with flowers; bouquets were at the end of each pew and on the altar, one at the side of the seats for the bride and groom, and two even bigger ones at the two ends of the steps leading to them. Although this building was grey in colour, it was also imposing, and the light that filtered from the large stained-glass windows created an atmosphere of elation. It had been designed by a famous Japanese architect.

John was waiting for Bea, dressed in an immaculate morning coat, when the music started announcing the entrance of the bride. It was not the music that Bea had chosen, but she had to admit that it was beautiful.

From that moment onwards, everything happened so quickly that the next thing they knew, Bea and John found themselves in their going-away clothes by John's car. Later that night in their hotel room, while hugging and drinking yet another glass of champagne, John said, "Darling Bea, you looked so beautiful when you entered the church that my heart almost jumped out of my chest."

"John, you exaggerate everything. I love the dress my mother designed for me, but I was not all that beautiful."

"Oh, yes you were, and you are!"

"The hotel delivered what we asked them, don't you think?"

"Everything was perfect and very formal," John agreed.

"I know I would have liked to have a little less formality and maybe a band to dance to, but the hotel did not accept that. In Argentina we would have danced until five in the morning."

"In England, weddings are varied. Sometimes you have the fun ones, but many are just drinks after the ceremony."

"In Argentina we are more relaxed; men do not wear morning coats as a norm, and we like to dance."

"Are we going to dance a lot, Bea?"

"All the time, darling John; I shall wait for you when you come back from the office in my dancing shoes," Bea said with a laugh.

The next morning they rushed to take the plane that was to take them on their honeymoon. Bea had been on location to Saipan on the island of Guam which is part of the Mariana archipelago in the South Pacific, and she had asked John to go with her to this paradise which was not all that far from Japan.

It was indeed a tiny paradise. They were able to go around the island twice in one day, but most of the time they took it easy—not because they did not want to be active, but because John had seen a half-sunken ship dating from the Second World War in the middle of the ocean, and he wanted to go and investigate. Bea stayed on the beach. The ship was further than John had calculated, and by the time he re-joined a worried Bea, he was glowing. His skin was deep red, and his eyes shone in an unusual way. When Bea touched him, he felt extremely hot but was shivering. That night and the subsequent two were not comfortable for John, but Bea proved that she could be a good nurse. It was not a very romantic honeymoon because John was literally untouchable, but it did not matter—they had time for that.

CHAPTER NINETEEN

Two months after they came back from Saipan one day Bea felt sick. She sort of guessed what was happening but did not want to tell John or her family before she was completely sure. When the doctor confirmed that she was going to have a baby, she realised that she and John had not talked about having children. She thought that most couples probably talked before embarking on having a family. She was a Catholic, and for her children either came or not, depending on God's wishes—but John was not a Catholic, and she did not know how he was going to take it. The fact was that they were just beginning to know each other, and it would have been good to have time by themselves a little longer before having to look after a baby. Despite all these negative thoughts, Bea was happy with the news and could not wait to tell everyone.

John first reaction was disbelief. "It has nothing to do with me!" he said, looking at Bea straight in her eyes.

"Who do you think it has to do with, then?" Bea answered, feeling hurt.

John kept looking at her and then took her in his arms. "My darling, darling Bea, I never thought about babies. I just thought about you and me. I cannot believe that we are actually starting a family. Have you told your parents?"

"Not yet. I thought I should tell you first."

"I must tell my grandparents. My grandfather was afraid that our family name would be extinguished after me; I am the last Fellow in our family."

"Darling John, your family name might be extinguished anyway, if we only have girls."

"I have a feeling that it will be a boy," John said.

"Will you be disappointed if it is a girl?"

"Of course not, especially if she looks like you."

Bea laughed while holding his face in her hands. "You are a nut case, John. I hope I will be able to give you a whole lot of boys and girls—all looking like you and me."

The baby was born one week after he was due. Bea had been sent for long walks, and it finally paid off. She started having contractions while strolling in her favourite temple near her parents' home.

"Mummy, are you in?" asked Bea, letting herself in with her key.

"Bea, darling, how are you?" Mercedes appeared from her room in the second floor and leaned over the banister.

"I think the baby is finally coming."

"Call the doctor! I will be down in a minute."

Bea did as she was told and waited for her mother, timing each contraction; they were getting closer and closer. "I would like to go and collect my suitcase."

"How far apart are they?" Mercedes asked.

"About ten minutes."

"We have time."

Mercedes followed Bea into their flat and picked up the small suitcase that had been ready for over a week. By now Bea's contractions were five minutes apart, and they had to hurry.

A nurse that was waiting for her took her to her room and then asked for a wheelchair. Bea had been brave up to now, but she said to the nurse, "I think the baby is coming." Bea was now completely concentrated on controlling the contractions in the way she had been taught. In Japan ladies did not scream, and Bea showed that she could do just as well.

The nurse had a look and said, "You are right. I am taking you to the delivery room. I'll call the doctor."

The little boy had a mop of brown curly hair and bright blue eyes that were wide open from the moment he came into this world. His eyes seemed to be saying, "I am here to enjoy myself. Now where is the fun?"

He was handed to her mother, who bonded with him immediately.

John had been called by Mercedes, and he was waiting in her room with his mother-in-law when Bea was brought back holding Charles.

Her first words to John were, "You can call your grandparents—the family name is safe."

She handed the baby to John, who was terrified of dropping him and held him with both hands, as if he was a flower pot.

"You must hold his head; babies can't keep their heads up by themselves until they are a few months old," Mercedes said. "Here, I'll show you." She took the baby from John's arms.

John was grateful and went to kiss Bea: "You are wonderful, darling."

"I hope I am—I have not had sleepless nights yet!" She laughed.

John suddenly realised how their lives had just changed, and he looked lost. Mercedes and Bea looked at each other and burst out laughing.

"Don't worry John, you will only have to get up and feed him at night when I stop breast feeding," Bea said.

John's face lightened up, and the two women laughed again.

Bea had asked Gaby to be the godmother and she had accepted with pleasure. John was not sure of what to do and Bea had to ask him: "Why don't you ask Angus; he is your best friend, isn't he?

"Yes, but he is in England."

"It does not matter; he can still be a godfather."

"If you think so"

"I know so, give him a call and ask him."

John did as he was told and was surprised at how happy Angus's reply was: "It will be an honour old chap; I can't believe you are going to be a father; I was at your wedding not long ago."

"I can't either; everything has happened so quickly!"

"I bet you do not even understand what caused Bea's pregnancy; you were always a bit absent minded."

"You have not changed; your sense of humour is still the same," said John laughing.

Bea had also talked to their parish priest and now she asked John to let him know that Charles had finally arrived.

He was christened the same day that they left the hospital, one week after his birth. It was a small ceremony in the presence of Mercedes, Alberto, a few friends, and Gaby, who was to be Charles' godmother. The godfather could not make it because of the short notice, but he sent a telegram that read, "I am looking forward to playing cricket with you, young chap."

Bea asked, "What is cricket?"

"It is sort of like baseball, only a little bit more complicated."

"I see," answered Bea, not understanding at all.

CHAPTER TWENTY

Alberto was called back home to Argentina six months after Charles's birth. Gaby had finished her studies and had gone to France; she had been offered a job at an art gallery as a restorer of valuable paintings.

John, Bea, and Charles were alone for the first time as a family. John and Bea had found that being parents was even more wonderful than they had imagined. Charles slept through the night after only two months and was on some solid food after four. By the time his grandparents left, he was a lovely little boy, crawling all over the place and giggling all the time.

The following six months were blissful, and when John received the news that there was a vacancy with a promotion in London, it was received with mixed fillings. John still feared that Bea might not adapt to living in London, but Bea felt that she would go to the moon for her beloved men.

"Darling, I told you I love London," she reassured him.

"How long were you there?"

"I know I was there for only two days, but I loved the city and met a lot of people."

John pointed out, "Bea, you met a lot of tourists."

"I met some English people, too."

"Yes—the tour operators and the concierge in the hotel."

"You are being negative, John. We are a family, and we are going as a family. I don't believe our life will change by being in another city."

"I am glad you are so optimistic, and I promise I will be there for you if you are not happy."

On that note they busied themselves packing the vast amount of things they had acquired since they were married. They had a mountain of wedding presents plus some furniture that Bea had ordered from Hong Kong. She had liked the tables that she saw while shopping with Florencia, and she had sent a letter to the kind man who had given her the figurine. Everything had arrived in perfect condition as soon as it passed customs, which had delayed it for some time.

Katherine was waiting by the rail that separated the arrivals from those who had gone to greet them. She did not look her best, and her complexion was grey. She was wearing her country clothes: boots, a skirt that to Bea looked Scottish by its design, and a Barbour jacket that Bea did not think much of but kept that to herself. They all embraced, and John introduced Charles to his paternal grandmother. Katherine bent down and said: "Hello there." The little boy smiled broadly; that made Katherine's serious face light up for a minute.

As they left the terminal to go to the parking lot, Bea noticed the weather: it was as grey as Katherine's face. Bea hoped for sun everywhere the next day; she could not let John see that she was anxious. She was going to make this work, and she held Charles' hand even tighter. The boy lifted his little face to look at his mother, and Bea's misgivings disappeared. By the time they reached the car, she was happy again.

John sat in the front with Katherine, and Bea and Charles sat in the back with some of the luggage that did not fit in the boot. Bea looked out of the window but did not recognise the landscape; it looked different from the train, or perhaps it was because then it was summer, and now it was almost winter. The thought made her shiver.

The house did not look the same, either—it was bigger than she remembered. But of course the last time she was there, she had only been shown the sitting room. Katherine had added a wing to it for John and the family; it could be reached by a narrow staircase that led from the kitchen. It was so cold inside that Bea kept her coat on and did not take Charles' off, either. Then Katherine decided to air the house and opened all the windows. Bea thought that, perhaps, this just might warm up the house—it felt colder inside than out.

The house dated from the sixteenth century and had been a pub in the very beginning; it still had the huge fireplaces of the time. One of them, the one in the dining room, was now occupied by a table that Katherine used as a side table. The windows were little squares that hardly allowed in the light from outside, lit the cold rooms. The walls were made of very thick stone. There was a big sitting room, a large dining room, and a family room or study close to the kitchen, where Katherine spent most of her day. The study was the only room that had a heater; there was no central heating.

John and Bea were shown into their living area that had three bedrooms and a bathroom. The largest bedroom and the bathroom had already been there; Katherine had used it as a guest suite. The other two rooms had been built in the same style as the rest of the house because it was a listed building and could not be changed in its appearance. Fortunately the bathroom, which had been renovated, had an electric heater.

Outside, the garden stretched far beyond what could be seen from the house. Katherine was a good gardener, but now that she was getting on, she had neglected some of the land. But in any case, at this time of the year, there was not much to look after.

"Katherine, do you mind if I go upstairs and unpack?" Bea asked.

"Of course, not—take your time." Katherine wanted to have time on her own with her only son, whom she had not seen since the wedding. She still felt uncomfortable with Bea.

Bea went upstairs with Charles and started unpacking their things. Katherine had put a cot in his room, which Bea felt was thoughtful. There was also a bed, a chest of drawers, and a table. She still did not take his or her coat off. She went to the bathroom, turned on the electric heater on the wall, just above the door, and ran a bath for Charles, who was in his room playing happily with the toys Bea had just given him. When she felt the room was warm enough, she took him there and undressed him in the bathroom. She had prepared his towel, pyjamas, sleepers, and dressing gown so that he would not be cold after his bath. Mother and child played for a while with some of the bath toys, and after the bath, she put him in his cot with his dressing gown on and fetched some socks from the drawer. Then she went down to ask Katherine if she could warm up the baby food and milk that she had also brought down with her.

"Are you going to feed him upstairs?" Katherine asked.

"Well, he is in his pyjamas."

Katherine insisted, "You must bring him down."

Bea hesitated. "It is a little bit cold for him here."

John took over the conversation and said, "Perhaps we could turn the heater on in the study, Mum." He went and turned on the heater without waiting for an answer.

As usual Charles was no trouble; he ate what he was given. Then Bea took him back to his room. She had taken her coat off while bathing and feeding him, but now she felt a chill and put it on again while she read to Charles and prayed with him before turning the light off. He had said good night to his father and grandmother before going up to bed.

Bea went down again wearing her coat; she was so cold she forgot to take it off.

"Do you always wear your coat indoors?" asked Katherine.

"Eh? No, it is just that I feel the cold," Bea replied.

"I did not realise it was that cold in the house."

"Mother, you are used to these temperatures. Bea is not, and I am afraid I'm not anymore, either. Where are your other heaters?"

"In the sitting room," answered Katherine in an offhand manner.

John fetched another heater and put the one in the study together with the one he had just fetched in the dining room.

Katherine had prepared dinner in advance and they went into the dining room, which still was freezing cold despite the two heaters. John placed one near where Bea sat, and she took her coat off but could not stop shivering. The soup that they had was very welcome.

"This is delicious, Katherine. You must teach me how to make it."

"Don't you know how to cook at all?" Katherine said.

"I can cook a few dishes, but I never really learned how to cook. We always had a cook."

Katherine raised an eyebrow to John and did not comment.

"Darling, it is difficult to find help in England, so we tend to do everything ourselves," John explained.

"I will learn," Bea said, smiling at both of them.

After dinner they washed the glasses and silver and put the rest in the dishwasher. At least Katherine had a dishwasher.

Bea went up to continue unpacking their things while John had a drink with his mother in the study. She went down again and asked Katherine if it would be all right to take one of the heaters to their room.

"You have an electric blanket in your bed," Katherine replied.

Bea looked bewildered, and John explained. "We put electric blankets under the sheets to keep us warm at night; you can turn it off if it gets too warm."

Bea's look turned into semi-horror now. She would be terrified of sleeping on something that might give her an electric shock. Either way, she was sure that nothing would make her feel too warm in that house.

John realised this and added, "Mother, I am sure you will not mind if we take a heater upstairs with us."

"If that is your wish."

Bea did not sleep that night. The bed felt damp, and although she was bursting to go to the bathroom, she could not bring herself to get up—the heater in the room was not enough, and the bathroom's heater was off.

The next morning John saw one of the signs that he had feared, and that Bea had never considered. She could not hide that she was beginning to feel miserable in the English weather, and she was worried that Charles might catch a cold and had dressed him for the Arctic.

"Mother, would you mind taking us to buy a car this morning?" John asked.

Katherine raised an eyebrow but simply said, "When would you like to go?"

"As soon as we are all ready, and then we can go to a pub for lunch. Bea does not know what a country pub looks like."

"What about Charles?" Katherine said.

"He will of course come with us."

"I do not know if children are allowed to go to pubs."

"Mother, we are not planning to fill his bottle with whiskey. I am sure we can find somewhere where he will be accepted."

Bea was quiet that morning. She was not only cold, but she was totally disoriented. It was still raining when they started that morning in search of a car. Again Bea saw something new. "I have never seen anything like it."

"Have you never seen a car dealer before?" John asked.

"Yes, I have but not like this. The ones I have seen carry only their make and are indoors. There are so many makes in this yard."

"These are used cars."

"Are we going to get a used car, John?"

"Darling, we are going to get a virtually new car—it is not worth buying a new car; they lose their value as soon as you have taken them out of the show room. This way we can keep up replacing it every one or two years, and we will not lose too much in the process."

They looked at several cars, and then John stopped by a dark blue BMW that looked in good condition. "What do you think of this one?" he asked his wife.

Bea and Katherine agreed it looked good, but Katherine said, "You'd better try it before you make a decision."

The salesman that had been following them gave the keys to John and said, "Take your time; it's quiet today."

The four of them, with Katherine sitting in the front, jumped in the car and went for a drive that they all enjoyed. They went back, and after the formalities, John wrote a cheque and said to Bea, "You go with Mother, and Charles I will follow."

"John, is there a pharmacy where I can buy some more nappies for Charles?" Bea asked.

"You do not buy nappies in pharmacies," replied Katherine.

"In Japan I always bought disposable nappies in pharmacies."

"What do you mean, disposable nappies?"

Bea said, "Nappies that you throw away."

"You will not find anything like that here," Katherine said a bit derisively.

Bea looked at John, and he said, "Mother, I am sure that there are disposable nappies in this area."

"I do not think there are disposable nappies in England."

Bea was growing more and more incredulous by the minute. How could it be that in a country like England, there were no disposable nappies."

"We will go to a chemist and ask about them," John insisted.

What Katherine had said was confirmed by the chemist: "You can buy Milton here, if you like."

Bea inquired, "What is Milton?"

Katherine turned to her and said, "Don't you know what Milton is?"

"I have never heard of it," Bea admitted.

The chemist interrupted, "You put one or two measures of Milton in a bucket with water, and then you put the diapers in it overnight. In the morning you can wash them in the washing machine at a high temperature."

Bea was happy to hear that at least there were washing machines in England. "But I do not have any diapers—I have only bought the disposable ones in Japan."

The chemist went to fetch a bottle of Milton and gave it to Bea. "Start by buying this; then you can go and get a bucket and the diapers. There is a babies' shop not far from here where you will find them." He gave John directions, and they left. Katherine had a broad smile on her face.

John said, "I am hungry. We will go and find the diapers after lunch." In the restaurant, John asked his mother, "Would you look after Charles for a few days while we go flat hunting?"

"If you get a nanny, I will."

"I thought that it was difficult to find help in England."

"There are nannies and cooks and butlers in England, but they cost a lot."

"We will get a nanny until we settle down," John said reluctantly.

CHAPTER TWENTY-ONE

That evening Katherine hosted a drinks party to introduce her new family. Bea was used to socialising, and she charmed all the guests who had been warned that Bea was a foreigner and might not know how to behave with the English country gentry.

"Would you know where I can find a nanny to look after Charles?" Bea asked a younger woman who had children at school—her name was Dorothy and she and Bea were to remain friends for the rest of their lives.

"There are many agencies," the woman replied, "but there is a girl who lives near me who might want to help you for a few weeks."

"Do you think she might want to come to London with us and look after Charles there?" Bea had been thinking that she would prefer to take Charles with them.

"I don't see why not. I will ask her to get in touch with you in the morning."

That night Bea slept—she was exhausted. But early the next morning, they were woken up by Katherine, who came out of the cupboard opposite their bed.

Bea was even more perplexed than she had been the previous day when she learned about the nappies. Had Katherine spent the night in the cupboard?

John said, "You should not do that, Mum. I am married now." Bea still did not understand and kept looking from mother to son while they talked. John explained, "This was my old room before it became the guest's room, and Mother used to come in from her side of the house to this one through this cupboard. Her room is on the other side."

Bea did not think there was any point in saying anything, and she kept quiet.

Katherine announced, "Dorothy has just rang, and she asked me to give you the nanny's telephone number. She is waiting for your call, Bea."

Bea got up and put her dressing gown on. She then took the piece of paper from Katherine's hand and went to make the call.

"Hello, is this Lucy?"

"Yes."

"I am Bea Fellow."

"Oh, yes! Dorothy told me that you are looking for a nanny."

"Yes, it is for a few weeks while we look for a flat in London. Would you be prepared to come with us? We will be coming back for the weekends so that you can see your family. We will make it worthwhile for you."

"That's fine. When do you want me to start?"

"We would like to go to London tomorrow, if that is all right with you."

"Sure. Would you like me to come and see you today?"

"That would be great; could you be here in about an hour?"

Bea ran to get Charles changed and to experiment with the new diapers that the saleswoman had showed her how to fold. Then she had a quick shower and went down for an even quicker breakfast. She was ready for Lucy when the nanny knocked at the door.

"Hello, Lucy, I am Bea, and this is Charles," Bea said while she presented Charles to Lucy.

"What a lovely boy you are," Lucy's said to Charles, who extended his hand with a broad smile on his little face—as he had been taught to do—and shook Lucy's.

"John, this is Lucy; she is coming with us to London tomorrow."

John greeted Lucy, not understanding the situation. Neither did Katherine.

"Katherine, this is Lucy. She will look after Charles in London while we look for a flat. I think that it will be better because he does not know you very well."

Katherine reply was, "I hope you are not going to spoil Charles."

"I am sorry, Katherine, I should have told you before, but everything was organised so quickly, and I was so tired last night that I forgot to tell you."

"She forgot to tell me too, Mum," John said.

"I am sorry, John. I just do not think it is fair for such a small child to be left so suddenly."

"You are right, Bea. I hope you don't mind, Mum. We will be back for the weekends so that Charles can start getting used to the house." He stopped himself from saying "your house".

"It is fine with me, but I do not think it would be so terrible for Charles to be left with strangers every once in a while."

"Oh, he is used to strangers, but in his own home. These surroundings are not familiar to him yet." Bea said. She then took Lucy, who had heard enough about the family saga, to see Charles' room and to show her the new nappies.

"Do you know how to change these nappies?" Bea asked.

"Yes, of course!"

"All this is new to me; in Japan we used disposable nappies."

"I believe that there are some around, but they are not so easy to get hold of, and they are very expensive."

"In that case, you know about the Milton, too."

"I do," said Lucy, smiling.

"Well, I think this is all that I wanted you to know. Can you be here tomorrow at about ten?"

"Of course."

Bea surprised Lucy when she gave her a hug and said, "I am so glad that you can come with us. I was worried about leaving Charles."

Despite the fact that she was not used to this kind of emotional display, Lucy hugged Bea, too.

In the meantime John had gone to ask the hotel if they had another room; fortunately the hotel could accommodate them in a suite with two bedrooms, which was going to cost a fortune.

"Bea, darling, I know you are used to living comfortably, but now that we have a family we should be careful with what we spend."

"I still have some savings; I will pay for the hotel, darling."

"I don't mean that—your money is yours."

"Then your money is yours, too." Bea replied, hugging him. "I promise to be thrifty, you will see."

Bea had gone on working part time after she had Charles, and she had saved enough to be able to afford some luxuries, but she knew that she had to be careful because money tended to disappear very quickly when one was not paying attention.

It was a comfortable ride in the new car. It also gave Charles time to bond with Lucy, who showed that she was good with children.

John had lined up several estate agents to visit about buying a flat, and also to rent one, while they waited for the two months that it took to get over the formalities of purchasing property in England—and they also had to wait for their belongings to arrive from Tokyo.

Finding a flat to rent was easy; they found one almost immediately, in central London. But buying was a completely different kettle of fish. Flats in central London were too small for the amount of money that John was prepared to pay, so they had to look out in the suburbs. By the end of the week, just when they thought that they would have to go on looking the following week, they found what they wanted. It was a quiet neighbourhood with trees down the sidewalks and lots of open spaces for Charles to play. The apartment building had its own garden. Transport was also good for John's work, and it was a direct drive to the country. They made an offer that was accepted and told the agent that they would be sending the deposit through their solicitor.

Bea asked Lucy, "Will you stay until we are settled in the new flat?"

Lucy had got on so well with the family that she accepted immediately. "I would love to; it will give me the opportunity to get to know London better."

They went back to Katherine and told her the news, which upset her. "I spent a fortune in your wing of the house so that you could come and stay with me," she said to John.

John hugged his mother. "Mum, we will come on the weekends."

Lucy went back to her home to tell her parents that she would be staying in London for a few months, and to prepare her luggage. "I am being very well paid. Bea is a kind person to work for, and Charles is adorable."

"We are happy for you, darling; it is time for you to leave home." Lucy was only eighteen, but she was a responsible girl. Her parents were happy that she had found a job.

Katherine had organised another party that evening. She liked to socialise, and although Bea was not what she had wanted as a daughter-in-law, she could not find any fault with her.

CHAPTER TWENTY-TWO

The next morning Bea felt sick. She was not sure what was wrong with her, but she guessed that perhaps she was pregnant again. What worried her was that she did not have a doctor, and she hardly knew anyone in England.

"Darling, you are looking pale today. Are you well?" John asked.

"I might be catching something, maybe a cold."

"I knew that you would say something like that," said Katherine, who had overheard the conversation.

John said, "Please, Mother."

"I am sorry, Katherine, if I have caught a cold it is not here, but in London," Bea said diplomatically.

"Most probably—the air in London is not good. You should look after yourself," replied Katherine a bit less aggressively.

"Hello, Dorothy."

"Hello, Bea, how did it go in London?"

"We found a flat to buy and also a flat to rent until all the paper work is done for the one we are buying; Lucy is coming to give me a hand until we are settled."

"That is great news."

"I wanted to thank you for introducing her to us; she has been marvellous with Charles."

"Yes, she is a good girl; her parents have brought her and her brothers up well."

Bea hesitated for a second before saying, "Dorothy, may I ask you another favour?"

"Yes, of course."

"I need to see a doctor."

"What is wrong?" Dorothy asked, concerned.

"Please don't tell anyone, but I think I might be expecting again."

"I see. Would you like me to make an appointment with my gynaecologist?"

"Do you think he might be able to see me next week?"

"I have known him for years; he looked after me and delivered all my babies. I will tell him that you need to see him soon."

Bea replied, "I will tell John that I would like to stay here next week."

"I will call you back as soon as I find an appointment."

Bea went back to the kitchen, where John was feeding Charles under the supervision of Katherine.

"Katherine, would you mind if I stay here with Charles and Lucy next week?" Katherine was surprised at this request and was slow to answer. John looked at Bea, not understanding. "It is just that Dorothy has invited me to her house, and she has been so kind. I did not want to turn her down," Bea improvised. "Darling, do you mind?"

John said, "I am delighted, Bea. Charles can get used to this house."

Katherine finally said, "That will be fine with me."

The sun had come out, and although it was still very cold, John and Katherine took Charles out into the garden. The toddler ran around, pursued by his father, and they also played hide and seek; even Katherine took part in this game. By the time they came in for lunch, they all had rosy cheeks and were puffing.

Dorothy had rung back Bea with the news that her doctor could see her on Tuesday. Bea was not feeling sick anymore and was much more relaxed. She had busied herself with making beds and doing a wash of Charles diapers in the washing machine that Katherine had in the garage.

"Katherine, what can I do to help you with lunch?" Bea asked.

"I have some soup already made in the fridge, and we could make sandwiches to go with it."

"May I make the sandwiches?"

"You will find ham, cheese, and tomatoes in the fridge."

"Good, I will deal with everything."

Katherine smiled. "John, would you like a drink?"

"Sure, Mum. Darling, would you like a drink while you are dealing with the food?"

"I am all right, darling. Do you mind if Charles eats with us at the table, Katherine?"

By now Katherine knew that Charles was a well-behaved child and answered, "That will be fine."

John looked at Bea with an understanding look and then kissed her on the cheek. They both thought they had won one battle against Katherine.

But that evening during dinner, Bea asked where she could go to church, the following morning being Sunday.

"I think there is a Catholic church in the next town, but you can always come with us."

John had been going to church with Bea since they were married, and now he found himself with yet another problem. "Are you planning to go to church tomorrow, Mum? You do not always go to church on Sunday," he said.

"I will go for your sake, John."

"I could go with Bea."

"Or perhaps Bea could come with us. Our church is much closer."

Bea had never been to a church that was not Catholic, but she knew that if she insisted, there was going to be yet another row. "That is fine, Katherine. We will all go to your church tomorrow."

John looked at Bea, who smiled. She would pray in church for her family, and she was sure that God would not hold it against her if she tried to keep peace with its members.

John had to go back to London that Sunday evening. He was going to a hotel for the first few days, and then he would be moving to the rented flat.

Bea had alerted Lucy that she was going to be staying with Katherine, so she only needed a few things for that week. There was room for her either with Charles or in the other bedroom, which was unoccupied. Bea felt protected having Lucy around, who helped Bea interpret the way the English did things.

On the Tuesday Bea told Katherine that she was going to see Dorothy with Charles and Lucy. That suited Katherine, who had a game of bridge organised for that afternoon.

Bea did not drive. In Japan it was difficult to learn to drive, and because public transport was so good she had never felt the need to do so. Fortunately Lucy had learnt how to drive a few years before, and she knew all the country lanes by heart. John had taken the train to London and left the car for Bea; it was the only way of transport in the county.

Bea had to confide in Lucy about her appointment with the doctor since Lucy was driving, but she asked her not to tell anyone yet. Lucy was thrilled with the expectation and took Charles to her home while Bea was at the doctor's. Lucy wanted her mother to see for herself what an adorable child he was. Charles had taken to Lucy and did not mind being left with her.

As Dorothy had said, the gynaecologist was a charming old man who confirmed that Bea was indeed expecting another baby. "You are about six weeks along."

"How strange—I had a period last month."

"Sometimes you can still have periods for one or two months after conceiving."

"I did not know that."

"Not many people do."

Bea sighed and said, "I will have to find a gynaecologist in London."

"I can refer you to one. If you wait a minute, I will give you his address and telephone number. I will also write a note to him."

"Thank you very much."

Bea dialled the telephone and said, "Dorothy, I am here at the gynaecologist."

"What is the verdict?"

"Positive."

"That's great! Come and have a cup of tea with me," Dorothy suggested.

"I will call Lucy to come and collect me, and we will be with you in about forty minutes."

Bea rang Lucy who was also thrilled with the news but told her mother not to say anything to anyone yet.

"Are you happy?" Dorothy asked.

"I am always happy to have a child, but I sincerely do not know how John is going to take it. We have just bought a two-bedroom flat."

"I see what you mean; it might be a bit tight for you all and Lucy."

"I think we are going to have to move in and then out."

"Couldn't you cancel the purchase?"

"I don't know."

"Have you paid a deposit?"

"No, not yet; John has just got in touch with the lawyer for all the searches and things you do here in England before buying a property."

"In that case, you must ring him tonight and cancel," Dorothy said. "You can tell the estate agent that you need a bigger property—I am sure that he will be delighted."

"All this is new to me, Dorothy. I feel a bit lost," Bea confided.

"Don't worry. You will get used to life in England; you can always count on me."

Bea got up and gave Dorothy a hug, which took her by surprise, but the woman understood that that was the way Bea was.

"Why don't you ring John now," suggested Dorothy, showing her the telephone. "I will go and get the tea."

Bea dialled, and when John picked up she said, "Darling, it's me."

"Is there something wrong? You sound troubled."

Bea sighed and said, "I am."

"For goodness sake, what is wrong?" Now John was the one who sounded concerned.

"Remember I was not feeling so well at the weekend?"

"Yes . . . ?"

"Darling John, we are going to have another baby."

153

After a short silence John said, "How did that happen?"

"The usual way, John—how else?"

That made John laugh. "What are we going to do? We have just decided to buy a flat that is not going to be big enough for our family."

"I have been talking to Dorothy; I am at her place now. She thinks that we can cancel the purchase and ask the estate agent to look for a bigger place; perhaps a house would be better."

"I know . . . but that will mean a much bigger mortgage."

"We would eventually have had more children; we might as well provide for them now."

"How many are we planning to have?"

"How would I know, John? I am not making the babies by myself," Bea teased.

"You are wonderful, Bea. I did not know that I was marrying a rabbit."

"Well, it seems that you have, so you'd better find a big house."

"I will call the estate agent right away."

"Thank you, darling. I love you."

"I love you too, very much."

Bea hung up and went to see Dorothy, who had stayed in the kitchen in order not to pry in the conversation. "John will call the estate agent right away; he thinks I am a rabbit," she said.

Dorothy laughed and said, "I like that."

Bea, Lucy, and Charles arrived back at Katherine's after six. Charles had been fed at Dorothy's, and he was tired because he had not had his afternoon nap. Lucy took him up for a quick bath and put him to bed while Bea went to talk to Katherine.

"You have been a long time," Katherine said. "Charles must be exhausted."

"Yes, he is. Lucy has taken him to bed. I was not completely honest with you, Katherine." Katherine lifted an eyebrow as she usually did when she was annoyed. "I have been to the doctor; I am expecting another baby."

Katherine was speechless for a few seconds and then said, "But you have just bought a two-bedroom flat."

"I know. I rang John from Dorothy's, and he said he would ring the estate agent. He called me a rabbit."

At that Katherine laughed. "It seems that you are!"—Katherine believed that one only had a sense of humour if one was able to laugh at oneself—but she did not really like anybody else laughing at her.

Bea said, "Everybody thinks so. Do you mind if I call my parents? I will, of course, pay for the call."

"Please do. I will go and get us something to eat." Katherine departed.

When Bea heard someone pick up on the other end, she said, "Mummy?"

"Bea! How wonderful to hear you, how are you."

Bea filled her in with all that they had been doing the past week and then said, "You are going to be grandparents again."

"That is great news! I will tell your father when he comes back. How are you feeling?

"I felt a bit sick the last two days, but today I am fine."

"When is the baby due?"

"In about seven and a half months."

"Darling, your life does not have a dull moment."

"It does not seem so," Bea answered with a laugh.

CHAPTER TWENTY-THREE

After a month of looking everywhere for the right house to buy, the estate agent rang one afternoon to inform them that he had found the perfect place for them and wanted to know if they would like to see it the following day. John and Bea were full of expectation when they turned up in front of a Victorian house on a tree-lined road in an up-and-coming neighbourhood. According to the estate agent, it had just been modernised by its owner, who was an architect. The outside certainly showed that it had been refurbished by the newly painted door with stained-glass panels, a polished brass letter box and knocker.

They were led to the sitting room, which was on the left of the staircase that led to the bedrooms. In Victorian times it had been a smaller room, but now it had been opened into the next room as well, and they could see a small garden at the end. This long room connected to the dining room via a pair of double doors. The kitchen was next to the dining room, and it had a door to the garden. Bea loved this part of the house and was eager to see the upstairs, which consisted of two large bedrooms and a study, a large family bathroom, and an en-suite shower room in the main bedroom. On the third floor there was a huge bedroom and a good size bathroom. She knew that it was well above the price that John wanted to pay, and she did not insist on buying it, but John had also fallen in love with this property, which was perfect for three or four children and had easy access for transport and the club of which John was planning to become a member.

John managed to get a bigger mortgage, a loan from his mother, and another loan from his godfather. He said, "Bea, I do not know how

I am going to pay for all that I have borrowed, but I will make ends meet."

"I could work," Bea offered.

"And what would you do?"

"I could teach Japanese to beginners."

"I know, but you are needed here." He gave her a kiss on the forehead and added, "Everything will be all right."

Two months later they moved in. Bea's tummy was quite big by now, and she walked like most pregnant women, with her legs slightly apart. Charles, who was nearly two now, enjoyed walking behind his mother copying the way she walked and making all those who saw them laugh.

A few months later, Bea felt a contraction but did not pay much attention to it, because Charles had taken his time arriving. She went shopping that morning, but by tea time she knew that she was in labour. She called John, who hurried home to take her to the hospital, but in all the rush he lost his way. When they arrived at the hospital, she was taken straight to the delivery room, where Ernest was born a few minutes later. He did not have his eyes open like Charles; he only seemed to want to sleep. As with Charles, Bea handed Ernie to his father who had learnt how to hold a baby and was amused by this little bundle of flesh. When Ernest finally woke up, his eyes were green, a beautiful emerald colour that with time became hazel like Gaby's. Ernie, like Charles, was a contented baby who did not cry as long as he was fed. On the other hand, Charles was into everything—he especially enjoyed finding screws that he could unscrew. How he did it was a mystery, but he managed to dismantle whatever he found with his little fingers. It was a good thing that Lucy had decided to stay with them for the foreseeable future; she had become a member of the family.

One day Bea said to Lucy, "I have been inquiring about courses that are subsidised by the government; they are virtually free. Why don't you take one, too?"

"I would not know what to take."

"What would you like to do when you leave us?" Bea asked.

"I would like to get married and have children."

"You could take a course in economics; that way you can economise when you get married."

They both laughed at that, but in the end Lucy followed Bea's advice.

Bea wanted to help with the house bills once she finished her course on Interior Decoration, but she found that she was again pregnant. Now she was almost ashamed—John had called her a rabbit before, and it was definitely confirmed.

"At least we have enough room for everybody," John said as he kissed her. "Do you think we will have another boy?"

John's grandfather had passed away soon after Charles birth and Bea said to John: "Your grandfather would have been happy to see that the name is now more than secure. It is such a shame that he is no longer with us.

"Yes, it is, but I am sure he knows it anyway."

Sebastian was born exactly twenty months after Ernie. This time Bea did not even realise that she was in labour until her water had broken. She had to ring an ambulance because John would not have been able to get to her on time. She was puffing regularly when the ambulance arrived and she was laid down on a stretcher. Two young male nurses attended to her while she gave birth just as they were approaching the hospital. Sebastian was a large baby with light brown eyes and no hair. When his hair finally grew, it was red, like Katherine's when she was young—something that would distinguish him from his brothers. Ernie's hair was lighter than Charles but not as fair as his father's. Sebastian was not as easy as Charles and Ernie—he would fall asleep while being fed and then wake up and be hungry again. But a few months later, he had become another contented Fellow.

"Darling, I have been asked to go and reorganise the Paris office; they want me there as soon as possible."

"Such a pity—Gaby has gone to work in the United States; it would have been great to have seen each other more often."

"I know; one of these days she might be able to come back and see us."

Bea was left with the three children, Lucy who was an angel, and a degree in interior decoration that she would not need for the moment. John was asked to be the chief executive of the French subsidiary, with a much bigger salary.

"Lucy, you know that I had to cut short my trip to Paris because my friend wanted to go to Spain," Bea said. She had often talked to her about her odyssey half around the world. "Well, now I will not only go sightseeing, but I will live there! How great is that," she said in her usual manner throwing her arms in the air.

"Do you speak French?" Lucy asked.

"Not really—I am going to have to take a course. And I think you should, too; we must be able to communicate with the people around us."

"From economics to French? I will end up being a professor of some kind," Lucy said with a laugh.

"And why not?" Bea said seriously.

Bea managed to let the house before the family joined John in Paris.

CHAPTER TWENTY-FOUR

John had found a beautiful flat in one of the fashionable neighbourhoods in Paris, near the Place Victor Hugo. It was an old and elegant building with large flats. He had waited for Bea to arrive before moving in.

As soon as they were settled and had found schools for Charles and Ernie, Bea went in search of a course in French. She tried two before she finally found the one that suited her; it was free, and now that she had one or two words of French already in her possession, it was perfect for her. This course was for immigrants from different parts of the world who wanted to live permanently in France; some of them did not even know how to write in their own language. The main attraction for Bea was the fact that she was not only going to learn French but also the way the French lived.

She had a busy life with John. They were invited out often, and she had to entertain, which meant that she had to be on the run all day long. Lucy was a great help, but Bea wanted to see her children and be part of their lives. Then one day she started haemorrhaging and lost a lot of weight. She had to go and see a doctor. Up to now she had only been to the doctor because of the babies—but this was different.

The doctor said, "You have a lot of fibroids; they bleed a lot. You should have a hysterectomy."

"Don't you think I am too young? I am only twenty–eight," Bea protested.

"If you do not have a hysterectomy, you must avoid getting pregnant again—it could be very dangerous for you."

This was a problem that she had never envisaged. She did not believe in contraception. How could she ask John to abstain from sex? It would be the only way to avoid getting pregnant again.

That evening when they were getting ready for bed, John asked, "What did the doctor say?" He had been worried about Bea; she was already thin, and she was even thinner now.

"She found fibroids and recommended that I have a hysterectomy."

"Aren't you young too for that?"

"That is exactly what I said to her."

"And?" he prompted.

"She said that if I get pregnant again, it could be dangerous for me."

"In that case, you must have a hysterectomy."

"Darling, would you consider abstinence?"

"Abstinence?"

"Yes. I could start checking when I am fertile, and we will not do it on those days."

"Won't that be too complicated?" John asked.

"We can try."

"Darling, if that is what you want, so be it."

"Thank you, John."

Life went on as usual, Bea's and Lucy's French got better by the day. Lucy made a few friends in her class, and one of them became a special one. He was Dutch, and they communicated in French, although his English was almost as good as hers. He was in France learning the language, sent by his company.

One day Lucy came back from the park with the boys; they were in an exuberant mood and went on playing ball in the lift. The result was that the ball got stuck in between the lift and the shaft, so that the old machine stopped midway. The fire brigade was called, but the boys arrived home feeling deflated because the ball had had to be punctured to get the lift to move again.

Bea waited for John to get back from work before telling him about the children's adventure. "The concierge had to call the fire brigade. All the neighbours came out of their flats; some of them were quite upset."

"Boys are boys, after all," was John's comment. He looked tired and apparently did not want to hear about complications in the building.

"I think we should move to a house with a garden," Bea said, changing the subject.

John sighed. "There are not many houses with gardens in the centre of Paris."

"We could move to the suburbs nearby."

"That would mean a longer journey for me in the morning. You know what traffic is like at that time around the Champs Elysees?"

"We have to decide on a school for Charles, too. He is learning how to read and write in French; don't you think that it would be better if he went to an English school?"

"That is a point I should have considered; he will be going to boarding school eventually."

"Will he?" Bea said worriedly.

"Of course—they will all go to boarding school."

"We had not talked about it."

"Darling, I explained when we met that in England, children go to boarding school. Dorothy's children are at boarding school."

"I did not think ours would go."

"It is the only way to have a proper education, especially when we are moving from country to country. It would not be fair on them to keep changing them from school to school."

"I suppose you are right, but I will find it very difficult to part with them."

"We will see them during the holidays," John promised. "They can come to wherever we are, and you can also go and see them at school every once in a while."

"I'd rather not think that far ahead now; what I think is important is for us to move to a house and for Charles to learn how to read and write in English."

"All right, we will put his name down at the British School; you can start looking for a house."

"Can I borrow your driver?" Bea asked.

"Yes, you, of course; I hope you will find something not too far out."

"I will try."

They moved just before the following school term started. The house was not too far out, as John had asked; in fact, it was quicker for him by underground, with only a few stops to the Opera and then a change to the station nearest his office. Nevertheless, he kept using the driver; he took advantage by working in the back of the car.

Bea had kept having periodical check-ups to make sure that the fibroids were kept in control.

"Your tubes are blocked," the doctor said one visit.

"What do you mean?"

"It means that you cannot conceive."

"Are you sure?"

"I can see they are."

Bea was so happy that she almost kissed the doctor. She went back home, and that night she cuddled up to John. "We don't have to be careful anymore," she announced.

"How come?"

"My tubes are blocked—the doctor said I cannot conceive."

"Oh, my darling, that is great news."

Two months later Bea missed a period. She worried and asked for an appointment with the doctor, even though it was not yet time for another check-up.

The doctor looked troubled. "You are pregnant."

"It cannot be possible! You said I could not conceive."

"I do not remember saying that. I do not have here that I made the test."

"You told me that my tubes were blocked."

"They appeared to be blocked, but obviously they were not completely blocked, because you are pregnant," she said matter-of-factly.

Bea was worried. "What am I going to do?"

"Because of your condition, I could perform an abortion."

"No—I would never have an abortion."

"We will monitor you and the baby, and if we see that there is any danger for any of you, we will tell you."

Bea went straight to John's office; she could not wait until the evening. All sorts of horrible thoughts were going through her mind, and she could not face her children, who could be motherless in a few months.

"This is a surprise, Bea. You never come to visit," John said. Bea was pale and sombre. John got up, went around his desk and put his arms around her. "What is wrong, darling Bea?"

"I am pregnant."

"But you said . . . ?"

"I know—she is saying now that they were not completely blocked."

"What are we going to do?"

"She suggested an abortion."

John said, "If that is the safest solution . . ."

"No, I will not have an abortion. She said that they will monitor me and the baby closely, and if there was a serious problem, she will tell me."

"I find that most irresponsible—how can she make such a mistake?"

"I should have asked her to perform another test before believing her."

By the seventh month Bea was enormous; the baby was not that big, but there were two fibroids that were growing at the same time as the child, and she looked as if she was having triplets.

The doctor told her, "I think you should have a caesarean before you come to term. The baby is being squashed by the fibroids, and it will not come out normally. I suggest we do a hysterectomy at the same time—it is not safe for you to go on like this."

Two weeks later John took Bea to the clinic. She said good-bye to her children with a lump in her throat. Was this the last time that they would see each other?

She spent that night alone in her hospital bed, waiting for her operation in the morning. She did not sleep and prayed all night.

After the birth she woke up in her bed again. John was by her side and had a minute baby in his arms. Richard was not even two kilos, but he had very defined features and looked like John. She wanted to hold her son, but she was in a lot of pain; she had been given an injection to induce labour. She had been taught how to control the pain in Japan, but that was to have a baby, not to shrink back to normal; she found it difficult to breathe at this moment. Her legs were numb, and she could not move. Two huge tears came out of her eyes, and John put the baby down in the cot next to her. He hugged her until she was able to stop sobbing.

CHAPTER TWENTY-FIVE

Bea was finally feeling like herself again. It had taken her six months to recover from Richard's birth and her operation. She was now given hormones to replace the ones that her ovaries used to produced, but while she was nursing Richard, she had to do without them; it had been the hardest of the four pregnancies, but she loved him just as much. He was still small, but he was healthy and cheerful.

Alberto and Mercedes had come to visit, which had been a great help for Bea emotionally; she felt sheltered again. The children did not know them and found Alberto's jokes most amusing. It was good for them to know that they had other grandparents. Katherine had visited them at Christmas every year, and they knew her well. Alberto, who was still working, could only stay for a couple of weeks, but Mercedes stayed until she saw that Bea was better.

Then suddenly everybody was getting married. Gaby had rung her to let them know that she had found the man of her dreams—an American who had an art gallery. She said that they had been working together for a while, and they wanted to get married in Buenos Aires.

Then Lucy announced that her boyfriend had proposed to her. This was a blow to Bea and John, who relied on her for so much. Nevertheless, they were happy for her. She wanted to go back home to organise the wedding, and she begged them to attend with all the children. Her boyfriend had finished his French course and had left for work as soon as he proposed.

They would have to take the children out of school from Friday until Tuesday for Lucy's wedding, which was on a Saturday. Fortunately, Gaby was getting married just after Easter, so they would still be on holiday.

"I know my parents have been to visit us recently, but it will be good to go back to Argentina; I have not been back since I left twelve years ago. Only those of my relations who came to the wedding have met you."

John said, "It will be good to go and see the country you were born in, and to meet the rest of the family. The boys are getting very excited with all this news."

John left Bea to go and phone his mother.

"Hello, darling, how are you all?" Katherine said. She was now almost used to Bea; she had seen how she ran her household and could not find many faults with it.

"Can you accommodate us for a long weekend?" John asked.

"When will that be? That is a surprise."

"Lucy is getting married, and she has asked us to the wedding."

"That is another surprise. What are you going to do without her?"

"Don't ask—it is a sensitive subject," John admitted.

"I can imagine; you must tell me all about it when you are here."

The children ran out of the car and went to hug their grandmother. Katherine was happy to see them; she thought that they were sometimes a bit too boisterous, but that was the way children, especially boys, should be. Otherwise they were well behaved, and they could be taken to restaurants without making a mess.

"How are you, Katherine? Sorry to be imposing on you like this," Bea said.

"This was the reason for the extension—there is enough room for all of you there. I left the cot that Charles used to sleep in for Richard. Perhaps Charles could share with him; the bed is still there."

"Thank you so much. I hope we have not given you too much work."

"You know I like to cook in advance; the deep freeze is full of food, and we won't have to worry about cooking. You are here for such a short time that I thought I would take advantage of every minute."

"Thank you, Mum." John went to give her a hug after unloading the car. "The wedding is tomorrow afternoon. Lucy wants the boys to be her pages."

"Have they got special costumes to wear?" Katherine asked.

"Yes. The three boys will be wearing dark green velvet trousers and waistcoats, white shirts, and bow ties."

"I am looking forward to seeing them; she has also invited me."

The wedding was exactly what they would have expected from Lucy and her parents. It was a simple country wedding, but it was also demurely elegant. Lucy looked beautiful in her long silk dress and chiffon veil. She entered the old church that had been decorated with an array of flowers. The boys behaved well, walking just behind her holding her train, and Richard did not make a sound in his mother's arms through the service.

The party was in the barn, which was also decorated with flowers and candles on the tables; it looked lovely, and there was dancing afterwards. "This is the closest thing to an Argentine wedding I have seen abroad." Bea commented to John and Katherine.

"Weddings like this are common in the country; people like to eat, drink, and amuse themselves." Katherine explained.

"It is wonderful. I am so happy for Lucy."

John said, "So am I, darling. But what are we going to do without her?"

"We have been using babysitters for the past month."

"Yes, but we have had a few bad experiences."

Bea recounted to Katherine, "We found a babysitter that, according to Charles and Ernie, would go every half hour to see if the children were asleep, and she woke them up when she turned the light on."

"You don't want that anymore, do you? You should try 'London Nannies'; they are expensive but reliable," Katherine said.

"I will give them a ring before we leave." Bea was grateful for the information.

"By the way, have you chosen a school for the boys?"

There was a silence, and then John said, "We haven't yet done so, Mum."

"Oh, but you must! It is difficult to get them into the right school."

"I had not thought of sending the children to boarding school, Katherine," Bea replied.

"If they don't go to boarding school, they will never be able to get in to a good university."

"Yes, that is what John has told me."

"Honestly, Bea, you must put their name down immediately."

John interrupted, "We will talk about it as soon as we get back to Paris, Mum."

Bea tried to forget that conversation and made an effort to enjoy the stay in the English countryside but she was as cold as ever and longed to go back to her warm home. Nevertheless, she did call 'London Nannies' and asked them for someone who would like to work in France.

The Easter holidays were upon them, and the excitement grew by the minute. The boys had not been in an aeroplane yet; up to now they had always travelled by car when going on holiday. It was easier to pack them all in the station wagon with three rows of seats than to wait hours for any other kind of transport. Unfortunately for John and Bea, this time they could not do so, but John did buy extra seats so that they could have two full rows of three for the family; otherwise the younger children would have had to sit on their parents' laps.

They shouldn't have worried. Charles entertained Richard until the little fellow fell asleep, then he watched a film and then he fell asleep, too. Bea, who was sitting in front with Charles and Richard, turned around and saw that Ernie, Sebastian and even John were also fast asleep, but she couldn't do so herself. It had been such a long time since she had been to Buenos Aires. She had only kept in close touch with very few people, and she wondered how much everything had changed.

The plane was on time, and because they had so many children, they were given preferential treatment and were out in no time at all.

What they had not anticipated was that half the family would be waiting for them in the airport—even Bea's grandmothers were there.

It was a bit disconcerting for John and the boys to be kissed and hugged by so many people that were strangers to them. Then they all trooped in their cars and went to Alberto's and Mercedes's flat. Bea went to take care of Richard and left John with the other three boys to get acquainted with everyone. Later on Alberto announced that he had reserved a table at his club for lunch. Again they all got in their cars and went to the club, where they ate, drank, and talked for three hours. By the time they went to bed, they could hardly keep their eyes open—especially Bea, who had not slept the night before.

The next morning Bea turned to face John in bed and said, "Sorry, I had forgotten how things were here."

"Is this going to go on?" he asked.

"I am afraid so."

"I understand now why the Argentines like their coffee strong."

Bea laughed and cuddled up to him.

Every single day there was something prearranged for them. The boys enjoyed every minute of their stay; they had never received so much attention in their young lives. John and Bea would have liked to have a bit more time to enjoy the city and perhaps wander beyond, but they could not let down their family and friends.

Gaby had organised everything herself, and no one had a thing to say. It was a similar wedding to Lucy's, but for the fact that there were more people and that the party was held in the family's club after the church ceremony, which took place in a large church in the fashionable neighbourhood where her parents lived. Bea admired her sister for insisting that she would do it all herself, but then Gaby was ten years older than Bea had been when she was married.

CHAPTER TWENTY-SIX

Back in Paris, Bea was anxious that with so much entertainment, their children's discipline might had suffered, but school and homework took care of that. The London 'Nannies Agency' had been in touch and said that they were sending someone the following week. In the meantime John had broached the subject of boarding school again with Bea, who could not escape this time. She finally agreed on a school that was run by Benedictine monks in the north of England. She had chosen it because it was Catholic and had a good reputation, but also because Katherine's brother and his family lived nearby. She thought that the boys would be less homesick that way. She had forgotten to take into account that the boys hardly knew these relatives, who were strong Church of England believers.

The nanny arrived on a different train than they were expecting. She had missed the one she was supposed to take and had not bothered to let them know. Having waited for hours on the platform, and after ringing Bea, who had not heard from the nanny, either, John went back home to find that he had to return to the station because she had just rung from the "Gare du Nord".

John expected some kind of apology, but the only thing he got was, "That was a long trip. I am longing for a bath and bed."

John knew that this woman would not be the right person for the job. They needed someone reliable. He felt desperate for Bea, who had so much on her hands at the moment. She was even taking driving lessons because she could not take the children to their different activities and had to ask for John's driver.

Bea was waiting for them. The children were in bed, and she had something in the oven for John and the nanny. But this woman said, "I have eaten in the train. Could I go to my room? I am very tired."

Bea, being the person she was, immediately took her to her room, which was ready for her, as was her bathroom. "Is there anything that you need?" Bea asked.

"A cup of tea would be very welcome."

Bea ran down to prepare it.

John asked her, "What are you doing, Bea?"

"She wants a cup of tea."

"Shall we get a butler for her?"

"She is tired, John. We will see how she is tomorrow."

But the next day was not much better. The nanny got up late, after the three older boys had been taken to school and Bea had fed Richard. She appeared in the kitchen and asked, "What is there for breakfast?"

"There is orange juice and milk in the fridge, and cereal, bread, coffee, and tea in the larder. You can find bowls and cups in the cupboards."

"I usually have a cooked breakfast."

"We don't," Bea answered, now a bit annoyed. "Tomorrow you can make yourself a cooked breakfast, but you will have to get up much earlier. The day starts at seven in this household."

"I think I am jetlagged. I do not think I will be able to get up so early."

"There is only one hour difference between the continent and England. When you have finished your breakfast, I will show you the house and the children's things."

On the way to check on Richard, she took a peek into her bedroom and saw that there had been a sort of hurricane in there. There were things everywhere on the bed and on the floor. At this moment she should have realised that this nanny was exactly the opposite of what she needed, but she decided to give her yet another chance.

That evening the nanny was asked to give Richard a bath. Bea had prepared his little bathtub and all the things he needed, and then she had gone down to get the boys supper. After what seemed an eternity Bea, went up again and found the nanny cleaning Richard, who was on her lap, with a piece of cotton wool that she dipped in the water in the little bathtub.

"What are you doing?" asked Bea, perplexed at the sight.

"He is much too young to go in the bathtub."

"He is nine months, and soon he will be going in the big bathtub, as his brothers did. He will catch a cold if you go on doing that. Here, let me dry him and dress him." Bea was now cross. How could an agency send a person like this? This woman was not a qualified nanny.

After dinner, Bea told John what had happened. "She cannot stay," John declared.

"I know. Tomorrow first thing in the morning, I will tell the agency that we are sending her back."

"I am sorry, darling. What are we going to do?"

"I will manage with babysitters and the crèche by the station."

"You do not know how that crèche is—you have never tried it before."

"No, but I have seen many mothers and children there, and they all seem happy; it cannot be worse than this."

"No, it can't!" John admitted.

As agreed, Bea rung the agency the following morning and complained. "The nanny you have sent is not qualified. She does not even know how to bath a child!"

"We are sorry—we did not run a full check on her references. But she was the only one who wanted to go to France and we did not want to disappoint you."

"We are sending her back this evening. I have not spoken to her yet since she is not up, but I will do so now."

"We will send you a refund."

"Thank you."

Bea explained to the nanny that they needed someone more qualified than her to look after the children.

"I do not really care much for children. What I really enjoy is parachuting—there is a good centre in Paris; this is the reason I accepted this job."

"I do not think you will have much time for parachutes, living with us. My husband will take you to the station this afternoon."

"Fine, fine, I will pack my things.

That evening Bea had a bottle of champagne in the fridge.

"To a new life, John; from now on I will do things my way."

"To a new life, darling; may I know what your way is?"

"You will see," Bea teased.

"I hope you have not changed your mind about boarding school."

"No. Charles seems to have taken to the idea and is telling all his classmates about it. He feels very grown up."

CHAPTER TWENTY-SEVEN

As planned, John took Charles to the boarding school the following year for an interview. He was not due to start until his tenth birthday, in a few months. Charles was a gregarious boy who knew what he wanted, and he liked to organise his life—and sometimes others' lives—in a determined way. He created a good impression when he was interviewed and was accepted immediately.

"What would I learn here that I would not learn anywhere else?" Charles asked the headmaster.

Without blinking an eye the headmaster answered, "Our music curriculum is above average. We have a choir, and sometimes we go on tours. If you are interested in music, this is a good place for you."

"I have been learning the piano for nearly six years now."

"In that case you can take the Royal Academy's exams here and go on studying. What other interests do you have?"

"Well, I like languages; at home we speak three," Charles said.

"That is impressive! You can go on with them here, too, as well as the classics."

That threw Charles off balance: "The classics?"

"Yes, Latin and Greek. We excel in them. And there are also several sports you can choose."

After this conversation Charles could not wait to join the school.

But the day he left, Bea felt as if one of her limbs had been amputated. She could not bear the thought of not having Charles around, but she had the others to think about and she could not indulge in feeling sorry for herself.

A week later she received a telephone call from Charles. "Mummy, I miss you and Daddy and my brothers, and the food is horrible here." He did not sound grown up—he was her baby again.

She said, "I will ask Daddy to go and collect you; you don't have to stay there."

"That is not what you are supposed to answer," Charles scolded her. "You should say that I should go on trying and that I will get used to being here soon."

"But darling, you said you were miserable."

"I did not say I was miserable. I said I missed you and that the food is horrible."

"True, but I thought you wanted to come home."

"No, I don't," Charles said. "I just wanted to talk to you."

"I miss you very much, too, and I hope I will get used to not having you around."

"You will, Mum. I love you." Then they hung up.

Bea recounted this conversation to John that evening. "I think Charles is going to go far," John said. "You must not worry about him. I am sorry for you, darling, but boarding school is not as horrible as you might think. They are kept busy, and although the food is horrible, they are not malnourished."

"I know, I should be happy for him," Bea answered, not feeling sure of what she was saying.

Almost two years later came Ernie's turn to leave. Her big family was decreasing in numbers too fast and too soon for her taste. Ernie did not even have an interview—he was already known to the school from the various visits the family had paid them.

The only problem they encountered was when Katherine's brother and his family invited the children out. On one occasion they had been taken to an Anglican Church service, and they had been made to have communion by Katherine's sister-in-law.

The monks did not like this and wrote to Bea, but how could she deprive her children from going out with relatives, and how could she tell the relatives that the boys were not supposed to have communion in their church? Bea rang John for advice.

"I will call the school and tell them to tell the boys what they should do when they are invited out. You must not worry." That solved the problem to a certain point, because each time they went out, they did not go to mass on Sunday. Not even when Katherine went to see them would she take them to a Catholic church. That was another problem that Bea never thought she would have when she married John.

John's grandmother passed away that year. All her belongings were inherited by John and his aunts; Katherine had been left out of the will, and she did not like it when Bea said that she should have a share of the inheritance. "Who does Bea think she is?" she told John. "The inheritance should have come to me, and then to you when I die. Bea has no right to dispose of what is rightfully mine."

"That is what Bea thinks—this is why she wants you to have a share."

"I should not have a share—everything should be mine," Katherine complained.

"Mum, it is impossible to get the money out. The only thing we can do is go and spend it over there. What Bea is proposing is for all of us to go together."

"I want to go to South Africa."

"All right, why don't we go and spend Christmas and New Year in Zimbabwe, and then when we come back here, you go by yourself to South Africa on the money that is left?"

Katherine could not argue; it was a fair proposal. Even if she thought that Bea should not have any part of the inheritance, she agreed that her grandchildren should.

That was one of the coldest winters in France and in England. They left in the middle of a snow storm but arrived in Harare on a very hot day in the middle of a drought. There were signs everywhere that said, "Drink wine, not water." "Share a bath." "Wipe it, don't wash it." Bea found this amusing, but Katherine was still not laughing. Then came the most amusing part of their arrival: It was very early in the morning when they reached the hotel; there was nobody about, except all the staff who was lined up waiting for them. They had reserved so many rooms on the best floors that they were treated like royalty. The head porter counted, "One, two, three, four boys—strong woman!" Bea burst out laughing; she did not know that in Africa women who had boys were honoured. In Argentina, as far as she knew, it was the man that was praised. This deepened Katherine's bad humour, but nobody paid any attention to her.

They spent only two days in Harare—enough for John and Katherine to show Bea and the boys where they used to live, and the school that John's father and uncle had attended. Then they went to the Victoria Falls and had a wonderful Christmas; they celebrated it in the British style but for the fact that it was around the swimming pool. That evening there was a show of regional dancing, but when the family got together, Richard was missing: "We thought he was with you boys," John said.

"We thought he had gone to see Granny."

Katherine said, "I have not seen him since lunch time. Let's go and see in the swimming pool; he might be floating there."

"Oh, Katherine, please don't."

"Well, if you do not care for your children, something will happen to them."

"Stop it, Mum," John scolded.

But they all ran to the swimming pool, and there was no sign of Richard anywhere.

They went around asking everyone if they had seen a little boy, until by chance somebody who had been watching the show said, "I saw a little white boy with a little black boy watching the show from the stairs."

Bea said, "That must be Fungai, they have been playing together since we arrived."

Again they all went to see—and there he was watching the show with great concentration. It was such a relief that they stayed until the end, and then Bea went to him, "You must never, never, go anywhere without our permission."

"Sorry, Mum," he replied. Bea hugged him for a long time while Katherine shook her head.

To make matters worse, the next day when they were taken sightseeing to the falls, all the boys were wearing T-shirts, but Sebastian's got very wet with the spray, and he took it off. He got sun stroke and was badly burned; that night he was bright red and shivering. Katherine again found an excuse to accuse Bea of not looking after her children properly.

Bea felt like telling her how John had been during their honeymoon, but she thought better of it. There was no point in making things worse than they were. She would feel happier in South Africa visiting her friends. For Bea's part, she was very grateful to Gramp, as he was called, for giving them the possibility of visiting where John was born.

The boys could not stop talking about all the things they had seen and the great time they had had in the lovely warm weather. They enjoyed going down the Zambezi River, where they had seen crocodiles and had tea with the locals on an island. But what they recounted as the highlight of the trip was what happened one evening just before dinner. They had gone down for a drink, and each one had asked for a different one which confused the poor waiter, who did not speak fluent English and got them all wrong. When he was told that he had made a mistake, he scratched his head and said: "Oh, shit." The boys and even Katherine thought that this was very funny, and finally she changed her grumpy mood.

CHAPTER TWENTY-EIGHT

The following year at Easter, on Ernie's second holiday from school, the whole family went skiing. Bea still did not know how to ski; the experience she had had in Japan was enough for her. But even if she had wanted to learn, it was difficult to do so with the boys; somebody had to take them to their lesson and stay with the one who was too small to learn. This was the first holiday that she was alone for most of the day. The older ones either took lessons or went skiing with their father; Richard was in a class for children of his age. It was more a nursery than a ski school; they also painted and played when they were not skiing, and Richard loved it.

They had rented a chalet, and she took pleasure in cooking for her hungry family when they got back from the slopes. One evening just after Easter, they turned the television on after the children had gone to bed, and they were astonished by the breaking news. "Argentina has invaded the Falkland Islands."

They looked at each other but were speechless. The first thing that went through Bea's mind was, *It is your fault, Mother—you have jinxed us.*

John was finally able to utter, "This must be a mistake."

Bea could not control a sob. Since Richard's birth, she had been trying her best to go on with life as if her body was the same—but the hormones that she had been taking were not the same as the ones her body produced and made her feel weak. Then she had to cope with losing Lucy, who was not only her help but also her friend. When

Charles left, she had made herself strong for her other children, but after Ernie left she realised that she would be alone soon. In fact she was already alone—all her men left after breakfast, and she would sometimes meet them in the slopes for lunch, but most of the time they had lunch up in the mountains, and Richard was at the nursery. They came home exhausted in the evening and went to sleep as soon as they had supper. And now this; had her mother been right when she expressed her doubts about their marriage? Was this the beginning of the end? She cried until there were no more tears.

Shattered, John held her in his arms. What did this mean for them? He had not seen Bea like this before, and he did not know if he was going to be able to deal with it; he had been brought up by a woman who never expressed sorrow. Katherine dealt with sorrow by getting bad tempered. He could cope with that—it was much easier, and he could get cross with her, too. But he could not burst out crying, as Bea had.

They went to bed like zombies, hoping that the next they it would reveal that it had been a bad dream. But it was not a dream. The news was all over the newspapers, not only on the television.

John said, "We must explain this to the boys. They are going back to England, and they must know about this situation."

"You can do the explaining. I will call my parents."

But as Bea was approaching the telephone, it rang.

"Bea, have you all gone mad?" Katherine said to her.

"What do you mean, Katherine?"

"Haven't you heard? You have invaded our islands."

"To start with, Katherine, *I* have not invaded your islands; the Argentine government invaded them. But you were the ones who invaded them first. The fact that it was years ago does not mean that you did not do it. They are miles away from England but very, very close to Argentine territory. I do not appreciate your call." This was the first time that Bea had spoken like that to Katherine, or to anybody else older than her. She had been programmed to be respectful to her elders, but she was not being herself at this moment.

Katherine was taken aback. "I did not realise you felt so strongly."

"Neither did I, Katherine. I will pass you to John."

Bea gave the receiver to John, who was listening to the conversation with a worried expression on his face.

"What is the matter with Bea? She seems out of sorts," Katherine said to him.

"Mother, I do not know what you said to her, but this is a very sad day for our family."

"Well, I think the Argentines have gone mad."

"I don't want to talk about it, Mum. How are you, anyway? Did you have a good Easter?"

"Yes, I had a good Easter, but I just do not know what people will think, what with you being married to an Argentinean."

"Good-bye, Mother, I'll speak to you soon."

Bea soon called her parents, and Mercedes said, "Oh Bea, we are so sorry."

"You were right, Mummy—it happened."

"Perhaps I should not have mentioned it."

"That is what I thought yesterday, but today I am thinking that I should have prepared myself for this. I don't know what will happen to us now."

"I remember John saying then that you would cope with anything that came your way."

"I hope I will be able to cope, Mummy."

"You will. You have coped with so many things that were foreign to you."

"This is not foreign."

"Your father wants to talk to you and John."

Bea sighed and said, "Hello, daddy."

"Bea, we are devastated!"

"So are we. I could not stop crying last night."

"Remember, we are here for you always."

"Thank you, Daddy. John is right here."

Since the conversation that they had had just before the wedding, Alberto had not been too forthcoming with John but now he wanted to talk to him.

John said, "Hello, Alberto. Bea is very upset."

"I know. You said a long time ago that you would look after her. I hope you have not forgotten. She will need your help now."

"Of course I will. You must not have any doubts about it," John answered, despite his doubts the night before.

"Good. I count on you. I hope this has not spoilt your holiday completely."

Alberto's last words reminded John that they were indeed on holiday.

After he hung up, John said to the family, "Come on, boys, get ready; I am going to take you all to your classes, and then we will all have lunch together in the restaurant of the hotel. Darling, I will not ski today. I will take the boys to their classes and then we can go for a walk; the day is lovely." Bea was looking at John without seeing; she felt numb. "Come on, darling. There is nothing we can do. For the sake of the boys, let's go on enjoying the few days we have left here. If you like we could go swimming in the hotel's indoor pool. And don't even think of cooking again; we will go out as a family for lunch and dinner." He put his arms around her and held her tight.

Bea gave him an uncertain smile and went to change.

After lunch, Bea insisted that John ski with the older boys. "It is what they enjoy the most. I will go for a walk with Richard."

But the walk turned out to be an experience that neither mother nor son would forget. They were engrossed talking to each other when they suddenly found themselves buried in snow; Bea was up to her waist in it, but Richard had almost disappeared. They had astray from the path and had not seen that the terrain covered by the snow was uneven. The more she tried to get out, the deeper they sank. The only way out was to roll. Bea managed to pull Richard up and gently pushed him horizontally towards the path; then she did the same herself. Slowly the snow became shallower, but they remained hugging tightly, lying on the thin icy snow by the road. This was a revelation to Bea; she understood then that no matter what happened in the world, the most important thing for her was her family.

CHAPTER TWENTY-NINE

The family went back to Paris, and then Charles and Ernie took the flight that would take them to London, and from there they'd take the train to the north of England. The boys were used to doing all this travelling on their own and were quite independent; their luggage was sent in advance separately, and it was usually waiting for them at school to be unpacked.

Sebastian had one more term in the English school in Paris, and then he would be joining his brothers in England. But neither Bea nor John was sure that the boys would cope with this situation. Despite the effort of the teachers and head masters, at both schools, some of the children were being horrid to the three boys. In Paris Sebastian had his parents to go back to, but Charles and Ernie were being bullied; students destroyed Charles's watch and put toothpaste inside Ernie's bed. Ernie slept that night in the wet bed and caught a bad cold. Charles only told his parents about it but begged them not to say anything. "They are calling me Argy, Mom. I wish you were not from Argentina."

"Are you sorry that I am your mother?" Bea asked, feeling that her world was falling to pieces around her.

"No, I just wished that you were not Argentinean. If you weren't, this would not be happening to us."

John, who had been listening to the conversation on the other telephone, said: "Charles, these things happen at school. If your mother was English, you would have been bullied for something else. That is life, and I hope that all that you are going through now will make you stronger for the future. I believe you owe your mother an apology."

"I'm sorry, Mummy, I did not mean to offend you."

Bea, who could not control her pain and was crying again, managed to say: "I love you all very much," and she hung up.

A few days later Bea was queuing in the post office to send her weekly letters to the boys, and she saw a friend a few places behind her. She tried to catch the woman's eye, but the friend did not seem to have noticed Bea. After she posted the letters, Bea approached her friend and said, "Hello, Linda, how are you?" But again Linda pretended not to hear the greeting. Bea found it strange and got closer to her, but Linda turned her face away. Bea was stunned—she could not believe it. Could it be the Falklands war? They had a bridge group and played regularly, but then Bea recalled that just lately there had been cancellations each time she was supposed to play.

She confided in John, who was not as surprised as Bea. "Darling, nothing will be normal for a while. I hope you will be able to accept that a few of our English friends will not want to see us, but you have plenty of other friends from different nations. Forget the idiots!"

Bea did try to forget the idiots, as John suggested, but it hurt anyway. She was delighted when they were invited to a party at the British embassy, and she thought that perhaps things were going back to normal. She took even greater care in what she chose to wear. John had said that he would meet her there. By now Bea had learnt how to drive and, she did not need to be collected by John's driver. But John had been delayed, and when she arrived at the party everybody stopped talking and looked at her; she felt like Scarlett O'Hara in *Gone with the Wind*. She could even see herself dressed in the red velvet curtains that Scarlett had made into her dress, and that gave her courage. She went down the stairs towards the lawn in the garden, where everybody was gathered. She pretended that she was Scarlet and thanked the ambassador and his wife for the kind invitation, as if nothing had happened. "I am sorry John is not here yet; he has been delayed in the office."

She tried to engage people in conversation, but she felt that they were not comfortable talking to her. She wanted to leave but had to wait for John.

Then Bea heard someone behind her say, "She will never be British—nor will her children!" She turned around to see someone that she knew quite well pointing a finger at her. Bea could not understand how people could change from one day to another. She was still the same person they knew. The other person looked embarrassed and later said to Bea, "I was telling Caroline that I was the only non-Briton in the party when she spotted you. I am sorry you had to go through that."

After that experience, they declined any invitation involving the English community. John said, "We do not need them; I do most of my business with the French."

That summer was the last summer for them in Paris. The head office called John back to take the place of one of the directors of the firm, who had passed away. Sebastian had to go to school in England, and that was an incentive for Bea, but she loved Paris and was afraid to go back to London.

All the boys had been with them during the holidays, and for the first time they all went back together in the car. Two trucks with their belongings followed them to London.

It was early afternoon when they arrived, and the boys ran upstairs full of expectation. Charles, Ernie, and Sebastian had been too young when they'd left the house years ago, and Richard had never been there. Now they wanted to choose where they would sleep. Charles and Ernie went to the third floor and put their rucksacks down. Sebastian and Richard were to sleep in the room next to their parents.

The packers started unloading the boxes that were in the trucks and piled them up in the sitting and dining rooms, while John and Bea unpacked and placed everything in the right place. There was little furniture to unpack because the company had provided them with furniture in Paris, and theirs had been left in the house.

It was late when they all finally went to bed and fell into a deep sleep. But Bea was woken up by a soft hand rubbing her shoulder. She could not believe that John was feeling amorous after all the work he had done. As she moved, the light in the room went on, and she saw a stranger in a red pullover and brown trousers standing by the door with rubber gloves, holding a large wooden fork that they had been given as a wedding presents from the Philippines. Bea tried to scream, but no sound came out of her mouth. The man dropped the fork and ran downstairs; that woke John, who did not know what was going on because Bea was still not able to speak. When she finally explained to him what had happened, John ran downstairs, but the man had vanished, leaving the door open.

John went upstairs to check on the boys while Bea rang the police. In no time at all the house was full of uniformed men looking everywhere for clues. This man had collected a few items that he had planned to take with him, but he did not have time to do so. The police told Bea that she should be on the alert because she had seen him, and he might come back to silence her. They added that the man probably thought that she had been alone and ran away when he discovered John lying next to her.

From then on Bea was terrified. She would not stay alone in the house, but it was even worse when she was with Richard on her own. She imagined headlines in the newspaper: "Woman found dead with child crying by her body."

Normally John would have taken Sebastian to his first term at the school, this time with Charles and Ernie, but Bea said that she would go with them. The thought of spending a night alone in the house filled her with terror. For convenience they took the car, which was fortunate because Bea cried all the way back to London. Little Richard tried to console his mother, but she felt destroyed. Was there ever going to be any peace in her life again? In the last few months she had done nothing but cry. She sat in the back hugging Richard, who fell asleep in his mother's arms.

John asked for the most sophisticated kind of burglar alarm on the market to be installed in the house; every single window and door in the house was connected. It could be connected completely if they were going out, or partially if they were in. Bea kept it partially on all the time, but it was not a good solution because sometimes she forgot and went to open a window, or Richard would lean on them, and there was pandemonium all over the neighbourhood. She was so obsessed that one day she saw a man on the roof of a house on the other side of the road, and she immediately rang the police. The poor man was a builder mending the roof. She became notorious, and she even found it difficult to get babysitters when they went out. She was a wreck and knew it, but she could not help it.

John's new job kept him busy, which in a way was a blessing for him; he really found it difficult to deal with Bea. They had chosen him to take the place of the old director because he had done such a good job in France. He could not let them down and worked late at night. This did not improve Bea's state of mind; they didn't make love anymore. John had to go to the office during the weekend as well, and when he did not, his time was dedicated to Richard. Bea tried not to show her misery to the child, but she did not laugh much anymore.

One day Dorothy rang her to see how she was. Dorothy was surprised at how much Bea had changed. "Bea, are you all right?"

Bea could not control a sob. "I feel dreadful. I don't know what it is. I cannot get rid of this sinking feeling."

"Have you been to see the doctor?"

"No. With the system in this country, if I go to the general practitioner, I might be put in a strait jacket and be sent away for good."

"Don't you have a private doctor?" Dorothy asked.

"I only know the gynaecologist that you introduced me to years ago."

"I will try and find out about a private GP."

"Thank you, Dorothy."

A few days later, Dorothy rang again. "Bea, I have a name. I do not think he is English, but you don't mind, do you?"

"It might be better," Bea said sadly.

"That is what I thought."

CHAPTER THIRTY

Bea was at the consulting room of the doctor at ten o'clock that morning while Richard was at school.

"What can I do for you?" The man sitting in front of Bea had a kind face and gentle manner, but Bea still had not found out where he was from.

Slowly, Bea narrated to him all that had been happening to her in the last few months. But he wanted to know more. He asked, "What about your childhood?"

"I had a wonderful childhood."

"When did you meet your husband?"

Bea recounted just about everything in her life, and then he asked if he could have a look at her physically. After she was dressed again, he said, "Clinically you seem well."

"Why do I feel so rotten?"

"Because you are unhappy; you should leave your husband. A woman like you will never be alone." He then got up and kissed her.

The only thing that Bea thought of doing was to get out of his consulting room as rapidly as her legs would take her. She went to a coffee shop nearby and, still shaking, asked for a glass of water. Then she did something that she never did: she called John at the office. "May I come and see you?" she asked.

"I am about to go into a meeting," John said.

"Oh. It does not matter. I'm sorry I disturbed you."

"What is it, Bea?"

"Nothing. I just wanted to talk to you," she said sullenly.

John promised, "We will talk tonight." John had become used to Bea's depressive mood and did not pay much attention to her now.

When she got home, she laid down on her bed. She had to compose herself—Richard could not see her like this. The telephone rang, and she picked it up without thinking.

"Bea, how did it go?" It was Dorothy.

Bea remembered what had happened that morning, and suddenly she found it funny. She laughed and laughed, almost hysterically; each time that she wanted to say something, she laughed harder.

"What happened, Bea?"

"You will not believe it!" she said, and she laughed again.

"Come on, Bea. Tell me what has happened."

Bea finally stopped laughing and she was able to tell Dorothy what had happened.

"You must notify the authorities," Dorothy said seriously.

"Dorothy, when I left his room, I did not know what to do. But I have not laughed so much since . . . I don't know when. He might have cured me!" She laughed again, and this time Dorothy joined her.

"Are you going to tell John?"

"I called him when I left the surgery, but he was busy. Now I am not so sure that I want to tell him. It is good to feel that other men still think that I am attractive."

"Of course you are attractive—very attractive, and young. Don't you go feeling that you are an ugly old thing."

"That is exactly what I been feeling lately. Maybe I have menopause without knowing it. You know I had a hysterectomy after Richard."

"You are too young to have menopause. Perhaps you need a tonic or a holiday. Why don't you go and visit your parents?"

"You know, that had gone through my mind, but I did not think I should leave John alone."

"I think he is old enough to look after himself."

Bea said, "You are right. I will take Richard with me."

"Bring me a present!" Dorothy said cheerfully.

"I will, I promise."

Bea hung up and dialled her parents. "Mummy?"

"Hello, darling, how are you?"

"I was wondering if it would be all right with you if I come see you, with Richard."

"Of course! Is there a problem between you and John?"

"No, he is just very busy, and the boys are away. I thought that perhaps it would be nice to go and see you."

"It would be lovely for us, too. When are you arriving?"

"I will let you know. I will ring the travel agent and ring you back."

Soon Bea called Mercedes again. "Mum, I found tickets for Saturday. We will be there on Sunday morning."

"Everything will be ready for you, and we will be waiting at the airport."

"I am looking forward to seeing you."

"We are too, darling."

That evening Bea told John, "I would like to go and see my parents with Richard."

"What brought that so suddenly?" John asked.

"Darling, you are so busy, and the boys are away. I am feeling a bit lonely. I hope you don't mind."

"What about Richard's school?"

"I am going for two weeks only. I will ask his teacher to give me his homework. I do not think he will miss too much."

"All right then. If that is what you want."

CHAPTER THIRTY-ONE

Alberto and Mercedes were waiting for them at the airport as promised. Bea felt a knot in her throat; she was in need of love and care, and the sight of her parents made her feel very emotional. They hugged for a long time, and then all the attention switched to Richard. "My, how have you grown," Alberto said. "You will soon be as tall as your mother."

"I want to be as tall as my father," the boy replied.

"Of course you will, but first you will be as tall as your mother." They all laughed and got in the car.

This visit was exactly what Bea needed; she visited the family and rested. Her parents still had a live-in maid who looked after them, and Bea had time to go out and not think of babysitters. One day when she was coming back home from the hairdresser, she saw a sign on a new building block that said, "Agent on site: flats available for showing."

Without thinking she went in and asked to be shown around. It was a brand-new apartment block with a garden and a swimming pool. She was shown several flats, but the one she liked was on the sixth floor overlooking the garden; the balcony ran the length of the flat. It had three bedrooms and two bathrooms, plus a servant's quarters. The reception room was not enormous but was big enough. "How much does this one cost?" she asked.

She was given the price in dollars. She could not believe what she heard. "Seventy thousand dollars?" Her family could not even buy a room in London for that price.

She called her husband. "John?"

"Hello there, how are you all?" he said.

"We are great; the weather is marvellous, and I feel much rested."

"Good, good. I wish I felt rested, too."

"This is exactly why I am calling you. I have just seen a beautiful, brand-new flat with three bedrooms and a swimming pool, for seventy thousand dollars."

"It can't be!"

"I was surprised, too. Life here is so much cheaper than in England. I would like to make an offer."

"Let me think about it overnight, and I will ring you in the morning."

Alberto and Mercedes were excited, too. "It would be so wonderful if you come and live here."

"We would not live here all the time, but we could come over the holidays. We might bring Katherine with us for Christmas."

"You do not think she would mind a warm Christmas?" That remark from Alberto made everybody laugh.

"Daddy, Katherine is finally beginning to feel the cold. She has her fireplace going all the time now, and besides, she is used to warm Christmases in Africa."

The next morning John gave Bea the go-ahead. "How are you going to make the payment?" he asked.

"I am afraid I will have to go and collect the money and bring cash back here; the situation with the banks between our countries is impossible."

"But it is dangerous to take so much money with you."

She said, "I shall strap it around my waist."

"You are mad."

"No, that is the way the estate agent said they do business here."

"Yours is a funny nation," he teased.

"I know, but we have good weather."

"Darling, I think you are much better. I am happy to hear you so enthusiastic."

Bea returned to London with Richard and called Katherine.

"So you are back?" Katherine asked.

"Only for a few weeks. I am going back to buy a flat."

"A flat? I did not know you were doing so well."

"Katherine, property in Argentina is very cheap. I was calling you because I would be very grateful if you could come and stay with Richard for a week or so."

"When will that be?"

"I have to go back with the money next month."

"You mean to say that you are taking the money with you?"

"Yes, Katherine—that is the way they do it over there."

"I'd better not comment."

"I know, it is not easy to understand. Things are so different over there, even for me."

Three weeks later, Katherine arrived with enough food to feed an army.

"It is very kind of you, but I have left food in the freezer, and the fridge is full," Bea said.

"I was not sure, so I brought some along."

"I am sure John will like to have your cooking again."

Bea had prepared Richard's room for Katherine so that she did not have to go up two flights of stairs to reach her room. Richard liked sleeping in his brothers' bedroom; it made him feel grown up.

Bea said to him, "You'll be good to Granny and Daddy, won't you, sweetheart?"

"I am always good."

"Hmm, be better then."

Bea hugged and kissed Richard and Katherine while John put the suitcase in the car. They were going to the airport after the bank.

"I will be back soon, Mum," John said. "Look after Granny, Richard."

Bea had made a large pocket in her petticoat, and she looked pregnant when she emerged from the ladies room in the bank. The bank had not been happy with this arrangement, but Bea explained the situation, and they had to accept it.

It was very uncomfortable for Bea to sit with so many bundles of notes on her. The paper cut on her flesh, but she had no alternative but to bear it.

She had asked if she could sit in the first row of the plane, "To be able to extend my legs," she had said. Seeing her in her condition, they immediately complied with what she asked.

As soon as dinner was served and the lights were turned off, Bea got up as discreetly as possible and went to the toilet with her large handbag. She unloaded the bills in it and went back to her seat. Though she knew it was unlikely, she was worried that she might fall asleep and somebody might take her bag. The seat next to her was empty, and she had two blankets. She put one down on the floor with the little pillow that was provided with the blanket, and then she lay down on it, covering herself with the other blanket. Her bag was under the seat, and no one could take it without going over her. Everything was dark, and she could not be seen because she was covered by the dark blue blanket.

A passenger who had gone to get a glass of water decided to take a shortcut through that passage, seeing that no one was sitting there, but when he went over Bea, he felt that the floor was uneven and moving, and he let out a scream. Bea also screamed because the man was quite heavy and was hurting her. Everybody woke up, and the lights were turned on again. What they saw was the head of a woman emerging from inside a blanket, and a man standing on top of her holding a glass of water, half full now because he had spilled quite a bit on Bea. She was asked to sit, and the man was given a strong whisky. Fortunately, nobody noticed that Bea did not look pregnant anymore.

Just before breakfast, she went and put the money again in her pouch. She was not sure that she was going to recount the incident of the previous night to anyone.

CHAPTER THIRTY-TWO

All the papers were in order. The sellers were represented by their lawyer, as was Bea with her parents and their lawyer. The bundles of bills were in front of Bea, Alberto, Mercedes, and their lawyer, who had to count each one and then pass it to the other side to be counted again. This reunion had taken place in the back room of the sellers' bank; as soon as the bills were counted, they were taken to the till, where they were counted again by the teller. Then the papers were signed and counter–signed. The whole operation took about an hour. After that Bea and her parents left the bank with the keys of the new flat, and instead of the bundles of bills she had a folder with all the papers declaring her to be rightful owner of the flat.

"I need a cup of coffee," said Alberto, who had been uneasy with all the bill counting.

"That would be very welcome," agreed Mercedes.

"Where shall we go?" asked Bea.

"There is a café around the corner."

"It's my treat," announced Bea, feeling proud. "Let's go to the flat and make a list of what I have to buy afterwards."

"I have to go back to the office," said Alberto.

"I will go with you, darling; all this is so exciting." Said Mercedes

"It is, isn't it? Who, would have thought that I would be buying a flat in Buenos Aires!" Bea said.

"I just do not know how you dared to bring all that money on you."

"I do not know either, Mummy. I'd rather not think about it." Bea was remembering what had happened two nights previously in the plane, and she had a slight shiver.

"I think I will buy bunk beds for the boys. I will give them the biggest room so that they can all share. I need an extra room for Katherine or any other guest that might want to come and stay."

"Darling, you know that some of you can stay with us."

"I know, Mummy, but I think it will be less complicated if we all stay together while the boys are still young. The holidays are the only time when the family is together."

"I realise that, Bea. Do you find it very difficult?"

Bea, who had been so happy up to that moment, suddenly burst out crying and held on to her mother. Mercedes was surprised at this outburst; she did not know how depressed Bea had been. Bea had never shown any signs of it when they spoke over the telephone.

"What is it, darling? Are things that bad?"

"You were right, Mum. There are huge differences between our cultures. I have accepted everything that John has demanded, but having the boys away, plus the stupid war, has left me in a bad way."

"Have you seen a doctor?"

"Yes, I have."

"What did he say?"

"That I should leave John and start a new life." Bea did not tell her that he had kissed her—that would have given her mother a heart attack.

"That is ridiculous! I will make an appointment with my doctor."

"Do you think a doctor will fix my life?" Bea asked.

"He will not fix your life, but he might be able to *help* you, fix it."

"You are great, Mummy. You always find a way to do things. I remember when you repacked my suitcase before I went on that crazy trip of mine."

"Do you think it was crazy?"

"Yes, it was, but I would not be married to John if I had not done it; I learnt so much!"

"In that case, you will remain married to John."

After having made a list of everything the flat needed, in order to be ready for the following holiday, mother and daughter had lunch and then went shopping.

Bea had not put her skills as an interior decorator into practice yet. She realised at that moment that there was something else that she could do with her time now that most of her children were away at school. In no time at all her shopping was delivered to the new flat and it was time for Bea to go back to John and Richard. But Mercedes would not let her go without seeing her doctor.

"Do you want me to go with you?" her mother offered.

"Don't worry, Mummy, I have been doing so many things on my own that now I am not afraid anymore."

"I am glad, darling. We will go out to dinner tonight."

"Thank you. I hate saying good-bye to you again so soon."

Mercedes lowered her head but did not reply. It was clearly very hard for her, too. Both her daughters lived abroad, but at least she had her sisters and cousins near her. Bea had no one.

Doctor Aragon was kind and said, "Your mother is worried about you."

"I know. I am sorry I lost control and cried in front of her."

"It was probably the best thing you have done on this trip. If you lost control, it means you need help. Tell me about yourself."

Bea was with the old man for over an hour. He asked a lot of questions, but he also listened carefully. It was somehow easier for Bea to say everything that was in her heart in Spanish. When she spoke English, her personality was different; here she expressed herself in the way she was brought up.

The doctor said, "The fact that you have had hormones for so long is not good, although I do realise that you need them to keep you young. You must have periodical check-ups; they might affect you in more than one way. I will give you a mild antidepressant and will write to your doctor in England. You must not stop taking them, even if you feel better. Only your doctor can tell you if you are ready to stop."

"Why don't you give me enough pills until Christmas? I can come and see you then. I'd rather you did not write to my GP."

The old man smiled. "I will do as you wish."

CHAPTER THIRTY-THREE

The pills made Bea feel dizzy and disoriented, and she refused to drive; she would get Richard up earlier to walk him to school. John was annoyed with Bea's problems and could not understand what was wrong with her.

"Why do you have to take those things?" he asked.

"To feel better," she said simply.

"But you are not feeling better, are you?"

"As a matter of fact, I am. You are not being kind to me, but I don't care. Have you seen me crying lately?"

"Bea, you are being melodramatic."

"I think you are working too hard, John. You have changed."

But a few weeks later, Bea really started to feel better. She got used to the pills and was not dizzy anymore. She decided that she was going to start a business and bought a book on how to go about it. She got some flyers printed, and on the way back from school, she put them in the letter boxes of all the houses of the neighbourhood. She also placed ads in interior decoration magazines.

She was surprised at how quickly people started calling her, and by the time they went on holiday, she had three jobs lined up for the New Year.

No one except for Bea knew the flat in Buenos Aires, and they were most impressed by it—especially Katherine, who could not believe that it had cost so little. Everyone was made a fuss of by Bea's family, who invited them out almost every day, and the boys loved the pool and spent most of the day covered in suntan lotion jumping in and out of it. December was still mildly warm for Argentina, but for John and the boys it was hot. Katherine did not seem to mind, which was a blessing considering that she did not mince her words when she was not happy. In fact, on more than one occasion she showed that she was enjoying herself by taking part in conversations and even playing with the children.

When everybody said good bye to them, they said: "See you next year."

Alberto and Mercedes, who went to the airport with them, were thrilled that they would be seeing more of Bea and her family, and they waved until the family disappeared from sight.

Arriving in London on a grey and cold morning was not welcoming, but the boys were eager to go back to school and talk about their exotic holiday, as they had done when they went to Zimbabwe.

The bullying that they had experienced when the Falklands' war happened, was long forgotten by their classmates.

Bea for once was also eager to be back, because she had her jobs waiting for her.

Katherine was the only one who was not so happy; for her it was going back to a lonely house which was now even cold for her. She would have to organise one or two games of bridge soon, and a supper party. She would call her friends the next day because by the time she'd get home it would be late. She had left her car in the car park and would be driving home.

John had not really stopped working at all during the holiday. He had been on the phone almost every day, and he was again on the phone as soon as they got home.

Bea took Charles, Ernie, and Sebastian to the station, where the boys met up with several of their friends taking the same train back to school. Richard held her hand, making sure that he was not going to be sent away with his brothers. As usual, Bea had to hold her tears back when she kissed the boys, who pulled away, embarrassed by such a display of emotion.

Bea's business was booming. She was making a name for herself and felt happy. Doctor Aragon had told her that he would prefer it if she went on taking the pills for a bit longer, to make sure that she would not go back to the way she'd felt a few months previously, and he had given her enough to last her another six months.

Unfortunately, six months later John arrived back home to announce, "We are going back to Japan."

"What do you mean?" Bea asked, bewildered.

"The office is in trouble over there, and I am the only senior manager who speaks the language. I should be there in the next two months."

"What about us?"

"If you like, you can wait until the Christmas holidays and come together with the boys."

Bea said, "I thought we were going back to Argentina."

"I am afraid it is not possible."

"What about Richard's school?"

"He should be boarding next year. He could come to Tokyo with us for the rest of this school year, and then he will board with his brothers."

"And me? What shall I do in Tokyo?"

"You could always go back to modelling."

"Do you really think I could go back to modelling?"

John said, "Why not? You have not changed that much in all these years. You are still young and attractive."

"Do you think I am attractive?" Bea asked.

"Of course I do."

"I am surprised—you do not show it. You hardly ever touch me these days."

"I suppose it is because I have been so busy, and also because you were so depressed."

"And didn't you think that perhaps a bit of care and attention would have helped me?"

John sighed. "Please, Bea, I cannot deal with emotional outbursts."

"You know, John, I think I have been completely blind. My mother was right when she had her misgivings. The misgivings should not have been about me getting used to living in England, but you understanding me. Perhaps, it is all the same thing. I have accepted everything you have put on my plate, but you cannot accept me when I am down."

"Bea, I was brought up by a woman who suffered the death of her husband and raised me alone. She never showed that she was sad."

"I know I am not up to your mother's standards, but unfortunately, darling, I was not brought up like her or you. I cannot help showing my emotions."

"You never showed any emotions when we were young."

"Before you said that I was still young, and now you are saying that 'when we were young'. Which one is it, John?"

"I should have said younger."

"This is it—younger. I look almost as young as I did when we got married; you have aged more than me in appearance, but my insides are much older. I have had four children and a hysterectomy. My teeth have suffered, but yours are the same as when you were a teenager, and you have never spent one day in hospital."

"I am sorry if I have disappointed you."

"John, the only thing I have wanted is for all of us to be happy together. But even our boys are becoming strangers to me. You and they have a great time together as men; they hardly even notice me anymore."

"I am afraid that is the way it is with men. I bet that if we had had girls, I would not exist," John said defensively.

"Oh, yes you would, especially if they had gone to boarding school. Nevertheless, I do not want to argue about it. I do not think it is fair that I should leave everything that I am building for myself here to follow you to Japan."

"I thought you loved Japan."

"I do, but I have not kept in touch with all my Japanese friends. It is difficult to do so at such a distance, and our foreign friends are not there anymore."

"You will make new ones."

Bea said firmly, "I will stay here with Richard until the holidays, as you suggested, and then I will see what I do."

John looked at her. Bea always ended up surprising him. She had adapted so well to life in England and in France, and although she had been depressed, she had got on with it. Now he was not sure whether she would join him in Japan or not, and he did not dare ask her to explain herself. He still loved her very much, and the thought that she might want a separation filled him with horror.

CHAPTER THIRTY-FOUR

John left for Japan after the summer holiday; he had explained to the boys that they were not going to Argentina for Christmas, but that they would be spending Christmas in Japan. That excited them even more—one more country to show off at school. This time Katherine agreed with Bea: couldn't John find a job that would keep him in England? She was beginning to feel old and wanted her family near her.

Bea said, "You see, John, now your mother feels like me."

"She is much older than you."

"But when you and the boys leave, I will be even more alone than her—my family is far away."

"You should go and visit them."

"You know very well that I cannot leave Richard."

"In that case, send him to boarding school earlier," John said simply.

"You can be horrid, John! I think you do it on purpose."

And that was the truth. Deep inside, John was a boarding school boy who used his tongue to destroy the enemy. At this moment Bea was the enemy; she did not want to do what he was asking. And he knew that Bea did not have the tools to defend herself; in a certain way he was right, because Bea had never been bullied at school, and his childhood years had been free from stress, but Bea had something that he did not have to the same extent: faith in God. Despite her depression, she had been able to survive all the hurting, with having to part with her children and being rejected by people she thought were her friends, because in the end she gave her sorrows to God. John had not had the instruction that Bea had in spiritual things; Katherine was not spiritual, or at least, she did not seem to be.

As soon as John left, Bea rang her parents and told them what was going on: "Perhaps I could go and see you with the boys, and Katherine can go and see John for Christmas."

"No, your place is next to your husband," Mercedes said. "You can come and see us some other time."

"That will not be too soon; I cannot leave Richard."

"In that case you will come when Richard goes to boarding school. Bea, just do what you have to do, and don't think too much about it. We will miss you, too."

But Bea had also been thinking of moving; before John came with the Japan news, she had been dreaming of buying a bigger house so that the boys, who were now older, could have each their own bedroom. She started looking at houses and found the perfect one; it was a detached house, a little bit further out but in a very good neighbourhood. It needed tender loving care, and she had plenty of that to give.

She rang John and told him. "I have found a lovely house that needs total refurbishment; it is well within our means. I propose to go see you at Christmas with the boys and then come back and do it up while Richard remains in school here until the summer. By then I would have finished, and we can all go back to Tokyo."

"So you are planning to leave me here alone until the summer?"

"No, we can go and see you in the spring holiday, too."

"Thank you, Bea; that is very kind of you."

"Do you have a minute to be lonely, John?" You spend most of the time in the office and when you get back home you are tired.

"I know it is selfish of me but it would be nice to know that you are at home here waiting for me."

"I am here; you can call me any time you like."

"It is not the same."

"I am glad. I have the feeling that you don't care too much about me anymore."

"I am sorry I give you that impression; it is far from the truth."

"I think a little time apart will do us good. I will be there soon."

Bea bought the house with a mortgage before selling the house they were living in; she did not want Richard to change schools twice. She was lucky that John's family had had an account at their bank for generations and was willing to lend them the money for the new house. But she was going to have to put the house which they were living in on the market in the New Year.

Katherine joined them at Christmas, and they travelled together. The boys loved their grandmother; she was a boys' grandmother who understood their mentality—and even more, the mentality of boys who went to boarding school. She had also been to boarding school and knew the protocol. Bea found it difficult; she did not know how to behave in front of her boys anymore.

The company had provided John with a beautiful house that was big enough for the whole family, and it also had a garden.

"It is great," she said. "The boys are able to have their own room here, too. It will make holidays more comfortable."

John was very loving over the holidays; like the John that Bea used to know—but not even that made her change her plans. She had to go back to work on their new home and on the various jobs that she had lined up.

"I am sorry that you are not staying, Bea," John said.

"I will be back next holiday, and as soon as Richard goes to boarding school, I will come and join you. We still have a good time together, don't we?"

For an answer, John kissed Bea as passionately as he used to when they were in Japan years ago.

By Easter the house was nearly finished, and Bea and the boys went back to Japan, this time without Katherine. John had asked for some holiday time, too, and they went sightseeing in Kyoto and Nara. The boys were not too interested to start with, but then they saw the life of the temples, what people did when they called their god, and the offers they gave the monks for their prayers. The gardens were very beautiful, too; azaleas and peonies were in bloom. They also enjoyed staying in Japanese inns called ryokan, and they liked the bathrooms, called ofuro, where they learned how to wash themselves before getting into the steaming hot water. They never slept better, and they again had more things to tell at school.

For the summer holiday, the boys brought friends; each one had one, so there were eight boys all together in the flat, and John and Bea had to find daily entertainment for them. Fortunately, Tokyo was a very safe place, and the boys could go out by themselves. Although not too close to Tokyo, Disneyland became a popular place. It was expensive to have eight boys going to all the rides, but it was better than having them bored at home. After the holiday, Richard was going to join his brothers at boarding school; seeing how his brothers enjoyed it, he was now eager to board, too. The friend that he had invited was not going to boarding school; his parents had decided to keep him at home. Bea was beginning to see a change in the way the British were but it was too late for her.

CHAPTER THIRTY-FOUR

This time it was Bea's turn to take a son to his first term at school. Richard's trunk was packed together with his brothers' trunks, which were sent a couple of days before to wait for their arrival. Richard wanted to sit with his brothers and their friends, but Bea insisted that they should sit together, to have a few more hours with him. From the station there was a bus to take all the boys to school, but Bea hired a taxi that would take her and Richard there and then bring her back to the station. It was difficult for her to stop fussing; she realised that it was annoying Richard, but she could not help it.

At school he was shown by one of the older boys to his room. There were two bunk beds, four cupboards, four chests of drawers and four desks in each room. The cupboards made a sort of division in between the beds for privacy, but there was never any.

Bea had a chat with the schoolmaster and left; she had already said good-bye to all her children. She sat in the back of the car and cried her eyes out, as she had done when Sebastian went to boarding school; the taxi driver must have been used to taking mothers like Bea to the school, because he had a large supply of tissues with him. This time she felt freer without John's disapproving look. The taxi driver did not try to talk to her, but when he left her at the station, he said, "In the end, we get used to it," and he gave her a gentle pat on the shoulder.

Bea opened the door of their house and turned the lights on. She realised that her life had changed completely. From then on she had no more children; they would come and go, but the school was forming their personalities now. She was not in control anymore, and she prayed that everything that she had tried to teach them would have some effect later in their life.

She made herself a cup of cocoa and went to see about her jobs. She had to take her mind off her family. She would stay in London to finish what she had started, sell the house that was under offer, and then go back to John. It was still early enough to ring her parents:

"Daddy?" she said.

"Darling, how are you? We have been thinking of you. Richard went to boarding school today, right?"

"Yes, they are all gone now. I wondered if I could see you before I go back to Japan."

"It would be lovely, but isn't a long way around?"

"I thought that I could come back to London for half term."

"Isn't that too long to leave John alone?" Alberto asked.

"He is busy; when I am there, I hardly see him. I have a few jobs to finish and sell this house, and then I could go."

"Darling, I think your days are pretty full, too."

She laughed. "Yes, they are—here. See you soon, I love you."

Bea only had two weeks with her parents; all her chores had taken her a month to complete. It was such a welcome rest and an infusion of energy from going back to her roots. She loved her parents so much, and they were always such a source of encouragement. They helped her find tenants for the flat that was now going to be empty for at least a year, and they promised to look after it. By the time she left, she was ready for all that was waiting for her; she was going to take charge of her life. She went to see Dr Aragon and told him that she did not need the pills anymore. He advised her to stop taking them by gradually decreasing the amount she took each week until she stopped completely.

The boys had not seen the new house yet, but Bea had already allocated their rooms by placing their belongings in each one. They loved having their own room like they did in Tokyo, plus there was the attraction of a bigger garden; they had a wonderful half term organising the house and seeing their friends in London. Katherine came to stay, and for once she had nothing bad to say; she thought that it was good for the boys each to have their own room. She looked frail, and Bea worried that she was still living alone in the country; Katherine depended on driving everywhere, and distances were long.

John was waiting for Bea at the airport; he looked thinner but was just as handsome as when they met. Perhaps, even more so, now that he had a few grey hairs; it gave him a very dignified look.

Bea was also looking as beautiful as he remembered her, and they kissed passionately in the middle of the crowd, who did not pay any attention to them.

It was a good welcome; they went home and had an early dinner and an early bedtime, like when they were newly married.

The next day Bea took to reorganising the house. John had left a few engagements that they had that week written for her in the dairy that they shared for invitations and appointments, and he had also asked if they could give a dinner party for some clients. She liked that because she hated the thought of being bored. That afternoon she took some time off her chores to write to each of the boys a long letter; she had planned to go on writing to them every week, recounting all that she and John did. She wanted them to be part of their lives, even at such a long distance. She also wrote to Katherine and her parents, and every once in a while to Dorothy and Gaby, who was still living in the United States and now had two children, Lisa and William. Bea wondered if she was ever going to meet them; she had to do something about that. It would be so wonderful if they could have a reunion in Buenos Aires one of these days.

That Christmas the boys and Katherine came to see them without friends. John wanted to take them all sightseeing again and also go skiing. Bea had company when John and the boys went on the slopes, and it was good for the two women to talk. In eighteen years of marriage, Bea had not had the chance to speak to her mother-in-law for any long period. Katherine was now comfortable talking with Bea; she did not have to hide her feelings and that helped the relationship. In fact both of them finally were able to bond as much as was possible, considering the difference in culture.

The boys went back to London with Katherine, who wanted to take them to the station in her car, but it was much too small for the five of them and their luggage, so she had to content herself with saying good-bye at the airport. On the way home, she had a stroke and crashed her car. She was seriously injured, and John and Bea were called that night by the hospital. They left for England that evening.

When they reached the hospital, Katherine was conscious but could not move the left side of her body. John insisted in taking his mother to a private rehabilitation clinic before he went back to London. The clinic was near Katherine's house in Wiltshire, where Bea stayed for a while until Katherine started regaining the use of her left leg; her arm was not responding yet. But Bea had nothing else to do. Eventually even Katherine agreed that she should go back to John.

That Easter the boys went to see their parents, but it was a quiet holiday; everybody seemed tired, and the only thing they wanted to do besides eating was rest. They had a huge appetite, and they were growing so much—even Sebastian, who was only thirteen, was taller than Bea.

This was the final year for Charles at school, and he was busy taking exams and choosing universities. He had several interviews and was accepted in two of them even before he found out how well he had done in his ' A' levels. After that he was able to go and visit Katherine, who was improving slowly but needed a special car; she was also going to need help at home. In the end she made the decision to sell her house and buy a ground floor flat in an old peoples' home, which had direct access to the garden. She would be independent but looked after.

That summer Charles did not go to visit his parents in Tokyo, but he took a trip with various friends. He had also chosen to take a year off to do some work experience in different countries. Because he spoke three languages, he was able to work in France, Spain, and in England. On some occasions he also visited his grandmother, of whom he was very fond.

He was coming to the end of his year out of school when he received a call from the home where Katherine was staying—he had been left as her next of kin since John was in Japan. After hearing the news, Charles rang John and Bea.

"Daddy, Granny is in the hospital. She has got pneumonia and is unconscious."

"We will be there tomorrow," John said. "Thank you for looking after your grandmother."

But by the time that John and Bea, arrived Katherine had passed away, and Charles showed his skills as an organiser. He had already informed her lawyer and organised the undertakers.

Katherine had left a will leaving things to John and the boys; Bea was not included in the will, but she was not too upset by that. For Katherine her family had always been John and the boys, although after the last holiday that she spent in Japan, and during the time that they all went to the ski resort, she had shown that she was beginning to be fond of Bea. Katherine had also left instructions for the kind of service she wanted.

John had been shocked by the sudden developments and was finding it difficult to cope for the first time in his life. Fortunately between Charles and Bea, everything was done in accordance with Katherine's wishes. Bea had to admit that the service that Katherine had planned for herself was beautiful; the music was perfect, and there were lots of people who were willing to say a kind word about her. She had helped a lot of handicapped children with riding classes, and over the years she had made many friends—the church was packed. Then everyone went back to the home, where tea was prepared for them, while the close family went to the crematorium before joining them.

CHAPTER THIRTY-FIVE

Since Charles had not been with the family in Tokyo that summer, Bea suggested that he go with her to Argentina; university started a month after the boys' school. John was still a bit shaken with the death of his mother, but he agreed that it would be good for Charles to spend time with Bea's family; he deserved to be rewarded for the way that he had dealt with his grandmother's passing, and also because he had secured a job for after university.

As usual the family was all over Charles and Bea. Alberto and Mercedes could not believe that this man was their grandson. Charles was very mature and confident for his age, but he was not conceited; on the contrary, he liked listening to his elders. He spent many hours with his grandfather sharing his experiences and listening to Alberto's stories; in that sense he was still a boy. He preferred to talk to men. Charles also had the opportunity to go and see some of his relations in other parts of Argentina, which gave him the chance to go sightseeing. He loved his mother's country—he liked the people, the weather, and the food. Everything was so much more relaxed in this part of the world.

Bea went back to London with Charles and took him to his university in the north of England. Charles was adamant that he wanted to go alone, but Bea said, "I want to see where you will live for the next three years. Please, let me go with you."

"All right, Mother, but don't expect to find anything special."

As Charles had predicted, his room was nothing special, but he had secured a room by himself with a desk so that he could work from there without distractions.

"Darling, this is great. How did you manage to get this room?"

"Contacts, Mother, contacts."

Bea laughed—Charles was already talking like John.

But the place where the university was located was special: it had a river that ran through it and a magnificent, twelfth-century cathedral, as well as many green areas.

"Darling Charles, I am so proud of you. You have been such a help, and now I know that you will enjoy your time in this idyllic place."

"Thank you, Mum. I do not think I will be going back to Tokyo. Do you think I could stay in the house during the holidays?"

"Yes, of course; this is the reason I bought it. But won't you be too lonely in that big house?"

"If you don't mind, I might take one or two friends with me."

"As long as you keep it clean and tidy, there won't be a problem."

But Bea was already thinking that perhaps that Christmas they could come to London instead of the boys going to Japan.

"It is good to have you back, darling Bea." John had not called Bea "darling Bea" since they were newly married, and that pleased her.

"I had a good time with Charles," she said. "I think it was a very good thing for him to see how we live in Argentina. I think he understands me better now. He got along with my father like a house on fire."

"Everybody gets on well with your father."

"This was very special—he listened to everything my father said. He really appreciates older males."

"What about women?"

"I think he appreciates younger women more, but for a different reason," Bea said with a smile.

"Good! That's my boy."

"He is very much like you."

John said, "I think he has a lot of you, too."

"He is not coming for Christmas."

"Why not?"

"I think he wants to be independent. Could we perhaps spend Christmas in London this year?"

"I will ask the company; I have been thinking that it is time for us to go back to England. If there is a place for me at the head office, they might accept. Everything is running smoothly here now."

John and Bea went back to London for Christmas; he had had a chat with head office, and they had asked him to give them time to look for someone who could take his place in Japan, perhaps, the following summer. "They want me to be the director in charge of international operations, but they have to find someone to take over the Tokyo office. They think that we could come back for good in the summer."
Bea was so happy that she jumped into John's arms and kissed him. She wanted to be near her boys and also nearer her parents, who were looking so much older.

CHAPTER THIRTY-SIX

Ernie finished school with good grades and a place in the best university for science and technology; he wanted to be an engineer. The college was in London but not close to their house, and Ernie asked if he could share a flat with some friends near to where he had to study: "It is not fair, Charles lives in his university."

Bea said, "Of course he does; he is miles from us. You have a perfectly good room here."

"It will take me ages to go and come back every day, and I will waste precious time travelling rather than working."

"Fine, we will give it a try," John finally conceded.

Engineering was not a subject that was studied by the elite in England; it was not considered important. But Ernie knew that it was. John found a company that would sponsor the boy; he had to work a month a year in their factory in Wales, and then he could count on a job at the end of his studies. But Ernie did not like Wales; he was sent to live with an old man who still worked part time for the company and was a dreary character. His grades were not good that year.

"What is it, Ernie? You could be doing much better."

"I think I made a mistake; I like engineering but not the life of an engineer."

"Not all engineers live the same way."

"Still, I have lost interest."

"What do you propose to do?"

"I don't know," Ernie admitted.

"Well, we think that you should go on studying, and when you finish, we can talk about it."

Ernie had lost interest in his work but had gained interest in partying. He was having a great time living with his friends in the middle of London, and he was hardly touching his books.

It was then that Bea put her foot down and said, "We are not going to go on paying for an expensive flat for Ernie so that he is close to his college, when he never works. He should come and live with us. We can buy him a car so that he can take his books with him all the time."

"Do you think he will agree to that?" John said.

"He will have to, if he wants to have a future."

Ernie was not happy, but as Bea had predicted, he had no alternative but to accept. Nevertheless, he still did not get up on time to go to his lectures. Bea decided that she would set her alarm clock for six in the morning and personally get him out of bed.

Just as Ernie came to live at home, Sebastian finished school and also got a place in a prestigious university, to read the classics. He had achieved extremely good marks in all his papers, and his parents were delighted with his success. A few months earlier, Charles had handed in his thesis and was having a good time waiting for his report; he was now enjoying a few weeks of relaxation with his friends before taking up his job in London.

Suddenly, after so many years of looking forward to having her family at home, Bea found herself busy looking after her men. She had missed the years that she would have enjoyed taking part in the education of her boys; now she felt that she was more of a housekeeper than a mother. Charles had his job and kept the hours that it demanded from him. Ernie had finally decided to work as hard as possible to recuperate the time that he had wasted during the first two years at university, and he was only interested in studying and eating. He would come home, go to the fridge, go up to his room, and only come back to share dinner with his parents when they were able to extract from him what he was doing.

"Tell us what you did today," Bea would prompt.

"You would not understand, Mummy."

"Probably not, but I would like to know anyway."

"I don't want to talk about it."

"Have you decided what you are going to do when you finish your studies?" John wanted to know.

"The only thing I know is that I do not want to be an engineer."

"So you have no idea of what you want to do?"

"I might want to go into banking."

"What kind of banking?"

"Investment, I think."

"Perhaps you should start calling the banks that you think you would want to work for, and you can ask them what you need to do in order to do so," Bea added.

"That is an excellent idea. Ernie, your mother is right."

"I will do that as soon as I finish my exams. I did not have a year out like Charles; I would like to have time to enjoy myself."

"That is what you did the first two years at university, my boy," John said lightly.

Ernie shook his head and did not answer. But he did start looking around for banks that would be interested in his input.

"So?" Bea asked after listening to a conversation that Ernie had with a prospective employer over the telephone.

"They require that I should be good at numbers."

"Did you tell them that you are?"

"Yes. I have an interview next week."

Bea got up and hugged Ernie. "I am very proud of you, darling."

"Thank you, Mum. I have been feeling that I've let you down."

"Well, you haven't," said Bea, giving him another hug and kiss.

After the interview, John and Bea wanted to know, "How did it go?"

"I think I got the job," Ernie said.

Both of his parents got up. "I can't believe it!" they said in unison. "Tell us more."

They all sat down, and Ernie recounted the interview: "She asked me what my hobbies were, and I told her that I really enjoyed playing the piano. She told me that she loved music, and we started talking about composers. Then I cannot remember how, but I mentioned that

I spoke three languages, and that interested her. We then talked about all the countries that she and I had visited, and that was it."

"Did she ask you about your studies?"

"Not really; I think she already had had a look at what I'd sent her last week, and she just wanted to talk to me."

"That is wonderful news, darling." Bea hugged him and kissed him again.

John gave him a hug and a pat on his shoulder. "Well done, Ernie. I knew you would do well in life."

Bea not only had her two older boys at home, but Sebastian would come sometimes on the weekends, and Richard came at half term and during the holidays; sometimes they brought friends. Bea was exhausted; she had no help in the house and had given up working at what she enjoyed so much.

Mercedes called her one day. "Bea?"

"Mother! How are you?"

"I am well, darling, but your father is not. He did not want to tell you or your sister, but he has been suffering from cancer for a few years now."

Bea was worried. "I thought he did not look so well last time we were there."

"I think you should come. I have already rung Gaby."

"I will look for a ticket immediately."

But as it happened with Katherine, she was too late. Alberto passed away peacefully during the night in the hospital. Mercedes felt desperate; they had been so close for so many years. She felt terribly lonely and asked her daughters if they could come and live in Argentina.

"Mummy, I promise to visit you very often," Bea said.

"We should try and come at different times, so that she always has one of us with her," Gaby said to Bea.

"Yes, and we must try to come and spend the holidays with her, too."

CHAPTER THIRTY-SEVEN

What Bea would have liked to do years earlier—when she thought that she would never meet her sister's family, and when their father was still alive—became mandatory now. She called the tenants of her flat in Buenos Aires and recounted that her father had passed away, and that she would need her flat from now on to come and visit her mother.

Bea said, "Gaby, I know we said that we should come at different times, but our families have not met yet."

"You are quite right—it is unbelievable, isn't it?"

"Let's come here for Christmas and the New Year. I wanted to do this before Daddy passed away. We must do it while Mother is still with us."

"We always spend the holidays with Mat's family," Gaby said, a bit hesitant.

"All the more reason to come here this year; I am sure the children will like the change."

"They are teenagers—I never know what they like nowadays. But I will call Mat."

"And I will call John."

Bea called John. "Darling, how are you?"

"I am fine, but what is more important is how, you are."

"Sad, but Mummy is devastated. I think that we must all come here for Christmas. I have asked Gaby to ask her family, too. Do you realise that after all these years, we still have not met her children?"

"It is ridiculous. I will talk to the boys, but I do not know if their jobs will allow them to take two weeks holiday."

"Even if they can just come for Christmas—tell them that we will pay for their tickets"

"I will. I love you, take care of yourself."

"Bye, darling; I love you, too."

Bea was back in Buenos Aires at the beginning of December to prepare the flat for her family. John had succeeded in getting all the boys to go for Christmas, but Charles and Ernie had to be back before the New Year.

Gaby had talked Mat, Lisa, and William into going to see their maternal grandmother, whom they hardly ever saw. They were going to be staying with her because they did not have a flat in Buenos Aires, as Bea and John did.

Mercedes was still in mourning and had become lethargic and uncommunicative. She had also lost a lot of weight, and the sisters worried that she might not survive their father's death much longer.

"We must try to bring her out of this mood," Gaby said.

"I will go and see Dr Aragon; he will know what to do," Bea volunteered.

"Mummy, please come with me; he was so good when I needed help. I listened to you and went to see him—now it's your turn."

"If that will make you happy," Mercedes said absent-mindedly.

"Yes, it will. I have made an appointment for this afternoon. He is fitting us in between patients."

As with Bea, the old friend and doctor prescribed the same antidepressants that Bea took when she was unwell.

Bea said, "I will stay with you until you get used to them, Mummy. They might make you feel dizzy."

"I am going to go and have a lie down, darling. I am sorry I can't be more cheerful," Mercedes replied.

"Don't worry, Mummy, you will soon."

Mercedes gave Bea a hug and went to bed.

By the time that everybody arrived, Mercedes was indeed feeling more like herself, but she was still not completely recovered. The pills had not made her feel as dizzy as they had Bea, so at least she did not have to get over that, too. The prospect of seeing all her grandchildren lifted her spirits; she had gone around the flat with her maid making sure that all the rooms were in order for Gaby and her family, and she had gone shopping with Bea.

"What do you think your boys would like?" Mercedes said.

"Charles and Ernie are working now; I am sure an extra tie or shirt would be welcome."

"What about Sebastian and Richard?"

"It is cold in England; perhaps pullovers?"

"All that is very easy. And what do you and John want?"

"I have no idea, Mummy. Why don't you surprise us?"

Mercedes smiled and said, "I will ask Gaby."

For Bea's and Gaby's children, Mercedes was the ideal grandmother. She made a special effort and talked to all of them separately at every opportunity. She concentrated on Charles and Ernie at the beginning of the holiday because they had to leave early.

"Do you like your job, Charles?" she asked.

"I do, Grandma, but I do not think I will stay in the same job all my life."

"Why not? Your grandfather and father have stayed in the same company all their lives."

"That is the way it used to be; nowadays people change jobs at least twice in their life, to gain experience."

"I see. Your grandfather would have enjoyed listening to you. He loved you very much."

"And I loved him and remember how much I enjoyed talking to him, when I was here last."

"You were the only one of his grandchildren that he saw before he died," Mercedes said sadly.

Charles could not help but hug his grandmother, who had started sobbing again.

"Ernie, try to steer Grandma away from talking about Grandpa; she is still very emotional," Charles said as he left.

Ernie nodded and said to Mercedes, "Hi, Granny, how are you?"

They were all around the swimming pool in Bea's flat; no one else in the building was around.

"Darling, I wanted to talk to you about your life in London."

"I am glad I finished university; I quite like my job."

"Are you planning to move and find another one, like Charles is?"

"No, not for the moment, anyway."

"What do you like about it?" Mercedes asked.

"I like investing and seeing how the money grows; it is exciting."

"Aren't you afraid that you might lose it all, and your clients might be left without it?"

"That is what is exciting—I have to think ahead and make sure that it will not happen. Up to now, I have done quite well."

"It is a pleasure hearing you talk like that. Have you got a girlfriend?"

Ernie hesitated and said, "Yes, but I have not told anyone yet—you are the first."

"Are you planning to marry her?"

"Maybe, but we are still young, and I would like to be able to buy a house before I do so."

"Won't that take a long time?"

"I could actually buy a small flat now; the bank would give me a loan straight away."

"That is wonderful," Mercedes said.

"Please, don't tell Mum and Dad. I have been thinking that I should move out closer to my job, but Mummy likes us all living together."

"She missed you when you were growing up and wants to catch up with what she missed."

Mercedes did not know that Bea had realised that the past was the past and that her children were men now; there was no way for her to catch up with the past. She could only build a future, but it was difficult; it was again she who had to adapt to what life dealt her.

CHAPTER THIRTY-EIGHT

Bea was left alone in the Buenos Aires flat after the New Year; John, Sebastian, and Richard left at the same time, a week after Charles and Ernie. She wanted to be with her mother for a little while longer so that Mercedes was not alone all of a sudden.

She felt thirsty and got up to get a drink of water, but as she was swallowing, it got stuck in her throat, and she fainted. She woke up on the floor of the bathroom and remembered what had happened. She got up very slowly and went back to bed, feeling worried. As she lay down and put a hand to her chest, she could not believe it—there was a lump on her left breast. With both hands now she went over her breasts, but there was only one lump. As soon as it was light, Bea got up, had a shower, ate breakfast, and waited until it was time to ring the doctor. She knew his secretary well by now.

"Hello, Miriam, it is Bea Fellow."

"Hello Bea, how are you?"

"I am not sure. Do you think there might be a slot for me sometime today?"

"Let me see . . . I might be able to fit you in before the first patient of the afternoon, at two. Could you come at a quarter to two?

"I'll be there. Just in case . . . please don't tell my mother that I will be seeing the doctor."

"Of course."

Bea then went to see Mercedes and took her for a walk and a cup of coffee. It was a lovely day, and for some reason Bea thought it was even lovelier than normal.

"What a beautiful sky. Look, Mummy, there isn't a single cloud."

"That's right, Bea, we are having a beautiful summer."

"It is *really* beautiful. The jacarandas are amazing this year."

"Darling, you are so happy this morning," Mercedes noted.

"How can I not be? I am with you and the weather is great. Poor John and the boys are freezing to death in England."

"Shall we have a cup of coffee?"

"Sure, let's sit here." They were at a coffee shop with tables outside on the pavement. Bea called the waiter and ordered.

"Will you have lunch with me?" Mercedes asked.

"Not today. I have an appointment at the hairdresser for my legs."

"Do they need doing?"

"Yes, they do; you cannot see because they are tanned, but they need doing." Bea had found an excuse that would not be noticeable. "I will come to tea and another walk, or perhaps we can go out to dinner. What do you think?"

"You are really full of beans today. Come this afternoon, and I will tell you then if I am up to going out."

"Fine, Mummy. We will do whatever you want to do."

Bea was at the doctor's at one thirty that afternoon; she preferred to wait at the consulting rooms rather than wander around not knowing what to do. Fortunately, the doctor arrived soon after and asked her to come into his room.

"What is so urgent, Bea?" he asked.

"I have a lump on my left breast." She then recounted what happened the night before.

The doctor raised his eyebrows. "I think I'd better take a look."

He touched her very gently all around her breasts and also under her arms and around her tummy, and especially near the area of the liver. Bea rested on the bed with her eyes shut, trying not to think.

"You do have a lump," he said. "I would like you to have a mammogram. How long has it been since you had one?"

"About two years ago."

"With you taking hormones, you should have a mammogram every six months."

"I know . . . I used to, but I feel so well now that I go when I am called, every three years."

"Take this to the clinic," he said, handing her a piece of paper. "I have written that it has to be done today."

Bea went straight to the clinic, but she had to wait. She called Mercedes. "Mummy, I got a bit delayed. How do you feel about dinner?"

"Fine, darling—an early one, please."

"I will collect you at eight. Is that all right?"

243

"Sure. And let's wear something nice."

"I will reserve in the Posadas; I know you like it there."

"You are good to me, Bea."

"Bye, Mummy, see you tonight."

Bea was finally called at five. "Your doctor will have the results tomorrow."

"Thank you," she said.

Bea took her cell phone—a new gadget that she had recently acquired and had become indispensable; life had changed so much since she got married over twenty year before. She called the hairdresser; she did not want to go home. "Can I come in half an hour?"

"You are lucky; today is very quiet."

Bea thought, *I am lucky today—I might be all right after all.*

For dinner, Mercedes looked better than she had for a long time, and she was wearing a stylish black and white dress. She still had a good figure despite her age.

"Mummy, you are looking very glamorous tonight," Bea noted.

"So are you; you had your hair done, too."

"Yes, I thought since I was there, I might as well have my hair done."

Bea hesitated, and in the end she decided that she would wait for the results before calling John the following morning. She went for a swim and was lying in the sun when her cell phone rang. "Bea?"

Bea sat up and said, "Yes, Miriam?"

"The doctor wants to see you. Can you come in the next hour?"

"Sure. Thank you, Miriam."

Bea ran, changed, and was ready in no time at all.

"Mummy, I will come and see you this afternoon. I have to talk to John. Do you mind if I don't go this morning?"

"Of course not, darling. I might start sorting out your father's belongings. I want you and Gaby to have his watches and cuff links; your boys might like to wear them one day."

"Mummy, you are so thoughtful. I am sure they would love to."

The doctor was blunt. "It's cancer, Bea. I can only tell you the truth."

Bea's mind went blank for a minute; she knew deep inside her that she had cancer, but up to then she had not wanted to believe it. She looked at the man in front of her and said: "What do I do now?"

"The lump is not too big; we can remove it, but we will not know whether it has spread or not until we do more tests. I think you might want to have these done in England, since you might need treatment afterwards."

"What do you mean?"

"Radiotherapy and probably chemotherapy, too."

"I see. How long will all this take?

"Dear Bea, I do not know. It can take about a year of treatment, but then, it might not."

"I am going to have to get organised. Please, don't tell my mother. She is just beginning to get over my father's passing."

"I won't, but I am sure she will find out—you can't disguise cancer treatment."

"I will see what I do."

Bea went home, changed into a pair of shorts and a sleeveless shirt, took some orange juice from the fridge, and sat with a piece of paper and a pen. She had to call John, but before that she wanted to call Gaby. She wrote down everything she had to do and picked up the phone.

"Gaby?"

"Hi, how are you and Mum?"

"Mum is getting better; she is sorting out Daddy's belongings."

"Oh, I am so glad."

"Gaby, I have breast cancer," Bea said abruptly.

"What!" Bea explained to her all that had happened in the last forty-eight hours. "But hadn't you felt any pain?"

"No. Apparently breast cancer is not painful, but it does get painful when it spreads."

"You must have treatment as soon as possible."

"This is why I am calling. Could you come and replace me? Mummy is getting better, but if I leave suddenly, she will suspect that something is wrong."

"I will talk with Mat. I might tell her that I want to go back to summer, and then when the weather here gets warmer, I will bring her back with me. Everybody is self-sufficient in this household. I hope that will give you enough time to have your treatment."

"Thank you, Gaby, you are an angel. I will call John now. I hope he won't take it too badly."

Bea rang John and explained to him what was happening.

"I will call the insurance and our GP, and ask for an appointment. When will you be back?" he asked.

"Gaby is calling Mummy today to tell her that she is coming back. I will try to get a ticket for next week."

"Everything will be waiting for you, all prepared, my darling Bea."

CHAPTER THIRTY-NINE

John was waiting at the airport when Bea got back to London, and he had a worried expression on his face as he hugged Bea for a long time. "Have you told your mother?" he asked.

"No, I just said that since Gaby was arriving next week and she was busy sorting my father's things, I would come back to check how things were at home. I told her that three men living alone in a house could be dangerous."

John smiled. "I am glad you have not lost your sense of humour."

"Funnily enough, I am not worried; cancer treatment is very efficient today. My father did not catch his early enough."

"I have to be honest with you, darling. The insurance does not cover your treatment, but it does cover your operation."

"How come?

"I am so sorry darling, since we hardly ever used it I had it downgraded. Now it only covers doctor's appointments and surgery but not things like cancer treatment."

"Yes, I recall now, vaguely that we talked about it."

"We have savings and can pay ourselves."

"No, we need those savings. Sebastian is at university, and Richard is still at school. I will do it on the National Health; we pay taxes"

"National Health is not the same as private medicine."

"I know, but I think they are good with cancer."

Bea went to see her general practitioner the next day, and he referred her to an oncologist. "Here is the number and an explanatory letter. Make an appointment as soon as possible."

Bea rang the oncologist, Professor Davies, from her cell phone and explained that she would like to see him soon. She had the results of her mammogram with her and a letter from her doctor in Argentina, too. She was given an appointment for the following day after hours, at six thirty in the evening.

"I will go with you, darling," John said.

"It is not necessary."

"Anyway, I would like to be there."

Bea smiled at the sentiment. "All right, darling, as you wish."

Professor Davies was not that old, but he was serious. He read the letters with great attention and then said, "I would like to see where the lump is. Take your top off, please."

Bea went behind the curtain and called him when she was ready. He went over her breasts as Dr Aragon had done in Argentina.

"I found it; do you mind if I insert a needle in it?"

"Why do you have to do that?" Bea asked.

"To make another test; it should not hurt."

Incredibly enough, it did not hurt, but it did leave a bruise were Professor Davies inserted the needle.

"I would like you to go to the hospital—to the Nuclear Medicine Department. They will insert another needle that you should keep in place until I go through with the operation, the day after tomorrow."

Everything was going so quickly. Bea did not know that it was going to happen this fast, and she was suddenly filled with apprehension. She had not prepared herself for this; she had not even told the boys yet.

John and Bea went home in silence; the appointment at the hospital had been made by the professor's secretary for the next day.

John called Charles and Ernie and asked them if they could be home for dinner that night. "There is something important that Mummy and I would like to tell you." He hung up and then asked Bea, "What shall I do about Sebastian and Richard?"

"I don't really know, but I think that it would be better if I called them and told them myself."

Bea sat for a while trying to compose herself and then picked up the telephone to ring Sebastian.

"Darling, I am back; how are things?"

"Everything is fine, Mum—lots of work, but fine. We were not expecting you back until the end of the month."

"Dear Sebastian, I have to have an operation the day after tomorrow."

"What is wrong, Mum?" he asked, sounding concerned.

"I have a lump in my breast, and they want to remove it."

"Is it cancer?"

Bea could not lie to her children. "Yes, at a very early stage. I should be fine after treatment."

"I'm sorry, Mum. I will come to see you this weekend."

"That would be lovely, darling."

She then called Richard, who was even more concerned than Sebastian. "Mum, I would like to be there with you. I will ask permission to come down tomorrow."

"Darling, there is no need."

"Please, Mum, talk to Father Henry."

"I will pass you to your father."

John talked to Richard, and then Bea heard him talking to Father Henry. When he hung up, he said, "Richard will be here tomorrow afternoon. He insisted that he wants to be with you for the operation."

Bea had the needle in her breast when they went to collect Richard at the station, and she could not hug him as close as she would have liked, but she looked well and optimistic.

John had reserved at a restaurant for the five of them to have dinner, but when they got home, Sebastian was there, too. Bea could not hold back a sob. She was going to have dinner with all her men before her operation. She was sure now that everything would turn out well.

CHAPTER FORTY

The anaesthetist was there when she woke up. He smiled at her and asked, "How are you? Any pain?"

"I feel fine, no pain at all."

"Good."

At that moment Professor Davies came back from the operating theatre. "Everything went well. I have removed the lump and three nodes from under your arm. If they prove to be malignant, I will have to operate again and remove the rest of the nodes in about a month's time, when you feel stronger."

Bea nodded but did not reply. She did not want to think about another operation just then. She was taken to her room, and there they were, all her men waiting for her. This time she could not control her tears. She was emotionally drained. Despite the fact that her boys had had so little to do with her while they were growing up, they still considered her their mother, and that made her cry.

They thought that she was in pain and said, "Would you like us to call the nurse, Mummy? She can give you a pain killer."

She was finally able to say, "I am not in pain. I am so happy to see you all here waiting for me."

They laughed and went to kiss her. John was the last one and said to her, "You are being very brave. Professor Davies has already told us that you might have to have another operation."

"I don't want to think about it now. He said I could go home tomorrow."

Bea recovered well from that operation and did the recommended exercises to regain strength in her left arm. But unfortunately the nodes came out positive, and she had to have another operation. This time it was going to take longer to recover because they were going to empty her underarm: "Would you consider having a complete mastectomy?"

"No—I have grown attached to them," she said, touching her breasts, which made Professor Davies laugh.

"I like that. We will leave it for the moment. Once you have had chemotherapy and radiotherapy, we will see how you go."

"I will have to have treatment as well?"

"Oh, yes. When it expands to the underarm, it might have gone somewhere else as well."

"Can't you check if it has?"

"No. Sometimes it is too small to detect."

Bea looked at John. They had not told the professor that their insurance did not cover treatment. Bea finally said, "I am afraid that we will have to do the treatment through the national insurance."

"That will not be a problem. In any case, I will not be in charge of the treatment. I will refer you to the person in charge at the hospital. Nevertheless, I would like to go on checking you every once in a while."

After the second operation, Bea was in pain and could hardly lift her left arm. She practiced the exercises, but her arm swelled with lymphatic liquid, which made it even more painful.

"I will drain it," Professor Davies volunteered.

She felt better instantly and went back home feeling reassured that whenever her arm swelled it would be drained. Unfortunately when she went to see Professor Milles, who was in charge of her treatment, he refused point blank to drain it again. "It might get infected," he said. So she had to bear the discomfort until the liquid disappeared of its own accord.

Bea had her first chemo session exactly a month after her second operation. She did not feel sick, but she could not sleep well and lost weight. The left side of her chest became purple, and she rang the nurse. "Don't worry; it is probably the bruise coming out," The nurse told her.

By the time Bea had to have her second chemo dose, the discolouring had reached her waist. Bea asked to see the doctor. "I would like you to see my chest; I called the nurse when it started happening last month, and she said that the bruise must be coming out, but I do not feel very well."

The doctor had a look and asked Bea, "Have you had radiotherapy?"

"No, just the chemo last month."

"Wait a minute—I will call another doctor."

The other doctor had a look and said, "I would like you to have a scan straight away."

Bea was taken to the fourth floor, where the tests were carried out, and she was seen immediately by the radiologist. "Your blood has gone yucky," she said trying not to use the word septicaemia.

Bea looked at the doctor that had gone with her to have the scan. He said, "You'd better call your husband—you must stay in hospital until your blood gets better again. You have to have intravenous antibiotics and move as little as possible."

She rang her husband. "John, I have to stay in the hospital. Could you bring me a nightie and my washing things, please? I will explain to you when you get here."

John left his office not knowing what was going on, but he did what Bea had asked him, trying not to panic.

He was there when Bea arrived in the ward. This time it was not private, and she was allocated a bed in the intensive care ward. The doctor explained to John what had happened.

"But Bea rang the nurse when she started having the discoloration," John said angrily.

"I am sorry. She should have come to the hospital."

"She was told to ring if she had any questions."

"I can only say that I am sorry," the doctor repeated.

John was not happy, but there was nothing to do now but to accept that Bea needed antibiotics to get better.

She was in the hospital for a week with a needle in her arm; it was incredibly painful because the veins gave up, and it was very difficult to inject her. They put her arm in hot water and wrapped it up with a blanket, but still the veins in her arm had had enough. In the end they had to inject her in the veins behind the knee, which was agony.

John, Charles, and Ernie took turns to go and see her, but she was in so much pain that it was difficult to have a conversation. It was just as painful for them to see her in that state.

255

Finally her skin became normal again, and Bea was sent home, but she had to go on taking antibiotics for another week until she saw the doctor again. In the meantime, most her hair had fallen out, and John agreed to shave her head to even it up. They also went in search of a wig, not knowing that the hospital would provide her with one. She ended up having two. The boys liked playing with them and trying them on to make their mother laugh.

She had radiotherapy next, and Bea understood then why the doctor had asked her if she had had radiotherapy when her blood had gone bad: her breast became purple again, and she had to treat her skin with a special cream. She felt cold and weak, but she did not want to show her state of mind to her men. She knew that John was kind and considerate, but at the same time he could not be self-indulgent, and the boys were like him. She had to be strong.

When it was all over, Bea was called by the radiologist, who had been in charge of her for the last two months. "The hospital has been your home for two months now; you have been coming here every day."

"I know. I have got used to it."

"Most everybody does. This is why you must be careful not to get depressed now that you will not be coming to see us again—or so I hope."

"I am planning to go and see my sister in the United States, and my mother in Argentina."

"That is a very good idea. If you can afford a trip away from England, it will help your recovery."

"Thank you, Doctor. You have been most kind."

"All the best, be happy," he said.

CHAPTER FORTY-ONE

Bea had not seen her mother for over ten months. Christmas was approaching, and she had promised Gaby, who had been looking after Mercedes on and off during all this time, that she'd take over. Their mother had not been told that Bea had cancer; both sisters had agreed that it was better not to tell her. Gaby had been going back and forth to Buenos Aires, as well as taking Mercedes to visit her family in the States. Bea had told her that she had been given an important job that was taking longer than she expected. Her hair had begun to grow again, but it was still very short, so she decided that it would be better to take one of her wigs.

She had made all the plans to go to Argentina for Christmas as they had the year before, but when she talked to Charles, he said, "Mum, I did not tell you before because you were still having treatment, but now that you are better, I would like you to know that I have been seeing someone who has become special. I will not be spending Christmas with you this year. I hope that you don't mind."

"Oh, Charles, of course I don't mind. Will you bring her home for dinner before I leave?"

"Are you sure, mum? I don't want you to go into any trouble for us."

"Darling, it would be a pleasure."

That evening at the dinner table, Bea recounted her conversation with Charles to John and Ernie. "Charles surprised me today: he has a special girlfriend."

Ernie looked at Charles and his parents and said, "I had been waiting for you to finish your radiotherapy to tell you that I am also seeing someone."

John and Bea looked at each other and laughed. "I do not understand why you thought that telling me this would upset me," Bea said. "I am delighted! Ernie, you must also bring your girlfriend for dinner, before I leave."

"Darling Bea, I think we should all go out. You have enough with organising your trip," John said.

"Fine, we will go out—you boys, choose a good restaurant. It will be an early celebration of Christmas, too."

As they were getting into bed, Bea said to John, "I wonder if Sebastian will be coming to Argentina. This is his last year at university, and he might have something planned."

"We'd better call him in the morning, before we get the tickets," suggested John.

But Sebastian had no plans; the only thing he wanted was to take his books with him—he did not just want to pass, he wanted to pass with honours.

They were right to assume that Richard would be joining them in Buenos Aires, but they were surprised to hear that he also wanted to take his books with him because this was his last year at school. "Please don't organise too many outings; I really have to work," he said.

Bea replied, "I will let Grandma know. I am very proud of you."

The evening before Bea left, Charles and Ernie introduced Grace and Camilla to the family at a French restaurant in town. Since they all worked, including John, it was easier for Bea to go and meet them.

Charles was holding Grace's arm when he approached his parents at the table. "Mum and Dad, this is Grace."

"Pleased to meet you," said John, extending his hand.

Bea got up and gave Grace a kiss. "It is indeed a pleasure to meet you. Please sit here," Bea said, pointing at the chair next to hers.

At that moment Ernie arrived with Camilla, and the process of introductions was repeated. Grace and Camilla already knew each other, and they hugged, as had become the custom in London recently, probably brought from the continent. So many things had changed since Bea and John were married.

They had a most enjoyable time. The girls were in their twenties and had been working for a while. They had that air of independence that success brings, along with sophistication. They were self-assured but not arrogant, and it was a pleasure for Bea and John to have the chance to meet them.

"I hope you will come to visit us when I am back from Argentina," Bea said as they were leaving.

They both responded nicely and wished her a safe trip.

John took Bea to the airport as usual, but this time he was not sure that he should let her travel by herself.

Bea reassured him. "Darling, I am going to see Gaby first. It will not be such a long haul."

"Nevertheless, please rest as much as possible."

"Don't worry; I am sure that Gaby will look after me."

Gaby and Mat were waiting in the airport when Bea arrived. Gaby held her in her arms for a long time. She had been shocked to see her sister without her wonderful hair. Mat also had a bit of a shiver when he saw her, but he disguised it well.

"How are you, Bea?"

"I feel a bit tired, but otherwise I am incredibly well. Please don't worry about me."

Mat asked, "What are you going to tell your mother? She will notice your hair."

"I have a wig that looks just like my own hair. She does not have to find out."

Gaby's kids, Lisa and William, were at home waiting for them. Lisa had set the table, and William had found one or two books that might be of interest for their aunt and put them in her room. They did not know Bea well, but they thought that she was kind and thoughtful the previous Christmas, and they were sorry that she had had such a horrible time lately. Gaby had told them, "Your aunt has cancer."

"Is she dying like Granddad?" they asked.

"No, she has just finished her treatment and is going to see Granny for Christmas, like last year."

"Are we going, too?"

"No, not this year—I have travelled enough; maybe next year."

They ran to the door when they heard the key and were taken aback by Bea's lack of hair, but they could not hide it like their parents. Lisa said, "What happened to your hair, Auntie Bea?"

"I lost it with the chemo, but it is growing now. I have a wig that I will show you later. The boys like playing with it—they pretend to be me."

"May I try it on? Asked Lisa

"Of course; I don't wear it all the time because it makes me feel hot."

Bea enjoyed staying with Gaby and her family. They allowed her to rest and do things on her own time, but they had also suggestions for sightseeing and going out to restaurants and a play.

"We are sorry we will not be with you this Christmas, Auntie Bea. We had such a good time last year," said William.

Bea replied, "I'm sorry too, darling, but your mum has been wonderful looking after Grandma, and she deserves a rest. Maybe next year everything will be more normal."

CHAPTER FORTY-TWO

Bea took a taxi from the airport; she had not told Mercedes the exact day of her arrival, so that she would not feel the need to come and collect her. As soon as she got home, Bea rang her mother. "Mummy?"

"Bea! Where are you?"

"In the flat; I have just arrived."

"Why didn't you tell me you were coming today?" Mercedes scolded.

"I did not want you to go through the trouble of getting up at the crack of dawn to come and collect me."

"How did you get to the flat?"

"I took a taxi."

"Will you come to lunch?"

Bea said, "I would like to unpack and clean the flat. Would you mind if I see you this evening?"

"No, of course not; but aren't you tired after the trip?"

"I was able to sleep, and it was not such a long trip from Gaby's."

"I had forgotten you were not coming from London. See you this evening, darling."

Bea cleaned the cupboards before unpacking and was in the process of cleaning the bathrooms when the bell rang. Bea thought it was the caretaker who had some mail for them and went to open the door, despite the fact that she was in shorts and without her wig; she did not even bother to take her rubber gloves off.

But it was not the caretaker. Mercedes stood there with Rosa, her maid. "Mum! What are you doing here?"

Bea had been taken by surprise—but so had Mercedes. "What happened to your hair?" she asked. I have brought Rosa to give you a hand with the cleaning."

Mother and daughter embraced while Rosa, who had cleaned for Bea before, went straight to the kitchen.

"You should not have bothered, Mum. I was getting along fine."

"Are you all right, Bea? You are so thin and pale."

Bea could not go on lying to her mother—she had felt awful doing so all these months. "Mum, I had cancer treatment, and I lost my hair because of the chemo."

"Why didn't you tell me?" Mercedes shouted, clearly shocked.

"Gaby and I decided that it was better if you did not know. Daddy has only been gone for a year."

Mercedes looked now like the old Mercedes, in charge and in control. "I am sorry I was such a burden to you both. I feel stronger now. But how are you, dear?"

"I have finished the treatment, and it is great being here in the warmth. I feel the cold even more than before."

"I'm really glad I brought Rosa."

Bea went to the kitchen and embraced Rosa, who was like a friend of the family. "Thank you for coming to help," she said.

"I heard what you said to your mother. You must look after yourself. There is very little to do now that your father is gone. I will come and clean for you while you are here."

Bea could not control her tears. She had been controlling herself for so long in front of John and the boys. Now she could let go, and it felt good.

"I will make coffee for you and your mother," Rosa said. "I brought some along with some biscuits. I did not think you would have any in the flat."

"Rosa, you are an angel," Bea said, hugging her again.

Mercedes had been standing by the door, and now she approached Bea: "Come and tell me all that has been going on with you."

Bea recounted the past ten months in detail. "I thought that I could go on pretending that nothing was wrong. I have a wig that looks exactly like my hair."

"Were you planning to sit in the sun and go swimming with the wig on?"

"Actually, that is exactly what I had planned, although I know that it would have been very hot."

"Bea, you are just the way you used to be—mad!"

The two women laughed while they drank the delicious coffee and biscuits that Rosa had brought. Then Bea said, "Mum, since you are here with Rosa, do you mind if I go and have a shower and then take you out to lunch?"

"That is a great idea. Rosa, when you feel in need of a break, go back home. If necessary, come back this afternoon."

Rosa replied, "I think I can finish this morning; it is only superficial dust. I cleaned the flat after Mrs Bea left last time."

"In that case, take the afternoon off. I am going to have lunch with Bea, and then I will insist that she has a rest."

"All right, ma'am."

Bea reappeared with her wig on and with her face done up. She looked much better, which made Mercedes exclaim, "That is my girl. Darling, you look great."

For some extraordinary reason, that remark made Bea hungry. Suddenly she felt like having a good lunch with lots of wine to drink. "Come on, Mum, we are going to enjoy ourselves, and then I will sleep all afternoon."

Mercedes left Bea at the door of her apartment block. "You have promised to have a good rest," she reminded her daughter.

"I will, Mum, but first I have to ring John before it gets too late."

She entered her house and dialled. "John?"

"Hi there, are you settled in the flat?" he asked.

"More than that, Mum appeared on the door with Rosa, and she found out."

"Oh dear. How did she take it?"

"Incredibly well—she is back to normal. We have just had a great lunch, and I am going to have a rest before going to see her and Aunt Filomena for dinner."

"You sound so well, darling Bea; I am sure that the weather there will do you a lot of good."

"I think so, but I miss you. Come soon."

"Only a week to go."

John, Sebastian, and Richard arrived at the flat in the same way that Bea had. There was no point in getting up to collect them when there was hardly room in the taxi for four.

"You look great, Mum," Sebastian said.

"Yes, you do. I can see that you have been in the sun," Richard added.

"I have been having a good rest and sunbathing with Grandma almost every day. She looks well, too. Rosa has been a Godsend; she comes every day to see if something needs doing."

John said, "What a relief! You can't imagine how worried I've been. It is good to know that everything has gone back to normal."

That Christmas was quiet. Mercedes insisted on having them to dinner with two of her sisters. The boys were at their books at all hours, except when they went to relax by the pool. For New Year's they went out, and the boys danced with two girls that were at the next table, but this year they went to bed at a reasonable hour. The previous year they had danced until five in the morning, and then the girls had insisted on going for breakfast.

As Bea and her family prepared to leave Buenos Aires, Bea said to Mercedes, "Mummy, are you sure you don't want to come with us?"

"I am positive, Bea. We are having wonderful weather, and Aunt Filomena has invited me to her house by the sea in Mar del Plata. Don't worry about me—I miss your father all the time, but I have got used to doing things by myself. I will go to see you when it gets a bit warmer in London."

CHAPTER FORTY-THREE

Bea had stomach aches all through the holidays, but she did not comment on them; she thought that her family had had enough of her aches and pains. But the pain went on, and she had to go back to her GP in London. This time they found stones in her gallbladder, and she had to have another operation. Everybody joked that soon she would have nothing inside her body.

She was better by the time that Sebastian graduated from university, not only with flying colours but also with a job and a girlfriend. He announced to his parents that he and Ann would be moving into a rented flat closer to their jobs; she was going to work for a firm of lawyers and hoped to become one eventually. Neither Bea nor John liked the idea, but they could not interfere with this decision; Sebastian had been a wonderful son, just as the others, and he was now an adult.

"What are we going to do in this big house all by ourselves?" Bea asked.

"Would you like to downsize?"

"It might be an idea, but I still feel a bit fragile."

Richard also graduated with flying colours and a place at the same university that Charles had gone to. Just as his eldest brother, he was taking a year off; the school had found him a place in a sister school in Chile, to teach English.

"I will be able to pop over and visit Grandma," he explained.

Bea smiled. "She would love that, darling."

A few weeks later Charles came home one day to ask them if they would give him their blessing to marry Grace—he was still a little boy in some ways.

"Have you already asked her?" Bea asked.

"Not yet—I wanted to talk to you first."

Bea approached Charles and, holding his face in her hands, said, "I like Grace, and if she makes you happy, that is all that counts."

"I am glad that you have found such a nice girl, son," John said. He hugged Charles as the door opened and Ernie came in.

"What is going on?" Ernie asked. They told him the news. "You beat me to it again, brother! I had been waiting for the right occasion to tell you that I have proposed to Camilla, and she has accepted me. We have not told anyone yet."

It was Ernie's turn to be hugged not only by his parents but also by his brother.

"Have you set a date yet?" Bea asked.

"No, we were waiting to talk to our families before deciding on the date."

"Why don't you marry on the same day?" Bea suggested.

Both brothers looked at each other and shook their heads. "I don't think that either Grace or Camilla would accept that; this is supposed to be the brides' day, and they want to be the special one," said Ernie.

"I agree," said Charles. "I am sure that Grace would like to plan her own wedding—that is, if she accepts me."

They laughed at that. "This has been a year of revelations. What are we going to do in this big house all by ourselves?" Bea repeated.

Charles said, "Don't worry, Mum. I am sure we will come back with our big families to visit."

They laughed again, and Bea went to call Mercedes.

"Darling, I had just been thinking of you. How is the weather there?" Mercedes said.

"The weather is not bad, considering that it is England, but I have news."

Mercedes was delighted. "You must let me know when these weddings are going to take place. I have to renew my wardrobe."

"This house is going to be empty soon. Will you come and stay for a while?"

"I will go for the weddings, but now that Richard is near, I want to go and see him. The weather here is still nice; we are having a mild winter."

"Richard said that he will visit you."

"Good, we will see lots of each other. It was high time that this happened."

Bea then phoned her sister. "Gaby, your godson is getting married."

"How wonderful! When?"

"They only just got engaged. I did not ring you before in order not to tempt fate. But there is more news."

"Spill it out—don't keep me waiting."

"Ernie is also getting married, and Sebastian has rented a flat with his girlfriend."

"My, my; it is a good thing that Daddy is not around; he would not have approved. But I am very happy for Ernie."

"My dear sister, this is another world from the one we grew up in. I cannot keep up with all this technology and freedom—or no freedom, because you have to be politically correct."

"I know. Have they asked you to do anything for the weddings?" Gaby asked.

"I have been told that it is the bride's day."

"I remember your wedding, Bea. You were so patient with everyone."

"Mum wanted to design my wedding dress and organised everything for me. I did not want to deny her that."

Gaby laughed. "I'm afraid I did."

"I know, but you were older and had been living abroad for a long time. I was married from home."

"You went on that trip, though."

"That was the only thing I did on my own."

"You opened the door for me, Bea. I will always be grateful."

"I am glad I have done something right in my life," Bea said.

"Now, now, what is that?"

"The boys are good to me, but I have the feeling that they would have preferred it if I had been English. I cannot forget what Charles said to me years ago"

"All children prefer to have other parents, until something special happens, and then, they realise that you are perfect. In any case, as you say, Charles said that under special circumstances"

"I know; I should try to forget about it."

"Yes, you should!"."

"It is great talking to you, Gaby. You lift my spirits."

"Don't forget to let me know the dates of the weddings."

CHAPTER FORTY-FOUR

Having one wedding in the family at any one time was a cause for tempers to be raised, and disagreements would inevitably happen. Having two weddings was even more difficult.

The two brothers wanted to have their weddings that same year, but who was going to be the first one, and who would be there from their family? They could not ask Bea's old relatives to come twice in a year—nor the young ones, for that matter. People were busy with their jobs, and plane tickets were expensive. John's relatives were mainly in England, but some were abroad, and most of them were also getting old.

Neither Bea nor John, were asked their opinion on their sons' weddings; they were just told what they had to do. Bea and Gaby had over the telephone remembered how Katherine had arrived a week before Bea's wedding and had changed the only thing that she wanted to be in charge of—the music. But Bea did not want to interfere. She would have just loved to be part of the preparations as a mother.

In the end the weddings were organised for the following year. Richard was away and could not be back on time that year, and the couples did not want to get married in the winter. It was decided that Charles would marry first, since he was the eldest; his was in June and Ernie's was in September. Some relatives would go to one wedding and others to the next one—except Mercedes and Gaby and her family, who were going to both of them.

Charles and Grace decided to go to Argentina on their honeymoon, and they gave a big party for those who had not been to their wedding. Then they went on a two-week tour of the country.

Grace hugged Bea. "I love your country—it was almost as hot as it is here in the summer. We went to the Iguazu' Falls and saw the bird sanctuary. Then we went south and skied in the sunshine. It was amazing."

"It is a big country; you can go back several times, and you would still not go everywhere. I have to admit that I know very little of my own land."

Camilla was very interested in the places that Charles and Grace had visited and took note. They also wanted to go to Argentina on their honeymoon but had not told anyone yet. "We must try to go somewhere where they have not been," she said to Ernie.

"I will check which are the best places to visit in September," he assured her.

"Good, I have had enough with the wedding and my mother."

"We are lucky that my parents are not interfering with the organization."

"True, they have not shown much interest."

Ernie said, "My parents would not do anything unless you ask them."

"Ah, I see—mine always do."

Richard had arrived full of beans from Chile just before Charles's wedding and started university just after Ernie's. He had the chance to see his grandmother in England, too; they were very fond of each other and spoke Spanish when they were on their own. Mercedes stayed with

Bea and John from June to September, which was good for Bea who was feeling a bit left out by her children.

Mercedes, "Darling, you were very special. Not even your sister allowed me to do anything for hers."

"I don't really mind not being consulted, but I would like to share things with them. They keep everything as a big secret."

"They are young, Bea, and everything has changed so much."

"I know, Mother. There are no more linen diapers anymore—they are considered unhygienic. When I came to England, disposable nappies were rare. I had to learn how to fold the cloth ones."

"This is the way I did it with you and your sister; they were boiled in a special tub."

"At least I had Milton."

"Oh, yes, I remember you and the bucket. I thought it was more complicated than just boiling them."

"I wonder what the girls will do. Have they spoken about having children?"

"No, and I don't dare ask them; it is a sensitive subject. In any case we never talked about babies with you—I just had them."

Mercedes laughed. "I remember you were called a rabbit."

"John still jokes about it when we meet new people."

"You were a bit like one," her mother teased.

Soon after the weddings, and after Mercedes had gone back to Argentina, Bea went back to the doctor.

"The stomach ache has not gone," she said.

"You might have an ulcer. Have you been stressing lately?" the doctor said.

"Well, two of our sons were married in the space of three months, but I hardly had anything to do with the weddings."

"Ah, well, weddings are always stressful. I will give you a prescription. Come and see me in two months if it does not get better."

Christmas was approaching again, and this year it was going to be spent in England. Charles and Ernie and their wives had just been to Argentina, and Bea had also just seen Mercedes. It was time to have a cold Christmas, but that was yet another problem—the new wives wanted to spend Christmas with their families. Then Sebastian announced that he and Ann were getting married; they did not want a big wedding, but they were planning also go to Argentina on their honeymoon, and they wanted to spend Christmas over there.

Bea asked if they would at least let her give them a party. She was allowed to give a small party at their home for her third son's wedding; only close friends of the couple and relatives of the bride were invited. Not even Gaby came this time.

"Don't worry, Bea. I met Ann at the weddings, and I think she is great; I hope they might want to come and visit us soon," Gaby said.

Bea repeated this conversation to Sebastian, and they thought they could make a detour on the way back and go to visit their relatives in the States.

Only Richard was with them through the holidays, but it was lovely anyway. He had been away for a year, and then there had been the weddings and his first term at college. They had a lot to catch up with and went for long walks, to the theatre, and out to dinner.

"Richard's Spanish is perfect now," Bea noted.

"What about the others?" John asked.

"They did not have a year in Chile, but it is not bad."

"I wish mine was better."

"Darling, you are so good at languages—you speak all of them well."

"Not as well as you speak English," John said.

"I live here, remember? I have a lot of practice." John laughed and hugged her.

CHAPTER FORTY-FIVE

Grace and Camilla told the family that they were expecting almost at the same time; it was possible that the babies could be born on the same day. But again they went to their mothers for advice. They visited Bea and John when they were asked, but Bea had to fix those dates long in advance. Bea and John were seldom invited to their homes.

After the birth of Katherine to Grace and Charles, and Mark to Camilla and Ernie, both couples decided to move; their flats were too small for a family, and they had not envisaged that babies would take so much room. Their babies took up more room than the four that Bea and John had—the amount of things those little bundles of flesh had, were amazing. They had monitors in their rooms in case the children could not be heard from the other side of the flat—although the flats only consisted of two bedrooms. They had high chests of drawers with labels on each one for all the clothing they needed, plus several movable drawers with toys. Bea thought that they would be at least ten by the time they finished playing with them. And then there were playpens and basins to wash them in, and even a television and a computer for later use. Some of these artefacts went with them in the car all the time—they needed a bigger car with a luggage container on the roof for when they stayed with someone—and, of course, anybody who invited them needed a big house to accommodate them.

"I could help you, if you like," Bea ventured one day when they were all together.

"Thank you, Bea, but we know what we are looking for," Camilla answered.

"We will have a look, and then perhaps you can tell us if it would be a good buy," added Charles.

"I just want you to know that I am here in case you need me."

"Thank you, Mum," said Ernie

"I want to have the christening before we embark on house hunting," Grace said. She had kept quiet until that moment.

"I know you wanted your weddings to take place at different times, but perhaps it might be simpler to have one christening. I could have everybody for lunch here afterwards."

Charles said: "That is a good idea. What do you think Grace?"

"What do you think, Camilla?" Grace asked her sister-in-law.

Camilla said, "Thank you Bea, it would be a great help." Bea replied, "Shall I ask our priest? It would be easier for the guests if the church is close by."

They all looked at each other and nodded. Bea was finally allowed to do something for her grandchildren. "I hope Father Matthias can do it in the next month or so, before it gets cold. I will get a marquee so that we can seat everybody."

"Thank you, Mum," Charles said. He kissed his mother, and the others followed suit.

"You can start looking for houses; I will take care of the baptisms." Bea was truly happy to be allowed to have the honour of hosting her family for what she considered the most important event in a baby's life.

Richard finished university as well as his brothers, with flying colours. He also secured a job, but it was not in London, but Madrid. The fact that his Spanish was so good gave him the opportunity to find a job abroad.

The remainder of that year and the beginning of the next were busy for everyone. Bea organised a beautiful lunch party for the families of her children and the godparents of the grandchildren. There were pink and blue table cloths and ribbons on the chairs, as well as a blue cake for Mark and a pink one for Katherine, with all sorts of animals as decoration. Father Matthias had been invited as a thank-you gesture for conducting the baptism at such short notice. John got his best champagne from the cellar. It was not every day that they would be having this kind of celebration.

The couples finally found the houses that they were looking for, but both of them decided to give the houses their own touch by adding or merging rooms. Bea was consulted in a very discreet manner; the young couples wanted the design and construction projects of their homes to be theirs and nobody else's. Bea was full of admiration for the amount of time and energy that the couples were putting into it.

Bea had also been visiting Mercedes regularly; she was now quite frail, and Bea and Gaby took turns visiting her.

One day Bea got a call from Gaby. "Bea?"

"How is Mum?"

"This is why I am calling—she has been taken to the hospital. She had a minor heart attack last night."

"I will look for a ticket right away. I will try to be there tomorrow morning."

The only ticket that Bea found was first class and very expensive, but she bought it anyway. She wanted to be next to her mother.

Unfortunately, when Bea got to the hospital, Mercedes had already passed away and had been sent downstairs. Bea sat on a chair in the corridor opposite her mother's room with Gaby at her side; neither of them talked. Bea held her head in her hands and cried. Why was it that she was never there when her loved ones died? Neither she nor John had arrived in time to see their parents during their last minutes of life. Bea prayed, "God, please forgive me for all the things that I might have done or said to make my parents unhappy. Please, take them with you." She lifted her tear-stained face and hugged Gaby. "Did she suffer?" she asked.

"She had another heart attack after I talked to you, and she did not recover consciousness. She looked very peaceful and beautiful when she finally stopped breathing."

Both sisters were left by themselves by the hospital staff, to let out their grief, but soon after relatives started arriving. Their older aunts did not come, but their cousins did, and they helped put a notice in the paper and telephoned everyone to let them know about the funeral arrangements. Fortunately, the company that had arranged Alberto's funeral had been on alert since her first heart attack and they were able to organise Mercedes's very quickly.

Neither Bea's nor Gaby's family were able to attend the funeral, but Mercedes's family and friends were there; so many had passed away already that it was not as well attended as Alberto's. Nevertheless, two of Mercedes's nieces and nephews had wonderful things to say about her; Mercedes had indeed been very kind to the people she knew, and she was going to be missed.

CHAPTER FORTY-SIX

"What shall we do with Mother's flat and all the things in it, Gaby?" Bea asked.

"I don't know. I have to go back home—I have been away for ages."

"I can stay and deal with everything. I might sell my flat, too. I don't think that we shall be coming all that often, now that Mother is gone."

"I don't think that I shall be coming all that often, either. Looking after a flat at a distance is a hassle."

"I agree. Shall I put both on the market?"

"I think that would be the best. I wonder if we will be able to take the money out."

"I know I can take the money of our flat out but I don't think we are allowed to take more than ten thousand dollars at any one time from money originating in Argentina. We have an account in a bank here. Do you?"

"No, we don't."

"I had to open one in order to pay the flat's service charges."

"What shall we do?" Gaby asked.

"I think you should open a bank account and get a debit card, so that you can take the money out from wherever you are. I do not think we can do anything else."

"What about all the furniture and silver, and the car that has been in the garage since Daddy died?"

"Let's choose what we want, and then we can call family, friends, and charities to come and get the things from this flat and ours."

"This is going to be very difficult, Bea."

"I know, but I cannot do it for you. You can choose first, and then when you are gone, I will deal with the rest."

Gaby had to stay another week in order to open her bank account and deal with the things she wanted from her parents. Bea introduced her to her bank manager, and Gaby was able to open an account in no time at all.

Bea called her husband. "John?"

"How are you doing, darling?"

"There is quite a bit of work to do here. I can either stay until the flats are sold—and I don't know how long that is going to take—or I can go back to London and come back when both flats are sold."

"I think that the latter is a better solution. What are you going to do all by yourself in Buenos Aires?"

John had become much more caring since Bea's cancer and wanted to look after her.

"I do know some people here, but I miss you."

"I miss you, too. Come back soon."

Bea had already organised a shipment of the items that she and Gaby wanted, as well as some of the things that their husbands and children wanted. In the end they took most of their parents' belongings, but Bea donated most of the things in the flat, as well as the car; one of their cousins called it vintage and took it from her.

Bea sat in their home sitting room and stretched: "It is so good to be back. What have you been up to?" Bea asked.

John replied, "You know what I have been up to—we talked every day."

"I know but I want to hear it again."

"Don't be silly. You look tired, and I am going to take you out to an early dinner and then to bed."

"That sounds like just what the doctor ordered."

Bea's stomach aches had been coming and going, but lately they were there all the time. She ate because she had to, not because she wanted to. But she did not want to confide in John; she knew how much he worried, and in a childish way she hated the disruption her illnesses caused.

"I might have to go back to Buenos Aires more than once; it all depends whether the estate agent is able to sell both flats at the same time."

"Do you think that is likely?" John asked.

"I have my doubts, but you never know."

Three weeks later, Bea received a call from the estate agent looking after both flats. "You have had an offer for both flats, but the offer on your parents' flat is lower than we wanted. What shall I do?"

"I will call you back as soon as I talk to my sister," Bea said.

She called Gaby and told her what was going on. "If you like, I can wait to get a higher offer. It is up to you."

"Bea, I wonder if we will get a higher offer. It is a lovely big flat, but it needs modernisation."

"Shall I accept?"

"Yes, I think we should."

"Thank you, Gaby. That will save me another trip."

"Thank you for doing this for us."

"I might pop over and see you before I come back to England."

"That would be wonderful!"

"I will let you know how things go," Bea said, and she hung up.

Bea did not want to stay in Buenos Aires longer than necessary, and she asked the lawyer to prepare all the paperwork and the estate agent to make sure that everything was in order with the buyers before she went there. Everything went like clockwork, and Bea was able to leave a week after she arrived. She went to the bank and sent the money from their flat to their London bank account, and she deposited the money from their parents' flat half in Gaby's bank account and half in hers. She had kept the ten thousand dollars allowed by the government to give to Gaby, but she did not need to do so for herself.

"Gaby, everything has gone well. Your money is in the bank, and I am bringing ten thousand dollars for you with me."

"You don't have to do that. What about you?"

"I don't need to; I have just sent all the money from our flat to London. John will be happy; we made a small profit."

"When will you be here?" Gaby asked.

"I could be there the day after tomorrow. Is that all right with you?"

"Great! We all want to see you again."

"Give Mat, Lisa, and William a hug from me."

"I will. See you soon."

Bea arrived at the airport with two hours to spare. She had nothing better to do, and she thought that going through customs and security in good time would help her relax. Despite the fact that everything had gone according to plan, it did not take away the feeling that a part of her life was now over. It had been difficult parting with the flats and their belongings; she thought of her parents and felt a knot in her throat. She went to the bar after the departures checks and ordered vodka orange; she did not normally drink by herself, but this was a drink that she enjoyed, and she thought that the orange juice's vitamins would do her good.

"Could I have vodka with orange juice, please?"

"Do you want ice?"

"Yes, please."

The woman presented Bea with three glasses that contained at least half a litre of liquid in two of them and ice in the other one. "That will be twenty-one dollars."

"Twenty-one dollars!" Bea repeated in shock.

"Yes; the ice is one dollar."

This was the most expensive vodka orange that Bea had ever had—and the largest.

"How am I going to drink this?"

"You can pour a bit of vodka and orange in the ice glass."

"So, I should mix it?"

"That is right; here, have a stick, it will help you."

Bea carried the drink to the nearest table, but since she had no hands left, and it was not allowed to leave any luggage unattended on the floor, she had to kick her hand luggage along.

It took her exactly two hours to drink what she thought was rather tasteless to start with, since it was mainly ice, but as it melted it became more tasty. Bea found this new pastime more and more amusing as she drank. By the time she boarded the plane, she did not have a care in the world—she just wanted to sleep.

"Oh, good! I have someone to talk to," said her seat neighbour. As if in a daze Bea turned to face him and smile, but she said nothing. "I can never sleep on planes, and it is nice to have someone to talk to." He went on chatting away until dinner was served.

A stewardess asked Bea, "Do you care for some wine?"

Eating with water gave Bea indigestion, so she asked for a little bottle of wine. She remembered finishing her main course, but nothing else.

CHAPTER FORTY-SEVEN

Bea opened her eyes, trying to remember where she was. Then she realised that she had her head on her seat companion's shoulder. She straightened up with a start and said, "I am so sorry."

"I tried not to move in order not to wake you. You are obviously not used to drinks—you only had a few sips of your wine, and you fell asleep. We are about to land; you missed breakfast."

Bea did not want to explain and just said, "How were you able to have breakfast with me on your shoulder?"

"I used my left hand."

"I am truly sorry. I am not in the habit of sleeping on people's shoulders, let alone someone I have just met."

The man smiled and said, "No problem; in fact, I slept too."

"I'm glad," said Bea, beginning to have a horrid pain in her right eye, but she tried not to shut it in case he thought that she was winking at him. She had embarrassed herself enough.

They landed, and Bea said good-bye and thanked the man again. She had to catch a connection from Chicago to Newark. She had not been able to get a direct flight at such short notice, but she had to hurry because it was leaving in an hour.

With horror she saw the queues that stretched all over the airport and approached one of the security officers. "Can you tell me what the problem is?"

"The computers are down."

"When are they going to go back on?" she asked.

"I don't know; they have been down for a while now."

"I am going to miss my flight if I cannot get through in the next ten minutes."

"Don't worry, ma'am, I am sure they will be able to find another flight for you."

Bea did not want Gaby to have to wait for her or go back home and come back to the airport, which was quite a way from their home. She prayed, and as if by a miracle the lines started moving. The airport put more people on the desks, and the lines moved quite fast. Nevertheless, by the time she got to the other side it was almost time to board her next plane. She did not know where to go and was looking from side to side when she saw an airport worker with very long legs pushing a wheelchair. "Can you tell me where to go to board the plane leaving at ten thirty for Newark?"

"Jump on," he answered. "We will find out and get you there in no time at all—open your legs."

Bea, who was now sitting in the wheelchair, did not know what he was about to do, but she obeyed in desperation. He put her hand luggage between her legs and wheeled her through the airport at an incredible speed. Bea kept her legs tight, holding her hand luggage, and she had her hands on her hand bag. He got them to where all the flights were announced and found the departure gate's number without difficulty. Then he sped again down another alley. Bea put her hand in her hand bag and found whatever money she had there and passed it to him over her shoulder. Gratefully he said: "Bless you."

"We are almost there; the next gate is yours," the man said.

Bea jumped out of the wheelchair and thanked him. Everybody around them could not believe what they had just seen. Was this a real miracle—a woman in a wheelchair able to run? Even the stewardess collecting the boarding passes was surprised and hardly looked at the pass that Bea handed her.

The doors of the plane shut as Bea entered. She was the last passenger to board.

All sorts of feelings passed through her body and mind, but she felt relieved—she had made it. She remembered all the things that she had just been through: selling her parents flat and the flat she thought would be the place where she and her family would spend time with her family; the gigantic vodka orange; the fool she had made herself of in front of her travelling companion; and her ordeal getting to the plane. She did not know whether to cry or laugh. Suddenly her stomach ache was there again, but she also felt a sharp pain in her back. *I need a rest,* she said to herself. *I am getting old.* She was offered breakfast but declined; instead she did the breathing exercises that she had been told to do for relaxation, but they did not help much.

It was so good to see Gaby and Mat waiting for her. She almost ran to them. Both sisters hugged and cried in each other's arms; their parents had gone, and they felt that they only had each other. Mat did not move or say anything; it was hard for him to see his wife letting go in this manner.

Upon arriving at Gaby's home, Bea called John. "Darling, I am here with Gaby, Mat, and the children." The children were now in their twenties, and they looked at each other and smiled. "Everything is done. Could you check that the money has reached the bank?"

"I will. How are you, darling?"

"John, I know you hate it when I am melodramatic—as you say I am when I feel the way I do—but I cannot help it. I have just erased a whole chunk of my life, and I want to cry my eyes out."

John was really taken aback by Bea's outburst. It had been the first time that she had said something like this without crying, but her voice was so solemn that he was worried. "Darling, I am so sorry. I should have been there with you—you have done too much on your own."

"Maybe I have, maybe I haven't, but I feel lousy. I might need antidepressants again."

"Whatever you need, you will have."

"Bye, John."

Gaby and her family had heard Bea talking to John, and Mat had gone to get a large glass of brandy for Bea.

When Bea saw what Matt handed her, she burst out laughing in the way she did when she realised that she had let herself go. It felt good, and she laughed so much that the whole family was infected; tears were streaming down their faces by the time that they stopped. Bea then recounted the vodka orange experience, and they laughed again.

"I should call John again; he must be so worried."

"Leave him," said Gaby in her ear. "What you said is the truth."

Staying with Gaby was good for Bea, but also for Gaby. They promised to talk more often and see one another as often as possible. New York was not so far from London; they felt they should have seen more of each other over the years.

"It is just the two of us, and the families that we have raised. I am happy that we kept the big house—you must all come and visit," Bea said.

"There is not enough room in our house yet, but Lisa and William will be leaving soon. Or at least Lisa will, now that she is engaged."

"I did not know that!?"

"With all that has been going on, I forgot to tell you," Gaby admitted.

"When is the wedding?"

"They have postponed it because of Mother, but they will set a new date soon."

"John and I will certainly come. Don't worry about putting us up. It has been so good staying with you before I go back to my family; I needed an injection of my own background."

"My family is not Argentinean."

"They might not be, but *you* are, dear sister."

CHAPTER FORTY-EIGHT

"I will send you to a specialist. You have had this stomach ache for too long now. Are you insured for private medicine?" Asked Bea's doctor

"I think so, but I will have to ask my husband to be sure."

"Here is a letter and the specialist's telephone number. Try to make an appointment as soon as possible."

That night after dinner, Bea talked with John. "The doctor has sent me to a specialist; are we covered?" she asked.

"After you had cancer, I renewed our policy, and we are fully covered now. They said that you were not covered for cancer for the next five years, but it has been over six, hasn't it?"

"Yes, it has. I will make an appointment in the morning."

"Darling, I am so sorry that you have to go through more tests again."

"I am sure it is stress; I wish I didn't have to have more tests, but it seems that I do. I do not notice that I get as stressed as I do."

John hugged her, and they went to bed.

The doctor said, "We will take a scan of your abdomen. You must eat what is in the list for one day and then fast for one whole day before the scan."

Bea was also given some horrid liquid that she had to take while she was fasting.

The day of the test, the doctor said, "Please have a glass of water and take off all your clothes. Here is a gown." Bea did as she was told. "Lie down and stay as still as possible. I need to strap you around your feet and head."

Bea tried not to think, but it was painful in her tummy and her back, and the scan seemed to take forever.

"We will have the results tomorrow afternoon; we will give you a ring and send a letter to your GP."

"Thank you. Did you see anything abnormal?" she asked.

"I could not tell you at this moment; only after the head radiologist has seen your scan can we let you know."

The next thirty-six hours were like thirty-six days for Bea; she felt as if she had butterflies in her stomach. The telephone rang and she ran to pick it up.

"I have good news," the nurse said. "There is nothing wrong with your abdomen."

"Why do I have such stomach ache all the time?"

"I would not know; you have to ask your GP."

"I have already done so many times."

"Sometimes we imagine pain."

"I see," Bea said curtly. "Thank you." Now she felt even worse; she must be going mad. She wanted to occupy herself doing house work or going out or something, but she could not. She went to bed and fell asleep because she felt so tired.

John came home to find the house in darkness, and he thought that Bea might have gone out. But when he went upstairs and turned the light on in their bedroom, he found that Bea was fast asleep. He did not want to wake her and went downstairs to find something to eat from the fridge. That night he slept in the spare bedroom.

Bea came down when John was having breakfast. "Where did you sleep?" she asked.

"In the spare bedroom; I did not want to wake you."

"I am sorry, John. I felt drained."

John asked, "Do you have the scan result?"

"The nurse told me there was nothing wrong with me. She said that sometimes people imagine pain. I must be mad—I have been imagining this pain for over six years."

"No, darling, you are not mad. There must be a reason why you hurt so much."

"Well, there isn't," Bea said, annoyed.

John hugged her, and Bea would have liked to cry, but she controlled herself; there was nothing wrong with her, and that was it. Although she was still feeling tired, she got on with what she had to do and was pleased that she had done all her chores when the telephone rang.

"Mrs Fellow?" the voice said.

"Yes."

"I called you yesterday with the result of your test, but I am afraid that after having a second look, they have found a shadow in your back. I have made an appointment for you tomorrow morning for a bone scan."

"I see," Bea said. "Is there any preparation for this test?"

"You must come for a radioactive injection in the morning, and in the afternoon you must come back for the scan."

Bea broke the news to John. "It seems that there is a shadow in my back. They want me to have another test tomorrow."

"I will go with you," he offered.

"There is no need. I am used to doing things on my own."

"I will take you there, and then we can go for a walk and lunch before we go back for the test."

"Thank you John, that would be nice."

"I can take time off, Bea. I am retiring at the end of this year."

"I know, but you don't like doing so."

"You are the most important thing in my life, Bea."

The doctor noted, "You must have had a lot to drink. The picture is very clear."

Bea replied, "I had six cups of green tea; we had a Japanese lunch."

"Are you in pain?"

"I am always in pain. Did you find the shadow?"

"Oh, yes. There are three; I will show them to you in a minute."

Bea got up from the stretcher, where she had been for the scan, and approached the radiologist. There in the middle of the screen were three things that looked like suns flashing; the largest was just behind her stomach."

"This is what is causing the stomach ache. When was your cancer diagnosed?""

"Six years ago."

"It is common to get bone cancer from breast cancer. I am surprised they did not give you a bone scan before."

"So what shall I do now?"

"You will be called tomorrow by the specialist. He will tell you what to do."

CHAPTER FORTY-NINE

Bea and John sat in front of Professor Davies, who read the letter carefully and then looked at the scan in his computer. "You must have radiotherapy again," he said.

"Why wasn't my wife given a bone scan before?" John demanded. "We were told that it is common practice for people who have had breast cancer."

"*Now* it is common practice, but six years ago it was not."

"But she has been having check-ups regularly."

"Her blood tests came out negative, and she does not seem to have the symptoms."

John was still not satisfied and was angry, but there was no point in arguing.

"You must start taking anticancer drugs immediately; here is the prescription. The radiotherapy department has already been notified; go down and ask for an appointment. Is there anything else I can do for you?" Professor Davies asked.

"Am I going to go on having this pain in my stomach?" Bea said.

"I am afraid you will until the effect of the radiotherapy works, but I can give you a strong pain killer."

"A few years ago I was given antidepressants; I felt better then."

"You can go on taking them."

"Could you give me a prescription, please?"

"Of course. What is the name of the drug?"

"I don't know what it is called here; it was given to me when I was in Argentina. I brought the empty box with me."

Bea handed Professor Davies the box. He nodded and then wrote another prescription for the drug. "Come and see me once you have had the radiotherapy."

Bea was given five doses of radiotherapy in one go.

"For you it will be more effective than small doses every day. You might feel a bit uncomfortable for a while, but it will pass," explained the radiologist.

For a few days Bea felt well. The anticancer drug was not giving her any side effects, and the antidepressant was just what she needed to feel more relaxed. But five days later she had a sharp pain in her back, and her stomach blew up. She felt so sick that she had to go to bed.

John said, "Darling, I have made an appointment with Professor Davies."

"I do not know if I will be able to get dressed; I can't move my right arm."

"Here, I will help you."

Again they sat in front of Professor Davies. This time Bea did not look well, and she could hardly sit; she had to keep moving in order not to scream with pain.

"I want you to have an MRI," he said. He picked up the phone and asked his secretary to fix an appointment straight away. "You might have to wait a while, but I want you to have it today."

Bea looked at John in desperation.

"Can she lie down while waiting?" John asked. "My wife cannot sit for a long period of time."

Professor Davies picked up the telephone again. "Cecilia, could you find a bed for Mrs Fellow? There might be one in the waiting room." He turned to them. "Go down; my secretary will be waiting for you."

Fortunately it was not painful for Bea to walk; it was just her upper body that was in agony.

Cecilia had organised the MRI and was waiting for them, as Professor Davies had said. "I found a bed, but you will have to undress for the scan," she explained.

"I will help her," said John

Bea said, "Can I have a blanket, please? I feel cold."

Cecilia came back with two blankets, and she covered Bea while looking concerned. "I hope it will not take too long. When it is done, get dressed and lie down on the bed again. I will come down when Professor Davies has the result."

Five hours later they were collected by Cecilia. Bea had fallen asleep and felt disoriented.

"Darling, the professor has the results," John explained.

Bea shook her head, trying to find her bearings. Then she lifted herself but could not control a scream.

John helped her carefully, and the three of them took the lift.

"The radiotherapy has been successful," Davies said. "Unfortunately it has left a hole in your back."

"What do you mean?" asked a concerned John.

"The radiotherapy has destroyed the biggest tumour, but where it was, there is a dent in your spine now. This is why it hurts."

"Is there anything that can be done?" Bea asked.

"The hole can be filled; like a tooth, and that will make the pain more bearable. I will ask Cecilia to make an appointment for you to go and see Professor Smiley."

"Not now, please. I want to go to bed."

"She will arrange it and call you at home."

Bea was told that after the surgery, she could go home free of pain.

"John, I cannot tell you how much I am looking forward to tomorrow."

"I am, too, my darling Bea."

But when Bea came out of the anaesthetic, she was in worse pain than before. Professor Smiley could not understand and thought, like others had in the past, that Bea was imagining the pain. Nevertheless, he asked for another MRI and a room for Bea. She was not going home that evening, as she and John had so much hoped.

"The cement leaked. The bone in your spine is very fragile, and it cracked when I inserted the cement. I am afraid it has leaked on to a nerve. It will take a while for the pain to get better."

John felt like hitting the man. He felt desperate for Bea. "Is she going to be in this pain all the time?" he asked.

"I think the best thing for you will be if I refer you to a pain control specialist. I will ask my secretary to make an appointment for you tomorrow. In the meantime I will order an injection of morphine."

After the injection, Bea felt better and was able to talk a bit, although she felt exhausted. "I am sorry I am putting you through all this, John."

"I'm sorry that all this is happening to you. Nobody seems to do anything right!"

Bea was able to move her arm little by little as the pain decreased, but she was still not able to sit for more than an hour at a time, and she had to take pain killers every day. It took her a year to be able to lead an almost normal life again. In the meantime Ann had a beautiful little boy, whom they called Albert John.

"I think this adorable child is going to help me get better," Bea said to the proud parents. "I cannot hold him yet, but I am going to do my best to get this arm in top shape as soon as possible."

"You can hold him if you sit; here," Ann said, passing Bea her grandson.

The baby sort of smiled in his dreams, and Bea held him tight against her. Yes, this was what she needed to feel better.

Then Grace and Camilla announced that they were expecting their second babies—again at the same time.

John said, "Darling, look who is here."

Bea, who was in the kitchen went to the front door and saw Richard smiling by it. She ran to hug him. "What a lovely surprise!"

"Mum, this is Maite, Maria Teresa."

"Pleased to meet you, Mrs Fellow," Maite said in Spanish.

Richard said, "Mum and Dad, we are engaged."

This time Bea and John hugged them both. Bea said, "This is wonderful, darling! When is the happy day?"

"We were waiting to see how you were before choosing a date."

"Then do it soon. I am delighted that I will be able to speak Spanish to a daughter-in-law."

"Mum, Maite speaks perfect English."

"I don't care—I will speak to her in Spanish," Bea said. They all laughed at that. "Do your brothers know?"

"They know I had a girlfriend, but I wanted you to know first about the engagement."

Bea kissed Richard again. Then she said to Maite, "You must ask your parents to come and visit us."

"My parents want *you* to go and visit *them*," Maite said with a smile.

"Where are you planning to get married?"

"In Spain; my father has a *cortijo,* and we thought we could get married there."

"It is a vast place, mum," Richard added.

"I can imagine—I have seen them in films. There are a bit like *estancias* in Argentina, except that we have no bull fights there."

"We do have bull fights in our *cortijo*."

"I am sure you do," said John, who had been listening to all this in silence. "If you are going to get married in Spain, it is only fair that you should come here for the engagement party."

"Yes, please let us do that for you," said Bea, full of expectation.

CHAPTER FIFTY

For the first time Bea had the chance to have a relationship the way she wanted it with future in-laws. Maite's parents understood that parents on both sides should be involved in wedding's preparations.

Maite's parents, siblings, and grandparents came for an informal engagement party.

Bea said, "Richard, they can stay with us; we have plenty of room in the house."

"I know, Mum, but you cannot have that many people to stay; I do not want you to fall ill again. They like staying in hotels."

"All right, then. We have reserved the dining room in the club. Would you and Maite like to choose the menu?"

"I will ask her, but I am sure she will say that she trusts you to choose it."

"What do they like to eat?"

"They are not fussy."

"Good. I will try to choose something a little British, but not too much."

Richard laughed; he was happy that his mother sounded so much better.

At the party, John was worried that they were making too much noise and somebody might complain, but fortunately nobody did. Everybody got on well, and there was a lot of talking, eating, and drinking. John asked for the club's best champagne and wines.

The girls seemed to get on very well, and Maite was the interpreter between them and her mother and grandmother. Bea loved Maite's family already, and they seemed to love Richard's family for the way they were enjoying themselves.

A date was chosen for the following spring. By then Grace and Camilla would have had their babies.

"You must not worry about the children; we have plenty of help at home. Weddings in Spain last at least three days; you must come for a week so that we have time to take you sightseeing after the wedding," Maite's father told them.

Nobody had imagined how big and fantastic the *cortijo* was; it was like a small town surrounded by trees. Bea and John were given a suite in the main house, but the boys and their families were given small cottages that were scattered around the enormous grounds so that they could feed the children whenever they wanted. They were also allocated maids rather like Lucy when she first came to help the family. The boys had to be the interpreters between the girls and their wives, but the children did not need interpreters and took to the girls immediately. It was a rest for the mothers after a long trip; they had come by car, stopping once or twice on the way. Fortunately, they were all able to find rooms in the same hotels.

Gaby and her family were the only ones from Bea's side to attend; the rest of her family was either too old or young or busy. One of John's cousins came with his wife, but that was all the representation that Richard's family had. Some of Richard's friends had come, too, and they were all together with Richard in two of the cottages. On the other hand, there were over three hundred of Maite's relatives and friends.

The wedding, as announced, took three days, starting with a bull fight after breakfast on the first day and lunch afterwards. The dress was informal, but the waiters served the tables, and the food was magnificent.

The religious service was the following evening, when the sun was going down in the middle of the main garden. The priest was Maite's uncle, and he was thrilled to be marrying her. When she walked down the red carpet that had been placed in between the two groups of chairs where the guests were sitting, she looked like a Madonna from an old Spanish painting. She had a large tortoise-shell comb in her hair that served to hold a long lace mantilla matching her dress. There were exclamations of admiration all around as she walked to the music of ten violins.

After the dinner that took place in a huge converted barn decorated with flowers from top to bottom, there was dancing. It was welcome exercise because there had been eight courses—and the cake was still to come.

Maite opened the dance with her father, who soon gave way to Richard. The newlyweds looked so happy that Bea and John could not help holding hands and looking at each other. "We did not dance at our wedding, but we were just as happy, weren't we?" Bea said.

"My darling Bea, you have made me so happy that I cannot imagine life without you."

"Even after all I have put you through?"

"You have not put me through anything. We have just shared married life."

Bea put her head on John's shoulder and said, "Let's dance."

The third day was a farewell to the guests without Richard and Maite, who had left after the wedding party.

Bea and John, as well as Gaby and Mat, stayed with Maite's parents for a few more days, but the rest of the family had to go back to work or to school. Mat's Spanish was almost as good as John's, which helped with the constant conversations during sightseeing or at meal times. The families bonded and had a wonderful time together, but by the end of the week Bea felt a sharp pain in her back again. She tried not to show it, but John saw how pale she had turned and knew that something was not right.

"Darling, shall I try and see if they have a whole row of seats so that you can lie down?"

"That would be great, John."

They were lucky that the plane was not full, and Bea was able to travel lying down.

When they arrived home, John called the doctor. "I would like to make an appointment with Professor Davies as soon as possible, please."

"He does not have any time available before Friday."

"Could you ask him if he could see my wife sometime before then? She is in a lot of pain again."

"I will call you back as soon as he comes out of the operating theatre."

A short while later, they received a call: "He can see her this evening at about seven. He will be operating again, so I cannot be precise with the time."

John took Bea to the hospital, and fortunately they did not have to wait too long for Professor Davies. "Tell me where it hurts," he said while tapping gently down her back.

"Ouch! There! It is horrid."

"Have you been taking the anticancer drug?"

"Yes."

"I think that one of the other tumours has grown. I will see if they can give you an MRI straight away. If they can't, would you like to stay here over night?"

"I have not brought anything with me."

"That is all right, Bea," John said. "I can go and get your things. It will be better than coming and going early in the morning."

Fortunately, she was able to have the scan that night.

Davies said, "I want to have a good look and discuss it with some colleagues in the morning. I will ask my secretary to give you a ring."

The next day they received a call. "Mr Fellow, the professor would like to see Mrs Fellow tonight, at the same time as yesterday."

They went in at the designated time, and Davies explained, "The tumours in your back have grown, but the MRI shows that the cancer has spread to other parts of your body. Do your legs hurt?"

"A bit—they feel a bit heavy. What really hurts is my back and hands."

"I am afraid that it can go on being this way for many years. We cannot treat it now. You have been taking the anticancer drug, but it does not seem to be taking effect anymore."

John looked at him. "What do you mean?"

"There is no cure for bone cancer, especially not at this stage. But your wife can live for many years yet."

"In this pain?"

"We can give her stronger pain killers."

"The pain killers I am already taking upset my stomach," Bea complained.

"We can give you something for that, too."

"How long do I have?" she asked.

"As I said, you can live for many years. Try to rest as much as possible."

John and Bea left the hospital in silence. John had one of his arms around Bea's shoulders.

CHAPTER FIFTY-ONE

Bea and John did not talk much in the car either, but when they got home Bea said, "I am going to call Dr Aragon."

"That is a great idea. I will go and prepare something for supper."

Bea dialled and got the receptionist. "Surgery."

"Could I please talk to Dr Aragon?"

"Dr Aragon passed away last year. The Surgery has been taken over by Dr Silvester. Would you like to make an appointment?"

"No, thank you."

"Did you talk to him?" John asked when Bea came into the kitchen.

"He passed away last year. I should have gone to see him when my mother died."

"He was old, darling."

"He was very good to me," Bea said defensively.

"I know; he kept you going when you needed him most. I am sorry I was not there, but I am now. I am retired, and we will do many things together."

"I will try my best, darling."

John managed to get the family together that Easter. Bea was not well but was excited to see her children and grandchildren. Even Richard was coming with Maite, who was pregnant with their second child, and they brought two-year-old Lucas. Ann was also pregnant expecting, her third child; they had a boy and a girl. Charles and Grace had two boys and a girl, and Ernie and Camilla had a boy and a girl.

They all went to church in the morning and sat in the back of the church—with eight children, they had to be near the exit. For Bea it was also better to sit in the back; Father Matthias had provided her with a soft velvet chair, but if she got tired of sitting, she could get up and walk about in the hall of the church. She leaned on John's arm to get to the altar for communion. She did not remember feeling so happy for a long time.

At home John and Bea were ordered to sit with the children while their parents organised the meal that had been cooked in advanced by all the girls. John was very good at romping around with the little boys, while Bea played more subdued games with the girls, although some of them wanted to join the fun that the boys were having, rolling all over the carpet with Granddad.

After lunch, which went on for quite a while, Bea went to lie down on the sofa while the children, guided by their parents, went all over the house looking for Easter eggs. They all came back with their little baskets full of the small chocolate eggs, and they sat down to eat them. Their parents tried to put a limit on how many they were allowed to eat, but the elder children found a way to sneak a few more. They all got on so well and looked so happy. Bea saw her family with her eyes half shut on the sofa, and she smiled. Her boomerang had come back in the way she wanted it.

John looked at her and approached. He leaned over and asked, "How are you, my darling Bea?"

"I am happy, John, very happy."

"I am happy, too. It is wonderful to see you coping so well."

"Can I ask you something?" she said.

"Anything."

"Can I have the 'Ave Maria' when I am gone?"

"Oh, my darling, of course—but that is not going to happen just yet."

Bea breathed deeply, and then she stopped breathing altogether. John held her tight and sobbed uncontrollably.

The family saw this and approached their parents. They were not sure what was going on.

"Dad, what is it?" Charles asked his father.

But John could not talk; he just kept holding Bea in his arms. Charles lifted him gently. Then he held him in his arms also crying.

"What is going on, Daddy?" Ernie asked, suddenly gripped by fear at what was happening in front of him.

All the brothers had been talking to their children about death; they wanted to prepare them for this moment and they were glad that they had done so.

Grace went to them and said, "Grandma has gone to heaven. She is resting now."

One by one they approached their grandmother and gave her a final kiss.

"Good–bye, Grandma. Look after us from heaven, please."

The End

ABOUT THE AUTHOR

Jenny Guest was born in Argentina and travelled extensively with her father, who was a diplomat. In Japan, she met her husband, a British diplomat. They were married in 1970 and have four children. They are currently living in London, England. She always wanted to write, but only now in her sixties has she had the time to do so. The characters that she creates are composites of several people that she has met plus her own imagination.

ABOUT THE BOOK

Bea and John meet in Tokyo at the end of the 1960. He is immediately smitten by Bea, who is an extrovert Argentine brought up in the strictest fashion by her Catholic parents—despite the fact that she is a model and has a busy social life supervised by her father.

John is British, was educated at a boarding school, and comes from a Church of England family. His mother is not taken by this charming girl and influences her son in doubting that the relationship can survive the differences in their backgrounds.

John encourages Bea that it will be good for her to see what life is like in England, before they get married. She embarks on a trip that opens her eyes to a completely new world.

But could this trip help their marriage succeed when there is also a war between their countries looming in the future?

The poignancy of this tale of love, courage and occasional heartbreak is only revealed to the reader in the last turn of the boomerang.